THE BEST
November Man Book Yet!

The Infant
Of Prague

BOOKS BY BILL GRANGER

THE NOVEMBER MAN NOVELS
*The November Man**
Schism
The Shattered Eye
The British Cross
The Zurich Numbers
*Hemingway's Notebook**
*There Are No Spies**
*The Infant of Prague**
*Henry McGee Is Not Dead**

CHICAGO POLICE STORIES
*Public Murders**
Priestly Murders
*Newspaper Murders**
The El Murders

Sweeps
Queen's Crossing
Time for Frankie Coolin

NONFICTION
Chicago Pieces
Fighting Jane (with Lori Granger)
The Magic Feather (with Lori Granger)
Lords of the Last Machine (with Lori Granger)

***Published by
WARNER BOOKS**

BILL GRANGER

THE INFANT OF PRAGUE

A NOVEMBER MAN NOVEL

WARNER BOOKS

A Warner Communications Company

WARNER BOOKS EDITION

Cover design by Rolf Erickson
Cover illustration by OSYCZKA

Warner Books, Inc.
666 Fifth Avenue
New York, N.Y. 10103

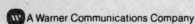A Warner Communications Company

Printed in the United States of America

This book was originally published in hardcover by Warner Books.
First Printed in Paperback: November, 1988

10 9 8 7 6 5 4 3 2 1

This is for Andrew MacElhone of Paris and John Lynch of Doonaha, Clare, Republic of Eire.

The Cathedral of Our Lady in the town of Chartres possesses a statue of the Virgin which is more than 500 years old and some believe it is a miraculous icon. In the course of Christianity, various icons, places or particular natural resources (springs, wells, even certain rocks) have been deemed by some to have miraculous properties.

In 1987 a Greek Christian church in Chicago claimed to possess a wood painting of the Virgin which wept.

Czechoslovakia is considered among the most skilled weapons producers in the Eastern bloc and has routinely supplied weapons to revolutionary groups in the West—notably, in the 1960s and 1970s, the Irish Republican Army.

Prague has gained favor in the West as a film production site because of the city's beauty and the favorable exchange rate.

On fire that glows
With heat intense
I turn the hose
Of common sense,
And out it goes
At small expense!

—W. S. GILBERT

ONE

The Age of Faith

Everyone in Chartres knows the story of the eccentric Englishman.

Thirty years ago, he came to the village southwest of Paris to see the wonderful cathedral. All the tourists came in their season. The giant continental tour buses pulled through the narrow market streets and clogged the curbing near the cathedral, and all the tourists went to the great church with their cameras and green and red Guides Michelin. All summer, the tourists mingled with the students and the pilgrims and took photographs of the cathedral and dropped coins in the box for the restoration of the cathedral. They could buy postcards depicting the church and little stickers for their car windows that showed they had come to Chartres.

The Englishman did none of these things. All that summer he would go quietly alone to the cathedral with a notebook and pencil. He made sketches and paced off distances in the church and wrote long passages about all he saw and felt and thought.

He studied the cathedral because it was a beautiful thing.

When it was autumn, the mistral began to blow down through France and touched the Côte d'Azur and colored the leaves on trees along the Seine and Loire and sent the tourists fleeing to their warm homes. Autumn cut down the farm fields around Chartres and autumn rain turned the bare earth black. And the Englishman stayed on past the season for visiting Englishmen.

Each afternoon, during the quiet time, he sat beneath the great rose windows of the cathedral entrance and contemplated the arching lines of the buttresses and the narrow, vaulted ceiling that soared so far above his head. Some said he studied the church so hard that he began to see the act of faith actually frozen in stone raised eight hundred years before, in an age when the earth was low and naked and even kings were often cold and hungry in their castles.

The Englishman knew the naked history of the place. How the old church in Chartres burned for a fourth time eight centuries ago, and how the people of the village found a blessed relic of the mother of God in the ashes and saw this as a sign to build the new, great church on the same holy ground. The bishop and the abbot approved this interpretation of the sign and the workers of Chartres began the work of a century, to lift a cathedral by cunning labor over the low, flat fields.

In time, the people of Chartres realized the Englishman would not leave the cathedral and they accepted him as part of it.

He stayed in the season and beyond it. Autumn gave way to the holy days of November, when death and the triumph of souls are honored in masses and benedictions.

The light shifted in the coming winter sky and the days were gray and brief. The light that came through the immense windows of the cathedral changed every day and made the shadows in the church reveal more of itself. The Englishman would sit and stare at the altars and the statues of the saints and the great nave and the chancel and the red lamp in the sanctuary and see everything past that had come to this moment of beauty.

After a time of silence and study, the Englishman began to speak of the cathedral. He would gather a few students or pilgrims or even tourists around him and he would let his hands soar to point out the glory of the flying buttresses that lifted the walls to the sky. It was wonderful to hear him speak of the cathedral and how it was made.

He is still there. In the afternoons, he speaks in the church with his light, English voice filled with affection and humor. He describes the past as if it were an old friend, and he reveals the secrets of the cathedral with his lifted hand. The listeners are always different and what they hear they hear for the first time. The Englishman has written several little books about the cathedral and they are sold in all the shops; he spends his days as a student and pilgrim and an explainer of beauty. It is a simple life, everyone agrees. When he speaks of the church, it is as though he describes his beloved.

The Englishman lifted his hand.

He pointed to the rose windows in the great stone wall above the entrance of the church. The gesture carried dignity, like the finger of Adam reaching toward the finger of God on the ceiling of the Sistine Chapel. The day was full of autumn clouds and sudden rains. The light fell delicately through the stained glass.

Hanley stared at the Englishman and held his green

guidebook in his left hand. He had been waiting for twenty minutes and he had attached himself to the small group of travelers gathered around the Englishman. He felt annoyed because his overcoat was heavy and wet and because someone had kept him waiting.

Then he saw him at the side door.

The second man moved from the brief opening of daylight to the shadows to the half-light of the candles on the side altar. The candles were lit as prayers. They illuminated the ashen face of the second man, and Hanley turned away from the group and crossed the center aisle of the church.

The second man stared at him. Hanley gestured back toward the group on the other side of the church. "He's been here thirty years," he said. "Studying the church, talking about it. Thirty years. It's hard to believe a man would give up thirty years for this."

"Did you learn anything?" Devereaux said. There was an edge of sarcasm that made Hanley frown.

"Nothing that I couldn't have read about in a book," Hanley said. "The English are strange. They're always producing someone like him."

"Why are we here?" Devereaux said. He and Hanley turned away from the center of the church and stared at the marble of the side altar. The candles made their harsh winter faces seem softer. Hanley put down the green guidebook on the metal poor box. When he spoke again, he scarcely moved his lips at all.

"I was wrapped in French security in Paris," Hanley said. "Then I received a signal and there's a matter, a simple matter really, that we have to act upon right away."

"So you dragged the reluctant pilgrim to Chartres," Devereaux said. His voice was low and flat and bleak as November fields.

"I gave security the slip, went out the back way of the hotel—"

"Hidden in a laundry basket?"

"Sarcasm," Hanley said. He had been pleased with himself for slipping the French security agents assigned to "observe" him while he met in Paris with the other members of the Western Anti-Terror Committee. It had been as enjoyable as a game in childhood and now Devereaux was trying to spoil his satisfaction.

"Are we here to pray or to merely observe the beauty of the church?"

"We are here because it is secure," Hanley said. His face was bland and round, as featureless as his voice. He was director of operations for Section and was no more at home in the field than Devereaux would have been in the bureaucracy in Washington. But the matter had come up suddenly, and even if it was simple, it had to be handled now.

"This is about a man who has interested us for a little while. He's a Czech and he wants to change sides. He has some bona fides to carry along with him and we think it's worth the chance."

"Worth the risk," Devereaux said. "Worth risking the neck of an agent."

Hanley frowned again. "There is no risk."

"Do I go to Prague?"

"No. Not at all. I said there is no risk. We've set up a simple train and you're the conductor. Your passenger leaves tomorrow night from Brussels. You conduct the train and the passenger to Zeebrugge. We'll have a boat waiting."

"Who set this up? Stowe?"

Stowe was the head of Eurodesk operations for the Section located in Brussels. Stowe was the logical connection for the business. Devereaux knew all this and wondered why Hanley insisted it was a simple matter.

"Stowe is not involved," Hanley said.

"You'll have to do better than that."

"I do not have to do better," Hanley said.

They waited for a moment. The statue of a saint stared back at Hanley's glare. Hanley lowered his eyes and his voice. "There is urgency and a need to involve as few people as possible."

"Who runs the train?"

"Perfectly reliable contractors in Brussels. They've been used before."

"Then why involve me?"

Hanley looked up. He seemed surprised. "But you're our man on the scene. That's obvious, isn't it?"

"Who's the defector?"

"Miki. Actually, Emil Mikita is the name. He's called Miki. A show-business sort of a person, they all have those kinds of short names. In Europe, I mean."

"Is he going to play you in the movie?" Devereaux asked.

"Humor," Hanley said. He felt compelled to identify remarks and moods of others in order to minimalize them. He never realized that Devereaux thought he was merely showing slowness of wit.

"Miki is the contact man between the State Ministry for Tourism and Promotion and a wide range of . . . Western entertainment interests," Hanley said. "He is the fixer, you might say, the man who gets things done. He's well known in some circles."

"How nice for him," Devereaux said. He rested his large hands on the communion rail that fenced off the small side altar. The candles reminded him; the lingering damp in the stone walls, the unblinking statues, the scent of burned incense in the church reminded him. The trouble with living into middle age was being reminded by all sorts of things of childhood, the time before you discovered the way things would turn out.

"He's in Brussels for an affair, something about the International Society of Filmmakers. He's supposed to get an award. Apparently, everyone makes movies in Prague now because of the costs and because the city looks . . . well, European. The way Europe used to look."

Devereaux said, "He travels abroad?"

"All the time. He's very connected. Sort of an impresario."

"Who works for the government."

"That's the way they do things over there."

"He goes to New York," Devereaux said. "Why doesn't he defect in Bloomingdale's?"

Hanley pursed his lips. "There are complications."

"I thought it was a simple matter."

"Your name was selected by . . . by the director." Hanley referred to Mrs. Neumann, the new Section chief.

"I'm flattered," Devereaux said. "How much more complicated does it get?"

"The complications are all outside, they don't involve you."

Devereaux turned. He stared at Hanley and his gray eyes glittered in the candlelight. There was something dangerous in those eyes and Hanley wanted to turn away but he could not.

"The complication is outside," Hanley repeated. "Our competition at Langley. Langley was interested in Miki before we were. Perhaps they tried too hard. Miki has made it clear that he doesn't trust Langley in this."

"But he trusts Section."

"Apparently."

"Is any of this certain? Or is Section depending on astrology again?"

Hanley winced. It had been an unfortunate matter and no one mentioned it anymore. Somehow, a clerk rose to GS-15 inside Section. He had complete clearance to the level of Q. And he was in charge of processing new code names for the permanent files of senior field officers. Instead of making random selections, however, he studied astrology charts and imprinted all the agents with names that—given their birth dates and other astrological data— "augured well for Section." So one became Aries and another became Tuesday and another was called Midnight. And the man who spoke to Hanley now was known on the permanent files as "November," though he used other names as well.

"There is a certainty that the risk of snatching Miki is small, compared with potential rewards. He's a top man in the Prague bureaucracy and he knows secrets and we want them. All Miki wants is a snatch—this is not a defection. He wants to be obliterated by us and buried in an empty grave."

Devereaux sighed. "A new name and identity. The country is going to become full of people with new names and new fingerprints, and no one will ever know who they really once were."

"Miki is afraid of Langley and that makes him all the more important to us," Hanley went on. "He hints he has a bit on Langley's dealings with the Czechs as well."

"Hints," Devereaux said. He used the word with contempt. He was tired of Hanley, tired of traveling. They had telephoned the number in Lausanne and the message had been waiting for him in a folded-up copy of the *Journal de Geneve* at the train station. He had traveled all night and all day, doubling back on himself to make certain he was safe. And Hanley had merely slipped out the back door of a Paris hotel to do the same thing.

"And what if it's not what it appears to be?" Devereaux asked. The tone of his voice had not changed, but Hanley felt on guard.

"There is no risk," Hanley said.

"Everything is a risk. Did Miki dictate the terms of his escape?"

"Not the terms. He doesn't know the train or the route. He only knows the time. Twenty-one hundred tomorrow at the *Grand Place* in Brussels. You'll be out of it less than two hours later. And back home to sleep in Lausanne."

"You want him for what he might have on Langley," Devereaux said, falling into the Section slang term for Central Intelligence Agency. "Just another bit of interagency competition."

"The pig that doesn't fight doesn't get to feed at the trough," Hanley said. "Everything is competition in the end."

"And what if the business fails? And Miki is part of a trap? Who gets the blame?"

"It can't fail," Hanley said. In the silence, they could hear the clear voice of the Englishman behind them. He was describing the work of lifting stones upon wooden scaffolds to the top of the church.

"Who gets the blame if it fails?"

"Whoever kidnapped Miki," Hanley said.

There it was between them. November was the sleeping agent, stricken from active files, and yet he was useful in a situation like this. Once a spy, always a spy; it was the rule and they both knew it could never be broken or altered in any way.

"Not Section," Devereaux said then. He had the truth at least. Stowe and Eurodesk Section were bypassed because what was about to happen in Brussels would never be traced back to Section if things went wrong.

"No, not Section," Hanley agreed. "We would never be involved in a business like that." He opened his Michelin guide and took out the instruction sheet written in clearspeak. He gave the paper to Devereaux. "You can drop this in the water font by the door. It's dissolvable."

That's holy water, Devereaux thought. The thought was not voluntary and he flinched from it. It was what he would have believed as a child. That was the cruelty of memory, to keep the faith of childhood alive even in the autumn bleakness of middle age.

Devereaux looked up from the candles and Hanley was gone and the voice of the Englishman echoed in the vast cathedral. He stared at the piece of paper. Then, almost with reluctance, he made his own way toward the side door. He paused at the marble font and stared at the stale water that was blessed by one of the priests. When the faithful came into the church or left it, they dipped fingers in the water and made the sign of the cross.

Devereaux opened the door to the last light of afternoon. It was raining. He had crumpled the paper up at the last moment and shoved it deep in the pocket of his coat.

TWO

The Age of Reason

The statue began to weep on Monday.

Wally, the church custodian, was the first person to notice the tears. Shortly after school opened, he crossed the concrete courtyard from the school to the church to make sure the heat had been turned down after the morning schedule of masses. Wally was a tall, shambling man who wore flannel shirts in summer and winter and always carried a black-handled screwdriver in the back pocket of his wash pants.

He was not a Catholic, but he had been attached to St. Margaret of Scotland Church for so long that everyone assumed he was. He had watched the change of rites and rituals over the years with the eye of a connoisseur: the Latin mass, with its bowing priests and whiffs of incense, had changed into an English-speaking, homey rite that involved much shaking of hands, playing of guitars, and a new, low altar shaped like a dining room table. Wally thought he did not like the new way as much as the old, and this thought was on his mind the morning he checked the thermostat in the church. At least, that is what he said later.

At first he thought one of the radiator pipes on the side altar had burst and sprayed the statue with hot water. Then he got close to the little statue and saw that the water was only on the painted face. No, it was more precise than that: Wally knelt on the base of the side altar and peered closely at the face of the statue of the Christ Child. Tears, he thought. The statue was weeping. The thought was so profound that Wally nearly fell backwards off the altar where he knelt.

Wally had few yearnings but one of them was an ordinary man's desire for fame, however fleeting. He always listened to radio call-in shows in his unofficial "office" in the basement of the church, and he frequently tried to call his favorite programs when they proposed some provocative question. His best moment had come one November when he expressed the opinion that Ronald Reagan was the best President since Franklin D. Roosevelt. He had held the airwaves for a full forty-five seconds that time.

Now, recovering from the miracle, he went to his office in the basement and began to make the calls that would lead him to fame. He called the *Tribune* and the *Sun-Times*, and at both places the response was unenthusiastic. They took his name and telephone number and said "someone" would check it out. The news radio station said much the same thing in different terms and so did the woman who answered the telephone at Wally's favorite television news station. By chance, he was connected with Kay Davis at a second television station on his sixth try.

Kay Davis did not believe him either, but it was Monday

morning after a gloomy, arid weekend and she sat at her desk in the newsroom and saw Hal Newt glaring across at her as she listened to Wally.

Hal Newt did not like Kay Davis very much anymore. It was nothing personal. Kay Davis was a mistake and they both knew it now. That's what he had told her in different terms at lunch Friday and she had chewed on the words all weekend.

She had come to the Chicago station with promise two years before. She had been a success in Des Moines, and when she left the Des Moines station for Chicago, they had written about her in the local paper. Hal Newt had brought her in and sold her to the station manager, who, in turn, oversold her success story to the director of the owned-and-operated stations of the network. As it turned out, Hal Newt had been too optimistic and the station manager, Al Buck, held it against him because his enthusiasm had made Buck lose face in New York.

Whatever sold margarine on the local news in Des Moines did not do the same thing in Chicago. Kay Davis, like the other starring faces on the local news, had a "book" that outlined her acceptability rating by the faceless public. Her book was a failure. Her book said men liked her but not in a sexy way—she came across as too cold and calculating. Women, on the other hand, found her too sexy for her own good. "If it was just reversed, we'd be looking at a whole different book," Hal Newt had said over lunch Friday. And Kay Davis had spent the weekend after that terrible lunch thinking bad thoughts.

Wally told her that a statue in the church was crying. She half-listened to him and stared across at Hal Newt and thought she would start screaming if she had to sit in the newsroom all morning.

And so she went to the church.

Two of the vans used by the news department—and dubbed "Actionmobiles"—were in the repair shop and a third had been dispatched to the Chicago Bears training camp in Lake Forest. So Kay Davis took a ride to the church in an ordinary car with Dick Lester, the technician with the camera and sound box. Dick Lester asked what kind of a story it was and Kay Davis said it probably wasn't a story at all. She just had to go someplace.

By the time they got to the church, Wally had gotten around to telling Father Hogan about the weeping statue. Frank Hogan had crossed the same courtyard from the rectory to the church and beheld the water stains on the plaster face of the Christ Child. When Wally told him about the lady from the television station coming to St. Margaret of Scotland, Frank Hogan was horrified.

He barred Dick Lester's camera from the church. "We can't have a circus going on here," he explained on the church steps, and when Dick Lester seemed intent on pushing the priest aside, Kay Davis intervened. She told Dick to wait and said she wanted to see the statue for herself. The priest, smiling at the pretty, familiar face of the TV reporter, asked her if she was a Catholic.

"Yes, Father," she lied and he let her into the church.

"You know the statue, of course," he said as he led her up the left-hand aisle to the side altar.

"Yes," she said.

"The Infant of Prague," he said. He looked worried. "The representation of the Christ Child as ruler of the world."

Wally stayed at the church door, instructed to keep Dick Lester out.

Kay Davis stared at the little plaster statue and saw the stains on the face. The Infant of Prague was a child dressed with lace cuffs and collar, holding an orb surmounted by a cross. The Child wore an ornate, bulbous, Eastern-style crown on his head. She stared at the statue and saw what she did not expect to see. She thought she saw tears at the eyes.

She blinked and did not speak.

"I thought it was the steam pipe, myself," Father Hogan said. "There doesn't appear to be a leak. But you have to be suspicious about these things. You know, something like this can reflect badly on the Church."

And on the priest who calls it a miracle, he thought.

A miracle, Kay Davis thought, thinking of Hal Newt and her bad book and the endless lunch last Friday at Arnie's. She had wanted to get drunk when Hal Newt explained about the book and about how it was probably his fault and that he had "rushed" her instead of "grooming" her acceptance by the public. As it was, she had polished off three very dry vodka martinis.

"This is wonderful," she said to Father Hogan.

"Well, it is certainly out of the ordinary," Father Hogan said.

"But it's wonderful," she said. "You have to let people see it."

"The church is open to all."

She shook her head. "No! I mean really see it. On television."

"That's where you would come in," he said.

"Why not, Father? I'm a Catholic," she said. And I need a miracle right now.

"I don't think . . . I think I need some advice on this. I better get in touch with the chancery office," he said. He thought about the Cardinal in that moment. The Cardinal was very big on social responsibility, racial justice, and the rights of the unborn. Somehow, he didn't see the Cardinal being overjoyed about a miracle at St. Margaret of Scotland Church. It was corny and flashy, something you might expect from one of those fundamentalists on television.

In the end, Dick Lester made do with shots of the exterior of St. Margaret and Kay Davis standing on the steps of the church explaining the miracle of the weeping statue. She also gave Wally fifteen seconds of fame on camera for being the person to discover the weeping statue. Father Hogan declined to be on camera because he was wearing his off-duty wardrobe, consisting of a green Izod shirt and yellow slacks.

It was just as well.

Kay Davis got a full sixty seconds on "News at Five," which perked her up. The station lost the segment for "News at Ten" but—miraculously, said a sly Dick Lester—it was revived and expanded into a ninety-second featurette on the morning news.

The Cardinal's liaison man was on the telephone to St. Margaret of Scotland rectory shortly after morning mass on Tuesday.

Had Father Hogan seen the news on television? asked the Cardinal's man.

Yes, the previous night, said Father Hogan.

Had he seen the statue itself? asked the Cardinal's man.

Yes, he had.

Well, what did he think of it?

Think of what? asked the parish priest.

The miracle, said the Cardinal's man.

Well, Father Hogan replied, it appeared there was a liquid-like substance to be seen on the face of the statue of the Infant of Prague.

And what part did Father Hogan have in alerting the news media to this phenomenon?

None at all, Father Hogan protested. He explained that

Wally the custodian had created the stir. He added that Wally was not even a Catholic, although that had not come out in the television report.

A silence lay between the chancery office and the rectory of St. Margaret's for a moment, and then Father Hogan had asked what he should do.

"Do what you think you should do," said the Cardinal's man.

"But can I get some guidance on this?" Father Hogan asked.

"In what way?" asked the Cardinal's man.

"Well, I was thinking, maybe the chancery could issue a statement," Father Hogan said.

The ball came smashing back to his own court: "The chancery was not even informed of the . . . phenomenon . . . until the Cardinal saw the news this morning on television."

So he watches TV news in the morning, Father Hogan thought. You'd think he'd have more important things to do than that.

"I certainly should have informed . . . someone," Father Hogan said.

"Well, that's water over the dam, isn't it?" the Cardinal's man said. "I think you're going to have to paddle in that stream by yourself for the time being, Father Hogan."

And that was that. Hogan heard the receiver click and said aloud, "In other words, it's up to me to twist slowly in the wind."

Kay Davis found Father Hogan kneeling on the side altar at ten in the morning. This time, Dick Lester was in the church behind her. He started shooting when he was less than ten feet from the altar and the bright TV lights announced his presence.

Father Hogan jumped down from the altar and the sound echoed through the damp, dimly lit church. At that moment, Dick Lester flicked the light bar off. "Too dark," he complained. "Can you turn the lights on, Father?"

"I can not turn the lights on," Father Hogan said. "What are you doing in my church with that camera?"

Kay Davis pushed her thin body between the two large men and touched Father Hogan's chest. The touch arrested him. He was among the minority of men represented in her book who would have said they found Kay Davis sexy in a kittenlike way. She had a wet-lipped smile and natural teeth that were so perfect they looked capped.

"Father, we really came back because this is a story that has to be told, a story of faith and hope," she said.

"Well, people can go someplace else for their faith and hope," Father Hogan said. "I'm not ready to be pushed around by the news media. I just got a call from someone at the Sun-Times, and for all I know this is going to be going on all day. I don't have time for this. You want to do something about St. Margaret's, why don't you write a story about how we need a new roof here on the church? Or the Ramirez girl over in the school, who won the northwest division spelling bee last year. Now that's good news."

"Father, you can't turn your back on a miracle," Kay Davis said in that very soft and sure voice that women in her book found so annoying.

"Maybe I can get a tight shot," Dick Lester said.

"Get outta my church," boomed Frank Hogan, and he pushed Kay aside and went for Dick Lester. With a cameraman's instinct, Lester flicked the light bar on and blinded the priest for a moment.

"Don't fight in church," Kay Davis said.

The two men paused and considered it. Frank Hogan's face was flushed.

He had tried to contact his rabbi at the chancery office after getting the call from the Cardinal's man, but he didn't get an answer. His rabbi had watched out for Hogan's interests downtown for a dozen years, from his first parish, Our Lady of God on the southwest side. St. Margaret's, while not a rich parish, was a step up the ladder of success. If Hogan didn't stumble here, he could look forward to getting a nice fat north suburban parish in a year or two. Which is why the weeping statue appeared to be more than a simple glitch in his plans. He had returned to the church that morning to see if there was some reasonable explanation for the stained, watery face. He had found none and uttered a heartfelt prayer: "Why are You doing this to me?"

"Father," Kay Davis said. "If you don't let us film the statue, someone else will. Some newspaper photographer will get in here or something. You can't keep the church locked—"

"I *can* keep the church locked," Hogan said. "And open it up for morning mass and put a couple of the parish men on the doors to make sure no one with cameras comes inside." He formed the plan as he said it.

"That's crazy," Dick Lester said. And it was, but it worked to keep cameras away from St. Margaret's one more day.

Which, in turn, led to a media frenzy to get inside the church and photograph the statue of the Christ Child.

On Tuesday night, Kay Davis described her own religious experience in witnessing the miracle of the weeping statue. To make up for a lack of graphics, Kay purchased a statue of the Infant of Prague in a religious supply store on the edge of the Loop, and the art department came up with a ten-second film clip of the city of Prague. She got a full sixty seconds both at Five and Ten and was interviewed by a stringer from *People* magazine. Suddenly, she was getting very hot and the memory of that painful Friday luncheon with Hal Newt began to fade.

"I didn't know you were a Catholic," Dick Lester said after watching the tape on the monitor.

"For years," Kay Davis said and never even thought of it as a lie.

Father Hogan got to his rabbi late Tuesday, just after the "News at Five" segment. He felt besieged in his rectory. Two photographers were sitting in unmarked cars across the street and the police department had dispatched a tactical car to keep a watch over the watchers.

"Get a friend in the media," his rabbi said in his close-to-the-receiver telephone voice. "You can't keep the lid on it by pretending it isn't happening. We're not in the Middle Ages, for Pete's sake. The Old Man is pissed off when stuff like this happens. He thinks you're hotdogging. He doesn't like hot dogs."

"I swear to God, Charlie, I don't want this any more than he does."

"Then lose it," said the rabbi.

"How do I lose it? I got the church locked and I got two of the men from the Holy Name Society said they would guard the doors tomorrow."

"This isn't Poland, Frank," the rabbi said. "You don't want guards around the church. I tell you, if I didn't know you better, I'd swear you were milking this. Why didn't you just get rid of the statue?"

"It's bolted down," Frank said.

"Unbolt it," said Charlie.

"I can't and I can't find Wally. I got pretty steamed up at him yesterday and I think he's taking a couple of days off to sulk."

"Get a friend in the media, Frank," said the older man.

"Get someone who is going to be reverent and solemn and all that. Don't make this look like it was put on by Baptists. Do the best you can."

Do the best you can. It was miserable advice, Frank Hogan thought sitting in his office in the rectory. He could smell Mrs. Clements' cooking from there. Corned beef hash again. He hated corned beef hash and she never failed to serve it on a day he really needed a lift from supper.

After supper, he called Monsignor Foley, the former pastor of St. Margaret's, who was now retired in Clearwater, Florida. He had to know about the statue in order to learn what to do next.

"I don't really recall." Foley chuckled on the phone. "We probably got it from some grateful old Bohemian who got his prayers answered. Used to have a lot of Bohunks at Maggie's. But I can't recall getting it, so it must have been there before my time. So you got a miracle on your hands, is that it, Frank?"

"On my hands is a good way of putting it. And the statue is bolted to the altar and I can't find Wally and you know me and tools."

"Clumsiest priest I've ever seen," Foley said. "Couldn't even take to golf."

"And the Cardinal is on my case about it," Frank Hogan said sadly, thinking of the corned beef growling in his stomach.

"Yeah, that's Bernie for you," Foley said. "He's gotten so very serious in the last couple of years, I think he's running for Pope. It's all those commissions he puts himself on. Me, I never was much for politics, especially church politics. They wanted me down in the chancery office at one time, but I was satisfied with Maggie's and taking the afternoon off for a round at Fresh Meadows. I can golf every day down here, you know. Maggie's suited me fine and I saw no point in giving it up to be a paper shuffler down at the chancery office. It was a big surprise when Cody made me monsignor, I never asked for it.''

God, Foley could ramble on and pretend he wasn't the slyest fox in the forest, Frank Hogan thought. Well, Frank Hogan wasn't going to be buried in Maggie's if he could help it.

The new line of action came to Frank Hogan after morning mass on Wednesday. The two ushers at the door had politely restrained the photographers; the children had been suitably impressed by the publicity. In fact, a number of their parents had come to mass that morning along with the children. All the people along with the news photographers and cameramen on the steps made it seem quite festive.

They locked the doors after mass and Hogan prowled the church grounds looking for someone in particular. When he saw Kay Davis alight from the white Actionmobile, he signaled to her and they both ducked into a side door of the church.

"I need your help," he began.

"Anything," she said. Her voice was husky. She could smell the aura of defeat about Frank Hogan. She would have to be very tough on him.

"The last thing we want is this to turn into a circus," he said.

"That's what it's turning into though, isn't it?" she said.

"I saw your report on the television news last night. I was quite struck by your speech there about how the apparent miracle of the weeping statue had affected you."

She saw the way it was. She lowered her eyes. "It was a personal experience for me. It was very moving."

"Yes," said Frank Hogan. "I didn't realize it at the

time when I was getting ready to kick out your cameraman."

"Father, can I make a confession?"

"Now?" Hogan said, raising his eyebrows. "It doesn't seem to be the time or place."

"No. I mean, I want to tell you something. I haven't been the best Catholic these last few years, but something about what happened here—what *is* happening here—has touched me."

"Well, that's why I wanted to talk to you. If we're going to have a miracle on our hands, I want it to be done right. I think I can get you your pictures if you can promise me that St. Margaret's Church comes out in a good light on this. I mean, we don't want this to be a freak show like that fellow on television who goes around curing people. We don't need a Lourdes here, is what I'm saying. This is just . . . well, like you put it, a religious experience. And I wish you would give credit to the Cardinal in this."

"Why the Cardinal?" she said.

Didn't the woman understand a damned thing? Frank Hogan thought. But he saw she didn't and tried another tack.

"What I'm saying here, Miss Davis, is that I can give your photo . . . opportunity, I guess they call it, if you would be willing to do me the favor of getting to the Cardinal on this and giving credit to the man and kind of . . . well . . ."

"Putting it on him," she said.

"In a manner of speaking," said Hogan.

"Then let's say that's what we'll do," she said.

"Can you guarantee it?" he said.

"Absolutely," she lied. Her eyes were bright and honest. She wore White Shoulders cologne and a Bill Blass silk blouse. She stood very close.

"Is the statue . . . is the Child . . . still weeping?"

"Yes," Hogan said in a sad, small voice. "There's stains on the collar now and the gown itself."

"Can you turn up the church lights?" she asked.

"Sure," he said in the same forlorn voice.

"Could we get a shot of you kneeling at the altar?"

Sure, he thought. It was why he wore his cassock today. And the celluloid white collar. He felt absolutely miserable and it wasn't just last night's corned beef hash. He had the feeling of something bad about to happen and being unable to do anything about it.

Her name was Anna Jelinak and she said she loved Chicago.

Previously, she had said she loved New York and Boston and Cleveland. In a little while, she was scheduled to love Kansas City, Phoenix, Los Angeles, and San Francisco.

When she said she loved Chicago, she was sitting on a stage in a television studio full of large women who clapped at her answer to the generic question: What do you think of America?

Anna Jelinak was a very beautiful fourteen-year-old from the city of Prague in Czechoslovakia. She was on a three-week publicity tour in the United States stressing the charm of Czech life, the beauty of its old cities, the culture of its museums, and the exciting world of motion pictures scheduled to be filmed in her native country. She, herself, was a motion-picture star in Czechoslovakia. She had appeared in two typical Czech films about small-town life and in one very long and gloomy French film which no one understood and which had won a major prize at the Cannes Film Festival the previous summer.

When Anna said, "I love Chicago," she sounded a little

like Greta Garbo and looked very much, as *Time* magazine had noted, like a "Pragueish Judy Garland."

Now in the studio, the black television hostess was dancing about her one moment and darting to the audience the next, establishing the repartee she was noted for. She was a large woman who carried a microphone in one hand and a trailing cord in the other, and she seemed to float when she moved, as though her feet were wheels under her long dress. Her hands fluttered with practiced gestures as she indicated first this and then that person was to speak to Anna Jelinak.

"What about pornography? What do we know about porn in Prague?" the hostess suddenly demanded and Anna sat very straight in her chair on the stage and stared at her. She had a good command of English and she had understood all the words, but they did not make any sense to her.

"You're in movies, what about sex in movies, in books, in magazines? In other words, how open is Prague today to Western values and Western morals?"

For the second time, Anna Jelinak answered with a blink of her pretty black eyes. What was this woman saying?

The hostess machine-gunned some more words at her and Anna finally caught a few. She blushed and put her hand to her mouth and a few women in the large audience tittered behind the smiling hostess.

"If there is such in my country or my city, I do not know of it," she said. Her voice was deep, and the way she carried the foreign words, they made a nice lilt. "In my country, I think it must be, children are permitted not to see the evil in the world. They are allowed to be children still."

Applause burst from the audience and the hostess flashed

her famous smile and Anna felt comforted by the applause. She craved applause which made her a good actress; she was warmed by the sounds of many hands clapping, even the applause of stagehands on a movie set. Most of the time she felt alone and frightened, but there was always the moment of applause when she was secure.

"Children should be allowed to be children," the hostess was saying. "What about us, Anna? What you've seen of America so far, do you think we exploit our children? Do you think we have become a permissive society?"

"Well, I think it is a good thing so many children can afford to have blue jeans," Anna said. Waves of laughter and more warm applause. She had won their hearts and she knew it. The Ministry for Tourism and Films would be pleased; Anton Huss, her temporary guardian in the U.S., would be pleased; even the sour old woman who pretended to be her mother in Prague would be pleased. It was a form of sweet revenge to be loved by these strangers.

She looked around the studio at the audience, her vision limited by the intensity of the arc lights that brightened the stage. Beyond the lights, behind the phalanx of cameras and booms, Anton Huss stood and watched her. He was a precise man who wore wool blue suits and starched white shirts. His clothes were cut in the European manner and he wore his hair a little longer than Americans did at that time. His sallow skin framed large, green eyes and he had an air of sadness and a little mystery about him. He listened carefully to all that Anna Jelinak said because there would be reports filed and evaluations made and questions asked, all the way up to the office of the Minister. He did not want this assignment any more than Anna wanted him as a guardian.

He was liaison at the embassy in Washington between the Secret Service and the other branches of the diplomatic mission. Essentially, the Czech mission was concerned with tourism, trade and espionage, but since everything is the province of espionage, Anton Huss made certain that his speciality was not overlooked by the other branches as they went about more mundane matters.

There are no mundane matters, the Deputy Secretary of the embassy had once told him: All espionage is the light of intelligence brought to examine what appears to be ordinary. In that special light, said the pompous Deputy Secretary, all that is ordinary is revealed to be something more than it seems to be.

Anton Huss shook his head at the memory of the aphorisms of the Deputy Secretary. He endured them just as he endured this foolish assignment, to guard Anna Jelinak as she toured the United States on behalf of promoting tourism and the Czech film industry. Guard her from what? She was a good enough actress to get her way around any difficult situation.

At first, in New York, where they stayed in separate rooms at the Plaza Hotel, Anton Huss was afraid Anna was practicing feminine wiles on him. She flirted her way through a long lunch and Anton's spirits had sunk. Was it going to be this bad through the whole tour? But no: Anna was just practicing, he decided after a while. She had no interest in Anton. She was merely a professional actress and she wanted Anton to love her because he was there. He decided to feign affection in a friendly avuncular way, and an amazing thing happened: Anna froze suddenly, her black eyes went cold. She said in her clear, precise Prague accent, "You do not like me. Very well, then. We can proceed on that basis and have as little to do with one another as is possible."

What did that mean? Anton Huss had thought. What complicated thought lay behind her sudden shifts in mood?

The Deputy Secretary would tell him to bring the light of intelligence to the subject to see it better. But then, the Deputy Secretary was an idiot.

Before Anton left Washington and the lovely, lingering autumn full of pretty leaves and pretty girls, he was given one final charge by the Deputy Secretary: "Remember, security is to be provided both ways. Anna Jelinak is a very important person to us, to the country, and it would not be the first time the CIA would attempt to subvert some . . . honest opening between our country and the United States . . . to purposes that were . . . well . . ."

Anton Huss understood the old man even before he finished. Defections. The Czechs had a sorry record in the department of defections. Sometimes it seemed Prague had a mission to train tennis stars who would mature into American refugees. No mistakes, Anton Huss: Make certain Anna does not let the light of apparent freedom blind Anna to her duties to the fatherland.

More applause, and it pushed his gloomy thoughts out of mind. Anton took a step forward and was boxed between two cameras. Anna was smiling and the black woman was smiling and he guessed this program was over. It was hard to be certain because this television business seemed a matter of stops and starts. There were so many times when the people onstage would not be on camera and the men in shirt sleeves would run around and tear pieces of paper from their pads or talk and joke with each other or just stand transfixed, listening to voices through earphones. It was maddening, he said to Anna. She had laughed at him and said, "You should see the way it is making films."

Yes, it was truly over. As always, Anton Huss stepped forward and put his hand in Anna's hand as though by renewing the physical contact he reminded her of who she was and what reality was. Reality was Prague, control, orders; it was difficult in the chaos of this vast, sprawling country to assert reality.

The cameramen stepped from behind the cameras and one of them smiled at Anna and said something in colloquial Bohemian that brightened her face. Anton looked suspiciously at him. It would be like the CIA to plant an agent provocateur as a cameraman. They had to hurry along in any case. He tugged her hand. She glanced up at him. "One more program, Anna," he said. "We have to hurry."

"I'm so tired," she said.

"One more and then we catch the airplane—"

"I'm so tired," she said again. They were treading their way through snakes of cables and the apparatus of backstage. "Can't we cancel this?"

But Anton Huss was a man of duty. The schedule must be obeyed. Even Anna knew that.

Hal Newt said, "This is fine, this is fine, Kay. Look at the light level. Dick does good picture. And this is ours? I mean, this is all ours exclusively?"

"Ours and that includes the newspapers, at least until tomorrow morning. The priest is in a bind, the way I told you." Her face was flushed. At the last minute, she had thought she wouldn't get the Cardinal at all, but he had done a nice little sit-down about faith moving mountains and some other blah-blah-blah. Kay Davis had worked her ass off on this and it showed. And she noticed Hal Newt wasn't talking about "book" and "public perception" and "grooming" and all the other bullshit he threw at her at Arnie's last Friday.

"Fine, fine," Hal Newt said, watching the monitor unroll the tape. They were sitting side by side in the control booth. Below, on the set of "News at Five"—the same as "News at Ten" except the cardboard skyline of the city was moonlit on "News at Ten"—Dr. Winkle the weatherman was sticking rainclouds over Minnesota and northern Wisconsin and otherwise preparing his map.

They had gone over the tape twice and Hal Newt had asked the serious questions that Kay knew the answers to. And they kept going back to the big scene, the one that made it all worthwhile. The whole town was talking about a statue that wept in a Catholic church on the northwest side—but no one except for a few who had gone to mass in the morning had actually seen the miracle.

"There," Kay Davis said.

They froze the tape.

"There and there," she said, tapping the monitor.

"It's clear, but you have to say what it is," Hal Newt said.

"Tears," she said. "Tears on the face of the Christ Child."

"I just wish it stood out more. Had more . . . you know . . . drama."

Kay Davis sighed. It was always like this. The inside people never understood a fucking thing. Stand on your head, balance thirty-two bottles of champagne, interview the President in his underwear, and you bring it back and shrink it down to twenty-one diagonal inches on videotape and someone says he wished it was more dramatic. Fuck them.

"You expected blood, Hal? I told you it was a crying statue, not a bleeding one."

"Well, just so we make it clear what we're seeing. Tell them what it is."

"Do a freeze-frame," she said. "Freeze it and blow it up so they understand what they're seeing."

"We want dignity though," Hal was saying. "No Geraldo Rivera on this, we got to keep it from turning into a circus.''

Kay Davis didn't say a thing. She was riding a good high and Hal couldn't bring her down from it. It's the high from being inside on a story, making the news instead of running after it. He couldn't bring her down from that.

"Other problem is time. We got eighty-seven seconds here and I can't figure where to cut. Let's lose the Cardinal,'' Hal said.

"I promised—''

"What?''

"The priest. Hogan. He's in a box on this. I think he thinks the church might think he was hotdogging on this miracle thing and I promised him I would slice in the Cardinal so that it looks more . . . well, like you said, dignified.''

"We've got to get this down to fifty-five moving and five seconds on the freeze frame.''

"It's 'News at Five,' Hal, not 'World News Tonight.' It's worth it, Hal.''

"Honey, the end of World War Two isn't worth eighty-seven seconds. People lose their concentration. You can't beat them over the head with this.''

"Hal, this is Chicago, a very big Catholic city, very religious.''

"Gimme a break, Kay,'' Hal said. "But maybe I'll talk downstairs with Big Tuna, see what we can work out.''

Kay felt chilled. Big Tuna was the Man, the Voice, the Presence, the $900,000 salary. He was Tom Day, smoked a pipe and boomed the news. No event happened until Tom Day said it had. Tom Day might just be able to give eighty-seven seconds—if he could worm his way into the story.

Kay got up then and walked up the stairs out the back of the control booth into the concrete-block hallway that led to the dressing rooms and Studio B. Here they taped all the public-service programs like the Sunday-morning winner "Leap of Faith," which involved religious discussions with aerobic exercises. Dick Lester was coming out of the tape room. He smiled at Kay. "What do they think?"

"Hal said you do good picture."

"I'm thrilled," Dick Lester said. "Are they going to freeze-frame the tears?"

"Yes. I think so." She felt distracted. It was a good story but now Big Tuna was going to worm his way into it.

"What did you think? I never asked you," Dick said.

"About what?"

"The statue," he said.

"What about it?"

"What about the tears? I mean, I've been thinking about it. You get these weird things sometimes, like that barn in Ohio where someone said he saw Christ on it. I mean, I was there and that statue was crying."

"Oh, come on, Dick."

"I looked all around—"

"Look, Dick. The roof leaks or something or there's undried wood under the plaster or something. Statues don't cry."

Dick flushed. "I know that. But I know what I saw. So what did I see?"

Kay Davis tried a bright, smart smile, the one that made men think she was just a bit too cool and too damned competent and was the reason she was not on her way to New York and might very well be going back to Iowa.

"You saw sixty seconds on 'News at Five' and, if we get lucky, a slot on the national news tomorrow night. That's what you saw, Dick."

Tom Day boomed: "Prague is in the news tonight."

Kay Davis, sitting to his right, nearly groaned. Only Big Tuna would make a connection like that.

The child sat between them in the guest chair on the set. The set was called The Bridge by nearly everyone because it was designed to look like the bridge of the Starship Enterprise. In the middle of the bridge was Anna Jelinak, a child star from Czechoslovakia. Tom Day, in his typically idiotic way, was connecting the girl from Prague with Kay's story of a weeping statue.

Tom Day was doing more than that and it made Kay furious beneath her Number 2 coat of pancake makeup. It broke all the rules: Tom was leading into her story and giving it away.

"And just how did you manage to get this remarkable film, Kay?"

He still said "film" instead of "tape." He even believed in the coaxial cable and thought instant replay was magic.

Kay was not prepared for the question and pushed it aside. "Tom," she ad-libbed, "this is an extraordinary story of a statue that apparently weeps, the statue of the Christ Child called the Infant of Prague. As you know, I've been the first person to see the statue and now I have tape tonight so that you can see what I've seen and judge for yourself."

Take that, asshole, she thought. Hal Newt was slicing his hand across his throat in the control booth and squeaking into Tom Day's earpiece, "Cut it, cut it, cut it, she's running over."

But the tape was running now.

Between the two newsreaders, Anna Jelinak sat still and watched the monitor off camera at the side of the set. The monitor flashed a shot of St. Margaret of Scotland and then cut to Kay Davis inside the church and then to a statue.

Anna Jelinak was very tired now but the English word "Prague" for her native *Praha* had alerted her. What was about *Praha* on the television?

They all saw the statue.

The camera pulled in and the tight shot filled the twenty-one-inch monitor with the plaster face and small blue eyes and the cherubic cheeklines. On the face were depicted tears. The camera froze and Kay's voice was soft: "The statue is weeping. That is what hundreds who have seen it now believe. As the Cardinal said, 'Perhaps it is a sign; perhaps it is an act of faith.' Whatever it is, it is a moving experience."

Anna absorbed the English words and a flood of memory. There had been such a statue in the little hall off the dining room. There had been smells of cooking and a strange man sitting at the table, talking in a soft voice, talking to the woman who said she was her mother. Anna knew she was an orphan, that her real parents were dead, that she had been raised by this sad, drunk withered woman and that the strange man would come to their rooms in the Little Quarter and drink brandy and talk and talk and talk. The statue was on the sideboard. The statue did not weep. The statue was her friend when she could speak to no one else. She would whisper to the statue, "I am an orphan and no one loves me." The statue would not speak to her. The statue was Christ in her heart. I am an orphan and unloved, she told Christ.

And Christ wept.

The monitor was frozen on the face of the weeping Child. For a moment, the rule about no silence on television was broken. Even Tom Day fell speechless. They all stared at the monitor. They saw the frozen tears on the frozen face. And then, slowly, the tape lurched from frame to frame in slow motion and they saw a tear slide down the cheek.

Then Anna Jelinak spoke. Curiously, she spoke in English.

"My God, oh my God," she cried.

Kay turned suddenly. Hal Newt barked into the microphone and his voice sounded tinny in Tom Day's ear. Tom Day tried to hear the voice and see who had spoken. It wasn't in the TelePrompTer script.

Anna stood straight up as though she had touched an electrical outlet.

"God!" she cried, her black eyes wide. She began to tremble. "This is a miracle!"

Hal Newt was screaming in the control booth: "Two, get me in close. Tight, tight. One, stand by. One, pan. Two, pull back, get me Tom's react. Tom, for Christ's sake, grab the kid, she's hysterical. Two, get me Kay, Tom is frozen out there—"

Kay touched Anna and felt cold flesh. How could she be so cold in this place?

"Anna," she said.

Anna turned and then said, "It is Christ."

Kay opened her arms. It wasn't for show, it was just a woman's instinct. She pulled the child into her grasp and held the cold, trembling body next to her. "It's all right."

But Anna shook her head and there were tears in her

eyes. "My mother is dead and my father and I am alone in the world and only Christ weeps for me." She said this in a flat, stubborn English voice.

And then Hal Newt saw Anton Huss at the edge of the set. Anton took a step forward and Hal said, "Number Three, catch the guy, get some lights on him. He's the goon who brought her here and killed her parents—"

Tom Day, still befuddled, caught the direction on his earpiece. He turned to see Anton Huss and shouted, "Murderer!"

Anton Huss stopped.

Camera Three came in close, the lights blinding him. He held up his hand.

Anna began to scream, pointing at him.

"Murderer," Tom Day intoned. Later, he couldn't explain why he came up with that particular word.

"Three, keep blocking the goon, good, good, and Two—"

Anton Huss felt the heat of the lights on his face and stepped forward, stumbling over a cable that pitched him to the edge of the desk on the set. Tom Day shrank back and Anton reached across the desk for Anna's hand. If only he could touch her, to make it real again for her, to let her see that this was all just illusion—

Kay pushed his hand away.

Without thinking, Anton Huss slapped her very hard across the face.

Kay Davis punched him then square on the nose. It was not such a terrible blow but it hurt.

And Dick Lester, with the mind of a cameraman running interference through a mob of other cameramen, leaped onto Anton's back and pounded him on the head.

Anton stumbled again and fell.

Kay was standing, the child clinging to her. Anna was

sobbing into her breast. Number Two camera focused and pulled it in tight. Two got Kay Davis stroking Anna's hair. Two got Anna's tears. Two got it all.

Tom Day said, "A miracle, we are seeing a miracle right here on live television."

And that, it seemed, was what it was.

THREE
Miki's Train

I t had rained because it always rains in Brussels. The cobblestones of the large square called *La Grand Place* glistened in the yellow lights of the ornate streetlamps. The moon danced in and out of the clouds scudding across the night sky.

All the lights were on in the baroque city hall that dominated the south side of the square. The party was not sponsored by the city, but the city was glad to host it because so many famous people had come together. There were film stars from America and Britain and France, and even the Russian director and his entourage who had spent the morning trying to convince a Flemish banking consortium that the Soviet version of *Huckleberry Finn* would find a ready worldwide audience. The hall was a glittering place tonight full of glittering people. And at the center of things, as usual, was the bright star called Miki.

Everyone knew Miki, even the Hollywood actress with

the sullen lips and spaced-out eyes who pretended not to know anyone. Miki was Miki, or he was "darling Miki" and "Miki dearest," and he was going to receive an award tonight from the international film community for all he had done for them.

He pushed through the glittering crowd and offered his lips to this cheek or that. Miki was reserved, a man of small delicate gestures in an arm-waving community. He seemed to smile just for you and listened to just your words. Miki understood things, as so many actresses put it. He had light brown hair and wore a leather coat and a silk shirt and a gold chain around his neck. It was not the usual ensemble of the Prague bureaucrat. But then, as Miki himself would have pointed out, he was special.

"I can arrange that perhaps," was Miki's most useful line. He could arrange discreet amounts of cocaine for the doped-out American television star making a spy movie in Prague. Or he could find very young girls from Hungary for the important film director who relaxed off camera with Johnny Walker Black Label, a large waterbed and hookers who pretended to be virgins. Not that Miki was a pimp; he was an impresario and a procurer to the stars.

The Czech Philharmonic was a triumph in America and that was because of Miki. And when the latest tennis star defected to the extreme annoyance of the Minister of Sports, it was Miki who smoothed things over by arranging an international tennis exhibition in Prague featuring all past Czech tennis stars who were now honorary Americans. This graceful acceptance of individual decisions to defect prompted *Newsweek* to do an admiring piece on Miki and his policy of "turning the other Czech."

"Miki, when can I make a movie again in Prague?" called the fruity-voiced producer from halfway across the room.

Miki turned, smiled, gathered his audience. "My dear man, you must go to Prague tonight, do not waste a single moment. Prague is empty, the stage set of the world, waiting for all you dear people to give it life."

Of course it was unbelievably humble of Miki to say such a thing, and no one in the Ministry of Tourism and Films would have permitted such an insult to Praha, but Miki knew his audience and knew just what to say. They laughed, they tittered, they accepted his gracious humility. They were rich people who did not notice the servants who removed the dishes but would certainly notice the servants who didn't.

Of course, Miki always thought, I am your servant, your pet, your little monkey, your pimp and your slave. Of course, I am whatever is useful to you.

The marvelous thing was that he never showed contempt, even in private moments. He watched, he saw everything, he knew secrets contained in secrets, and that was enough satisfaction for him.

And it would be enough tonight to know that in less than an hour, Miki would disappear from the face of the earth and that would frighten some people almost to death.

Nearly one hundred yards north of the city hall was a three-story building attached to a four-story structure next door. The facade of the building carried a date in ornate stone script: 1706. In three centuries of life, it had been many things, including a nineteenth-century version of a French-speaking Hellfire Club. During the Nazi occupation, the building had slipped into the hands of collaborators and was used as a club and whorehouse by German staff officers. Now it was simply a tavern that opened each evening at six and closed each morning at dawn. It was a place for men who made contacts. Many of the men were important.

The first floor held the narrow bar and a couple of tables, and Philip the manager worked the place. The second floor also held tables but was empty. The third floor was a large, empty room and a man stood there by the single narrow window.

Devereaux looked down at the square. He was barely visible at the window. He was dressed in black—black raincoat, black trousers, black turtleneck sweater. He wore a navy-blue watch cap on his head. Even the pistol in his belt was fashioned of dark steel and did not reflect the light.

Devereaux listened to the steps on the stairs and counted them. He had counted all the stairs in the narrow building and examined the garage beneath the first floor, and even then he had not been satisfied with the arrangement. He was the reluctant agent of R Section and he had been with Section too long to trust what Hanley said or even what Hanley implied by saying nothing.

The door opened and light burst into the room. Then it closed again.

Philip said, "Everything is set. He made the signal."

Devereaux did not speak. The train had been set up without him. He was the conductor because he was the man from R Section and that made him in charge. But Devereaux felt out of control. His status in R Section had evolved in the last couple of years and it was something he could live with: He was the outside man, kept on payroll and maintained in the records but only called in when the problem required a solution out of channels. That's the way Hanley put it in bureaucratese: Out of channels. But what was so special about conducting a defector to the

American side? Why involve him? Hanley had not answered and Devereaux had known from that moment in
the cathedral at Chartres that the matter was more important
than it seemed.

"Did the driver show up?"

"He's in the cellar garage, everything is ready. The
passenger should disappear in the next fifteen minutes."

Devereaux frowned in the darkness. Everything like
clockwork. As though none of it was real. He had worked
with independent contractors before and he never trusted
any of them.

"Don't be nervous," Philip said and almost giggled.
He was young with a pointed nose designed for a thinner
man set between two fat cheeks. He annoyed Devereaux
and knew it.

"We could have handled this ourselves, you know,"
Philip went on. "We do lots of work for lots of people.
We've done work for the CIA."

"You talk too much," Devereaux said.

"Just so you understand we know what we're doing, we
do lots of work for lots of people. I don't know if you've
done this kind of thing, but it's a piece of cake once our
passenger makes his departure. It's all up to him, you see.
He's got to make the first move, you might say."

"You still talk too much," Devereaux said.

Philip wiped at his lips and tried a smile. He wanted to
push it in a little more. "You don't speak French very
well, you know that? I mean, from your accent, you could
tell you were an American."

"Or just an ordinary Belgique trying to pass for a Nor-
man," Devereaux said. It was a nasty French slur.

Philip flushed then. "Next time, I hope they send someone else."

Devereaux turned. He stared at the square. He was tired

of Philip and the waiting. It was always a matter of waiting, even when you didn't know if anything at all would happen.

"You didn't have to be unfriendly. In the beginning, I mean," Philip went on. "You don't like homosexuals, is that it?"

Devereaux saw the moon on the square. It was a lovely square and a little sad in the moonlight.

"You didn't have to be unfriendly."

But Devereaux was watching now. There. Across the square. The man in the raincoat was walking very slowly, as though he were out for an evening's stroll. The square was empty because of the rain. Suddenly, a car flashed its high beams on the square and came around the corner from the direction of the Amigo Hotel. The lights picked up the pedestrian.

Devereaux removed the pistol from his belt. It was the weapon he had insisted on, a modified version of the Colt Python .357 with a skeleton handle and other alterations to lighten the weight. The ordinary Python was over three pounds but his version was less than two pounds. He had lost a little accuracy in making the conversions, but the reliability of the revolver and the devastating stopping power of the ammunition were what he wanted. All the people in hardware at Section insisted he should use a lighter, more sophisticated weapon, like the new Italian .9-millimeter automatic. He thought they were wrong.

The car's headlights swept the pedestrian but he did not turn to look at the lights. The car squealed around the square and the walking man was left in the dim light of lampposts again. He had a lot of guts, Devereaux thought. Or maybe it was all just theatrical to him, maybe he knew how to make entrances and exits.

And disappearances.

"He's here," Devereaux said as the man approached the building. Philip pulled at his long nose, turned, opened the door and started down the stairs.

Devereaux swept the square with the barrel of his gun. No one. The center of Brussels was all baroque emptiness. It began to rain again, softly as it always rains in Belgium, and the rain polished the cobblestones beneath the lamp lights.

The door opened on the third floor.

Miki blinked, stepped into the dark room. Philip was behind him. They couldn't see the third man.

Devereaux, in darkness, said, "Leave the door open, Philip. I want his pockets turned inside out."

"Who the hell are you?" said Miki.

"The Man," Devereaux said. He held the pistol. In the light now, they could see the pistol.

Miki turned out his pockets. He had a wad of mixed Belgian francs and Czech kovnas and a gold box of cigarettes with a matching lighter.

"Spread your legs, Miki, on the floor please. Hands above your head."

Miki stared at the darkness. He could begin to see the shape of the man who held the gun. He got down on the dusty floor and spread his legs and put his hands above his head.

"This isn't necessary," Miki said.

Devereaux stepped out from the shadows and pressed the pistol against Miki's ear. He started with each arm from the wrist down to the shoulder. He felt along the leather jacket. He patted down the length of each leg from crotch to ankle.

"How does he feel to you?" Philip said in French.

Devereaux stood up. "All right, Mikita."

"Miki. Everyone calls me Miki. Who are you?"

"Just The Man," Devereaux said. "We won't need you, Philip. Go back down."

"I was supposed to lead you to the garage—"

"Change of plans," Devereaux said. "Good night, sweetheart." This last was in English. Philip stared and mostly he saw the gun. He turned to the door.

Devereaux lifted the trap door. The trap door was cut irregularly into the planking on the third floor. Beneath the door was a set of wooden steps. There were thirty-nine steps which led down between a false wall of the club and the wall of the building next door. It was not the only secret of the ancient building. It had been added just after the First War.

"Go first, Miki," Devereaux said.

"It's dark."

"Yes. Try not to fall."

Devereaux closed the trap above him. He had a pencil-sized flashlight that broke the darkness of the stairwell. The well was small, enclosed. The walls pressed in, the ceiling was too low. They went down the steps as cautiously as old men.

"Open the door."

They were in a cellar that had the stale, damp odor of all old cellars. They could hear the click-click-click squealing of rats. Devereaux blinked the pencil light three times and they both heard the roar of the motor before they saw the car.

The headlamps of the Mercedes 560 flashed on the garage door that led up to the street. The driver was inside.

"Go ahead," Devereaux said. Miki moved to the car, opened the front door.

"Back seat," Devereaux said. He held the light and the pistol on the driver.

The driver did not look at him.

"Get out," Devereaux said.

The driver started to turn off the ignition.

"Leave the motor running. Get out."

The driver wore a chauffeur's cap and a black raincoat. He got out of the front seat and stared at Devereaux. He had a white face and a broken nose and a wide, thin mouth.

"Hands on the roof, spread your legs," Devereaux said.

The driver followed the instructions and Devereaux went over his body. When he found the pistol, he was not very surprised.

It was a .22 automatic, probably a Spanish-made knock-off of a Smith & Wesson. It was a gut-shooter's pistol. Devereaux put it in his pocket.

"I always carry a pistol on a job," the driver said.

"Not tonight."

"I always figure on something going wrong."

"Is something going to go wrong?"

"It never has but you have to be ready. Can I stand up straight now?"

"Sure. Get in the car. Turn the headlights off until we're in the street."

"It might be dangerous coming up without lights into the street."

"Take the chance," Devereaux said.

"It's your party," the driver said.

Devereaux settled in the backseat next to Miki. Miki lit a cigarette from his case and blew the smoke against the side window. The driver pushed the car into low gear and started up the ramp to the street. In the street, he flicked on the headlamps and pulled into the square. The square was still empty and Miki had now disappeared without anyone knowing it.

"I feel so strange," Miki said softly. "I feel as though I have stepped on the other side of my own death."

Devereaux stared out the windows. Now and then, he would look behind him. There was nothing following them. The weeknight streets were nearly deserted. They drove up past the Bourse and along the line of fashionable shops that reached up the hill to the edge of the Ghent road. Baroque old Brussels, crammed with odd buildings and the neon lights of American franchise hamburger stands, appeared solemn and dull.

"Where do we go now?" Miki said.

"Zeebrugge," said the driver. Devereaux said nothing. He watched the streets and kept his hand on the pistol.

"You know what I was? Back there?"

Devereaux turned to Miki. He had no interest in the other man but sometimes they had to talk, they had to make a friend at the point of defection when they left everything behind. Until the moment came, defection seemed one-way, a looking glass that led into a new wonderland of freedom. But there was always the naked moment when they had to step through the looking glass and leave that other, real world behind forever.

"I was invisible and they wanted to give me an award for my invisibility," Miki said. "I was the arranger and they all told me their secrets in the end, all the dirty little secrets that no one would be terribly interested in at all. I could tell you about a woman who makes love to her dog, a woman you would not believe this of in a million years. Do you suppose I wish to know that secret? But they all tell me everything. Because I am no more important to them than a servant. I am there to dress them, wash them, feed them. I arrange their beautiful lives for them. And not only those people. Even in the Ministry. I know so much, I know so much I wish I did not know. And now I am dead and at rest.''

Devereaux thought Miki was talking for the sake of his own comfort.

"Cigarette?" Miki said.

Devereaux shook his head.

"You are American?" They had spoken French from the point of meeting.

Devereaux nodded.

"Then I speak English. It is so much better than my French. The French, even these Belgiques, they always tell you how you do not speak their language."

"What do you know that interests us?"

The question had been formed from the first moment in Devereaux's mind and he had considered it for flaws. Hanley either knew or did not know and was willing to let Devereaux be the risk of a guess. In any event, a careful agent stays alive by reminding himself to know everything.

Miki smiled. "Perhaps that should wait."

"Perhaps," Devereaux said. "But why would we be interested in the secrets of movie stars?"

"Everything is politics," Miki said.

Devereaux waited.

"And politics is money," Miki said. "Do you understand that?"

Devereaux stared at the profile. His face was all angles and planes. There was a curious sense of good health, even of power, about him. Miki was a happy man because he had so many secrets.

"Everything is here," Miki said, tapping his head. "And when everything is down on paper and tape, then Miki will be disappeared. So I think it should be waited for,

for Miki to speak to the man in Washington or wherever he is.''

The long night road to the sea was illuminated by lampposts all across the little country of Belgium. The road fell away from Brussels and passed through the pleasant, rolling countryside and climbed up past Ghent. The dual roadway was empty save for the occasional elephant parade of tandem trucks the English call ''juggernauts.'' The trucks moved slowly toward the sea and the harbors of Zeebrugge and Antwerp and the long night's journey across the North Sea to Britain. It was raining all the time now and the single wide windshield wiper on the Mercedes whoosed back and forth, creating a rhythm that echoed the click of the tires on the road. The dull sounds, regular as a ticking clock, lulled them. Devereaux yawned and felt his hand relax in the grip of the gun. Maybe it would all be routine after all.

When they pulled off the road, Devereaux cranked the side window. He smelled the bare November fields and the chill odor of the sea. The narrow two-lane road brought them up past Bruges to the new port village of Zeebrugge. The wind rose. Devereaux closed the window. The wind picked up a howling sound from the sea.

All the holiday homes were clustered in a tangle of streets west of the concrete harbor. The homes were shut for autumn and the wide, windy beach was deserted. The wind prowled inland from the sea and offered a hint of terror.

Zeebrugge was an ugly village with a few shuttered cafés and hotels near the main harbor entrance. In the Middle Ages, the sea had come to Bruges fifteen kilometers away. Over the centuries it had brought silt and sand and rocks to the coast and the land extended more and more out into the sea, so that Zeebrugge became the new port and Bruges, lovely and old, became a place for the past.

"This is the place? What do we do now, take a ferry boat to England?" Miki smiled. He was very relaxed now and he spoke to Devereaux as though he were talking to a friend.

Devereaux stared out to sea. The sea was as black as the sky. The sands snaked from the beach across the road and piled up against the fences around the summer homes.

"What do you do?" he asked the driver.

"Make the signal. Three times. I'm supposed to go down the beach a little ways. You gentlemen are to wait up here."

"Why?"

"Sir, I don't ask those questions. That's what I was told to do."

Devereaux got out of the car and Miki scrambled across the leather seat to follow him. Devereaux felt the chill pluck at his face. The wind cut at him.

Miki shivered immediately. "Damned cold, damned cold," he said in English.

The Mercedes growled into gear down the street. The two men looked around them for shelter. There was the shuttered café across the road, but the wind was roaring straight at it. Perhaps in the lee of the harbor wall.

Devereaux saw the Mercedes turn to face the sea. He saw the signal. He stared out to sea and saw the answering signal at last. Then it was all right after all, he thought. For the first time, he let the pistol slip into his pocket and he took out his hand.

Miki turned from the wind and tried to light a cigarette. He saw it first.

He cried out and Devereaux turned and then he too saw the Mercedes bearing down on them. The big car was moving very fast.

Miki began to run across the street toward the café buildings.

Devereaux, alone on the sand, pulled the pistol from his raincoat pocket and fired. The bullet went high and he fired again.

The car nearly nicked him as it skidded on the sand and the brake lights flashed on.

Devereaux had leaped aside. Now he was on his knees in the sand, bringing the Python up in both hands, firing.

The glass shattered in the rear window.

Devereaux looked around for Miki and saw the two men emerge from the gangway between two buildings. They carried boxy Uzis in their hands and they were firing.

Devereaux shouted "Miki!" once and then returned the fire.

The one on the left went down hard, while the spray of machine-gun bullets plowed up the sand in front of the kneeling American agent.

Devereaux fired on until the hammer sounded hollow on a spent chamber. He pulled the Spanish knockoff out of his other pocket and fired at the man by the café door. And he saw the man had stopped firing and was grinning at him.

He saw the horrible grin.

Everything had been a setup, he thought.

And did not see the Mercedes backing up wildly in the sand toward the sea, the rear wheels spinning furiously. He did not even feel the impact when two tons of German steel caught him sideways and flipped his body up above the car and back toward the sand. Did not feel pain, thought, regret: only saw the face of the other man who had stopped firing, saw the familiar leering grin, saw what it had all meant in that final moment of life as he fell through a childhood nightmare without any sound but his own muffled scream.

FOUR

Julie on Line 2

Big Ben Herguth was. He wore size 52 jackets and 46 slacks. The slacks came in at $650; he picked up his clothes at a place in Palm Springs. He was always brown from the sun, even in the rainy season of Los Angeles. The other thing about him was that his eyes were flat and dead.

"I don't know what the connect is, Julie," he said. He rolled the cigar next to his unoccupied ear. The other held the receiver of a white Prince Oleg Cassini telephone. He had his boxy Sunset Strip office redecorated every year by the same decorator. He liked change but not too much change. There had been too much change the last couple of days.

"You want to know what I think, I think there is a connection because that is the way the G works. Remember all that shit about how Reagan was giving money to fucking Iran to get some hostages out, and then it was being ripped off two ways and going back to the contras? You come to me with that bullshit for a script and I tell you to walk. I mean, William Goldman couldn't make shit out of an idea like that. It just happened to be true though. So yes, I definitely think there is something going on between the fucking CIA and that little bitch in Chicago who decides to defect, and I think there is some shit going on by coincidence with the CIA and our old friend Miki, who disappears Wednesday night in Brussels. You fucking-A-do, I think that.''

Ben Herguth listened then. Julie talked in a soft voice all the time. He had soft hands. He would probably live to be a hundred, which was a lot longer than Ben Herguth figured he would last, but what the hell, Ben had fun. Julie never seemed to have fun. Except for the little girls and that was not Ben's cup of tea, but Julie was Julie and he was the most important man in Ben Herguth's large and important life.

Julie was saying, ''The first priority is Miki. Find out who took him and why. We got a lot invested here, Ben. We don't need a double cross from some cowboy at Central Intelligence.''

''I still say we end-run them,'' Ben Herguth said. ''This is all connected to that little girl in Chi. She musta been some kinda connection. A movie star, for Christ's sake, tell me that Miki didn't know who she is. This is some setup, and when the G starts setting you up, it's always some fantastic plot idea like this that nobody would believe in the first place. But why would they want Miki and why would they want to put the screws to us?''

''The reporter at the O and O in Chicago. Kay Davis,'' Julie said. ''I wish I had never heard of her. Apparently, she has an in with the girl. And the girl's attorney.''

"I looked her up with some of my friends in the shyster business. Her name is Stephanie Fields, she's a big do-good civil-rights-type broad. She is complicating it."

"I think this Kay Davis could work for us if she saw the right way," Julie said.

"All right, that's the subtle approach and I take off my hat to you, you always usually make it work. But I think this is a matter of time here. I mean, if the G has got Miki and he's starting to talk too much—"

"What are they going to do with it? They're in for a pound as much as a penny."

"That's it, Julie. I can't figure out their angle except they have to have an angle. All I know is fucking Miki goes to the ladies' can at the city hall place where they was holding this party and he's got a bimbo with him, he's going to give her a standup bang in the ladies' can—"

"Who was it?"

"Nobody with a brain, I checked that out. If she's working the CIA, then you can sell your savings bonds and start buying Russian. You know who it is, I forget her name, she was in *Zapata's Raiders*. She was the one they raped in the convent but not the nun. Sandra something, it'll come to me. I sent my boy to talk to her and she ain't hiding nothing, believe me. She just wanted a fuck. So Miki fucks her and stays in the john to take a pee. She goes back to the party and that's when he got out. The john is on the ground floor. But where did he go then? And who did he go to?"

"What do our friends in Prague say?"

"They are not happy people. First they lose all their tennis stars and gymnasts, and now they got a kid movie star defecting along with their number-one impresario. Prague must be getting like a ghost town."

There was a long pause that ate up the ether between New York and Los Angeles. Julie's voice was different now.

"I saw the tapes from the O and O in Chicago. The little girl. She's a cute thing. A real cute thing."

Ben closed his eyes. He saw the way Julie's voice was going. He sighed. "Yeah, well, Julie, for fourteen, she's got a nice can on her and the tits look real. But you can't tell. You can't tell at that age."

"Yes," said Julie. It was just what he wanted to hear.

"Nice can," Ben repeated for Julie's benefit.

"Definitely a derriere," Julie said. "Maybe it would have to be your way after all, Ben. Maybe we'd have to take her in to see what the government wants to do. Give us a card."

"Take her in," Ben said. "I could get you some tapes then. We wouldn't have to guess."

"Yes," Julie said. "I'd like that."

Ben sighed again. He knew Julie would like that. It didn't do a thing for Ben. Charlene in the outer office, she did a thing for Ben. Or two. Charlene was stacked and active and that was something Ben could see. But everyone was different, he reasoned. And it was just as well to humor Julie because Ben Herguth might be the biggest prick in Hollywood, but he wasn't shit if Julie didn't make him so. They both understood that.

"You keep me informed. On everything. On her. You put your own people on it, Ben. You got people in Chicago."

"I got people everywhere," Ben said.

"Then you keep an eye on things. On this Davis and this Fields. And on our little refugee girl. An orphan. She says she's an orphan. Isn't that darling, Ben?"

Ben said it certainly was.

FIVE

The Neumann Solution

R Section was funded secretly out of the vast Department of Agriculture budget. Under examination, it appeared to be an international crop reporting and estimating service of the Department. It counted grain in the Ukraine and the price of bread in Warsaw. In fact, it actually did some of these things. But in another part of Section, separate from the first, it did many other things that had nothing to do with the Department of Agriculture.

Agriculture occupied two squat, solemn buildings off Independence and Fourteenth Street in Washington, not far from the Fourteenth Street Bridge and National Airport across the river. In the bowels of the vast bureaucracy housed in the two buildings were the central rooms of R Section.

It had been called R Section simply because it had no other name. When it was first created as an intelligence agency during the Kennedy Administration, it was funded under a provision of paragraph R of the Agriculture budget. At the time, it was the ninth intelligence agency operated by various arms of the government including the National Security Agency, CIA, FBI, Defense Intelligence Agency, Office of Naval Intelligence, Army Intelligence, Air Force Intelligence and the Department of State's intelligence section. But its main rival for power and position was always the CIA, the Langley Firm. As Kennedy had said, "I don't ever want those bastards to be able to put me over a barrel again." He referred to the Bay of Pigs disaster, which he blamed on the CIA. R Section was the evaluator of CIA intelligence, the spies set up to spy upon the spies.

Or, as the present director of R Section put it, "We are the left hand seeking to know what the right hand is doing."

Mrs. Neumann's aphorism had created a positive feeling inside the bureaucracy of Section. The feeling was needed following the scandals involving the previous director and a White House liaison.

Mrs. Lydia Neumann, formerly in charge of the computer analysis division, had become the highest-ranked woman in the national intelligence community by dint of being available when she was needed. It had been a low moment for Section and Lydia Neumann had led Section out of it.

But today she did not feel triumphant or upbeat about anything. If she had been asked for aphorisms, she would have only thought of gloomy ones.

On this sleepy November afternoon of soft Virginia sun against the glittering phalanx of buildings on the river, Mrs. Neumann sat very still in her large office that overlooked Fourteenth Street and asked Hanley the same question she had asked him in the morning.

"Where is Devereaux?"

Hanley sat across the desk from her. The red leather chair squealed as he twisted in it. "We don't know."

"People cannot disappear."

"It was exactly what we wished Miki to do."

"And Miki has vanished as well."

"The ship received the signal from the driver. We're looking for him now. When the dinghy got to the beach, they were all gone. Car, driver, passenger, conductor. Everyone was gone. You remember Mason, the young man that Devereaux recruited? He was in London on station duty. I detached him twelve hours ago. He's been in Zeebrugge."

"He's inexperienced."

"But he's outside the scope of Stowe's people. I thought we still wanted to keep this out of regular channels."

"Perhaps we were wrong."

"Or right. Terribly right. If this whole thing was a setup by our friends at Langley to give us a black eye," Hanley said.

"What does Mason say?"

"He was in Zeebrugge. He found machine-gun cartridges in the gutter. Also some auto glass on the street. There might have been a fight. In any event, that's all we have without calling in the Belgium police. And we can't do that. I don't think they would appreciate us using their country as a staging area for defections."

"Damn," she said. She rarely cursed. Her voice was rough and raspy and she wore her hair in clumsy spikes fashioned twice a month by her husband, Leo. Leo had always cut her hair. He did so in the early years of their marriage as an economy. Now, like so many other things they did, it was an act of love. Leo was an accountant and Lydia Neumann was chief of a vast intelligence agency and they never talked about their work to each other.

Hanley understood. There were always frustrations but sometimes, even after a lifetime of frustrations, it was too damned much to bear.

"Is Devereaux alive?"

"If he is, he is held against his will. That means that he is across the wall now and it is time to cut our losses. I've gone through his 201. Most of his old business is neatly sealed. I don't think he can hurt us."

"He would hurt us?"

"Mrs. Neumann. If this whole matter was an elaborate ploy by the Soviet Socialist Republic of Czechoslovakia, it involved trapping an agent. If it was successful and Devereaux is not dead, then he will surely tell them everything they wish to know. Pain has no limits but men do."

"And the alternative is that he's dead."

"Yes. It's the preferable alternative."

"Was Miki worth it?"

She had asked him the question three weeks ago when he proposed using Devereaux to bring Miki across. He had probed Miki through an agent in Amsterdam the previous summer. Miki had only let one nugget drop but it was a beauty: It was a photograph of a Paris restaurant in the Trocadero district. Two men sat together at a table. One was the highest-ranking CIA agent in the Paris embassy. The second man was Miki himself. Miki did not explain the photograph but it was enough to convince Hanley. This was good enough to bring in Devereaux, to work outside the routine apparatus of Eurodesk.

"Miki was worth it if this was not a setup. If this was a setup, Miki is still worth it now because we will get him. Believe me, we will get him. This month or next or next year, but we'll get him and break him and bleed him and get rid of him."

Hanley's voice was still mild and flat and Mrs. Neumann frowned. "There are no sanctions, Mr. Hanley," she said.

"There are no rules," he corrected. "If they have set us up, then we will set them up."

"We will review our options," she said. "I don't want any cowboys working here. We have enough cowboys working over there."

She inclined her head and Hanley knew she meant the White House crowd.

"We'll find out about Devereaux. If they have him, they'll let it slip. If the real reason was to get Miki back —that they found out about the defection and moved to stop it—well, that's within the rules."

"Devereaux is dead," she said.

Hanley blinked. "Of course," he said. "One way or the other. If they have him, he's dead. If they killed him, he's dead. There are no other possibilities."

"But I want to know," she said, her horrible raspy voice barely breathing the words.

"I will put out trip wires and probes. Nothing will move until we find out."

"Put it back in channels," she said suddenly.

"Why?"

"Let Stowe know about it and put out some chasers. Find out what went wrong. This is my responsibility. If I have made a mistake, I'll acknowledge it. We just get in deeper when we keep fishing out of channels."

"Mrs. Neumann. I think it would be wiser—"

She smiled. She was a plain woman with a beautiful smile. She wore plain dresses to work and never wore jewelry. She saw things with frightening clarity. She saw the way it was now.

"Devereaux is dead. Or Devereaux is snatched over the

wall. If it's the latter, let's see if we can make a trade. If that seems likely, then I'll set up a conference with the White House people and see what we can negotiate. I may get a black eye but it won't come from Langley saying we didn't play by the rules. I can always ask about that picture and what their man was doing with Miki in Paris this summer. Meanwhile, put our Eurodesk on it directly. Find out what went wrong and why. And Mason . . ." She paused.

"What about him?"

"Do you suppose he was close to Devereaux?"

"No," Hanley said. "Devereaux probably never gave him another thought after he got him hired on. He was just someone who crossed his path one day." Hanley knew the day and the time: It had been Sunday and they were stealing David Mason's car from a parking lot in Bethesda and Mason had let them do it with a sort of bemused smile on his face. When the business had been concluded, Devereaux sent around one of the GS-12s and gave Mason his car back. And offered him a job because Devereaux had told Hanley, "Either he's completely stupid, in which case he'll wash out in two weeks, or he has the guts of a burglar and the same instincts. Section could use more burglars." Which is what it turned out to be.

"Devereaux's woman," Mrs. Neumann said. "Send Mason. Let her know as much as she has to know."

"We don't know he's dead."

"We know he's disappeared. In some countries, that is the same thing," she said. "Send her someone like Mason. Someone who can take the edge off what he has to tell her. Whatever Section has to do."

Hanley nodded.

"And you should go home."

Hanley was pale and very tired from the flight home

and the last twenty-four hours of waiting. He had not shaved in two days.

"Go home," she said.

"I'll signal Mason first. And then I'll take a nap on my couch. We still might get a signal." He meant from Devereaux. As soon as he said it, he felt foolish.

"You don't believe that," Mrs. Neumann said.

"It's possible," he said.

But Lydia Neumann shook her head. She stared at the truth of things and she thought she saw the truth now. Like all women, she was not a romantic. Hanley made wishes like a child; Mrs. Neumann could see the beach of Zeebrugge and the body of a man on the sand. The agent called November was now, finally, finished with.

SIX

Prague
Has No Tears

When he could not bear the pressure anymore, Cernan put on his overcoat and muffler and walked down three flights to the front door of the gray Ministry building and went outside.

It was strange that he found peace in the noisy clutter of Vaclavske Namesti. The streetcars ran back and forth full of shoppers going up to the main business streets at the top end of the broad avenue. What would they find today in the shops along the Narodni Trida or Prikopy? It was difficult to say, although things were not so bad in Prague anymore. Things had been much, much worse.

He shoved his hands deep into the overcoat pockets and started out along the street. It is called Wenceslas Square and there is certainly a statue of the great king astride his horse in the center. But it is a street, really, and not a square. Like everything else in Prague, Vaclavske Namesti was not exactly what it said it was.

Cernan frowned but did not realize he frowned. His face could frighten underlings in the Ministry when he was in this mood, and he took his solitary walks in moments like this because he had no wish to frighten anyone.

The spires of Prague were gilded in thin November sunlight and the city smelled old and closed for the coming winter. The sunlight glittered on cobblestones in the streets where the students had fought the tanks.

Cernan did not know where he was going—he was just walking to use up the frustration that had built in him— but he always followed the same path: down to the Charles Bridge, across the river and through the steep park up to the castles and cathedral on the Heights above the city.

On the Heights, the wind began and he felt chilled and that pleased him: Perhaps he would tire himself out this afternoon, perhaps he would sleep this evening.

Sleep had become the great difficulty in the three days since Anna Jelinak went before a television camera in Chicago and declared that she was an orphan and that she wanted to be given asylum in the United States because she had seen a miracle.

A weeping statue. It was incredible. It was so bizarre that Cernan could scarcely believe it was an accident. The agency had questioned Anton Huss in Chicago and the embassy had obtained the television tapes and even Cernan had seen them by now. But how could any of this happen? And how could Anna Jelinak suddenly declare that she was a misused, abandoned orphan when her mother was right here in Prague, living in the same house where she was born?

Cernan had gone to see Elena on the second day. Elena had been drunk on brandy. It was only noon and it had made Cernan angry. She said she had been visited by the police and then by two men from the Ministry. Cernan had not authorized that and later discovered the two men had acted on the authority of Cernan's deputy. Elena was beside herself.

Cernan listened to her for a long time, to all the boozy self-justification he had heard before. Anna had everything, Elena had nothing. Elena's youth and beauty had slipped away and all the years had been empty. Yes, yes, yes, Elena; Cernan nodded, felt uncomfortable, exactly as he always felt. But Elena knew and Cernan knew that he would not become impatient and tell Elena to stop blubbering and he would not walk out of the house. They both knew that Cernan must suffer.

The house was small and neat, which was extraordinary in that Elena was such a sloppy woman now and a heavy drinker besides. But something of what Elena had been showed itself in the four small rooms of the house in the Little Quarter.

"You will have to go to America. To get Anna back," Cernan had said.

"Oh, my God, I can't go there, I cannot even speak that language—"

"It will all be arranged. Anton Huss will be there. He is from the embassy in Washington, he can interpret for you and he will make the arrangements. They are holding Anna for court proceedings, to see if she can be granted defector status. It is important for you to be there and to claim your child."

Elena sobbed into her brandy. "How important is this for you? What do you care if Anna is there or here? She is lost to me, she was lost when she began to go with those film people, all of them perverts and sex fiends. . . . Oh, my poor little girl, do you think they have taken her?"

Cernan knew what she meant. Poor Elena. She kept her little house as clean as any and she had a little statue of the Infant on the sideboard and she had a crucifix on the wall above her bed. Elena clung to faith as she held onto her bottle of brandy, with a fierce and childlike belief that all would be well.

All would be well. For three nights without sleep, Cernan had sat in his own rooms in his own apartment, smoking one cigarette after another, waiting for morning, staring into the heart of the problem.

The problem was Anna Jelinak. What had induced this extraordinary display? Had Anton Huss failed in his job to guard her from contact by agents from the other side? Cernan was certain he had not. It was more than just a fear of reprimand or even punishment: Anton Huss had a splendid record, it was the reason he had been chosen to guard Anna. Chosen by Cernan himself. How did this make Cernan look? His deputy at the Ministry had dispatched two men to question Anna's mother on his own authority. When Cernan had raged at him, the deputy took it with a certain insolence, as though he were silently saying that this was all Cernan's fault in the first place and that Anna would not have defected if she had been more carefully guarded.

Anna.

Cernan saw the face of the child in memory. He did not need the photographs or the copy of the Beta tape. He saw her walking on the Heights above the city. She was very famous in Prague, and none of the newspapers had printed a word about her defection but they were already telling little jokes in the artist cafés and in the bar at the Inter-Continental where the foreigners gathered. Prague had no secrets if you understood where to look for the answers; Prague had no tears for Anna, for Cernan's dilemma, for Elena—Prague was always filled with a malicious sort of laughter, a mix of scorn and ridicule and satire. If Cernan fell on his face, so much better the joke for everyone else to enjoy.

The more Cernan knew of the case, the less he knew.

Anna Jelinak was now staying in the home of Stephanie Fields, the lawyer appointed by the American court to defend Anna's interests. He'd found out all about Stephanie Fields within twelve hours—the efficiency of the Service in the embassy in America never ceased to amaze him.

Stephanie Fields was an American leftist with vague socialist leanings that could not be counted on at all. She was not married and she was what Americans called a "feminist."

The embassy's law firm had sent a top man to Chicago to represent the rights of Anna's family and the court had been told that Elena Jelinak would soon be in America. Elena was taken to the airport outside Prague by two men from the Ministry and they described her as nearly hysterical and quite drunk. Another reason for Cernan not to sleep.

The only consolation for Cernan in the last three days was that the Ministry was in an uproar because of the disappearance of Emil Mikita. Anna Jelinak might be a problem and certainly she was a public-relations disaster. But Miki had disappeared and that was much, much worse. Thank God I had no part of that, Cernan had thought more than once in the last three days.

Not that he wasn't involved now.

Anna was in films and Miki was the great impresario. Was Anna's defection tied to Miki's disappearance? The question had been posed by Henkin and they had all thought about it for a long time and certain probes had been made in Brussels and even in Los Angeles and the result was that no one had any idea.

Henkin was Minister for Tourism and Films, an unlikely combination of interests but perfectly logical if one considered what the end product was: Preserve Prague and the illusion of a quaint, charming European city of another age. Certainly Prague was dominated at night by a great illuminated red star that rotated slowly above the spires in the old quarter. But that was to be expected; Prague was not ashamed of the Soviet Republic that had replaced the corrupt and brief rightist government after the war. Prague was in the business of making money and Henkin made a lot of money for the country, partially through the good offices of his agent and friend, Miki. Where the hell was Miki? What were the Americans up to now?

Henkin had rarely talked to Cernan in the past and now he seemed to need to talk to him twenty-four hours a day. He was part of Cernan's frustration. He was driving Cernan crazy with his endless questions and speculations. What was the point of guessing about connections until they could get some concrete idea of where Miki was and what the Americans wanted him for? Hearing that argument, Henkin became very cold and reminded Cernan that he was a Minister and Cernan was nothing but an upper-level civil servant. "Miki is a vital man with vital contacts and he has secrets, Mr. Cernan, that would be disastrous to fall into American hands."

What nonsense! Cernan glared and frightened a small boy playing in the park in front of him. When he saw what he had done, Cernan tried to smile and made it worse. The boy ran away, clattering down the broken sidewalk. Cernan shook his head. His thoughts were so gloomy and he had no wish to frighten anyone. But Anna Jelinak—

He stopped, blinked, remembered the summer afternoon again when they were making a film outside Hradcany

Castle and little Anna was dressed as a child of another century.

He had driven up to the site to see Anna. He watched her under the artificial lights that were turned on despite the fact that it was a bright summer afternoon. It had been very warm and he sat in the car with all the windows rolled down and watched her from a distance. He could see her clearly that day.

He stood now in November, in the chill, in the same place. He saw the castle, which was real and eternal like all of Prague, and he saw the illusion of the past. He could almost speak to Anna, it was so real to him.

Come back, child.

She stared at him.

Come back. You're only a little lost now. Don't go on any further. Come back.

SEVEN

The Messenger

Rita Macklin felt afraid when she heard the knock at the door. Her life with Devereaux was so singular, so private, that the door to the apartment on the Rue de la Concorde Suisse never admitted visitors. And now there was the knock of a stranger. Dread filled her.

She thought she had prepared for this moment because she had rehearsed it so many times in daydreams and nightmares. A time would come when he would go away, saying nothing to her, leaving in the silence of a midnight, and days later or weeks later there would be a stranger at the door of the apartment and he would tell her so little about what had happened. Except that something had happened. She had rehearsed the moment until she knew how she would react. Now the moment had come.

Rita pulled the robe tight around her and went to the door and opened it on a thin chain. She saw the tall man in the unlit hall. It was the middle of the morning in Lausanne and brittle autumn sunlight fell through the window at the end of the hall and illuminated the apartment.

"Rita Macklin," he said, not asking a question. She felt a moment of dizziness. She closed the door, dropped the chain, opened it again. Yes, she definitely felt as if she might be falling.

He must have caught her beneath the arms and dragged her across the room to the couch. When her green eyes opened, he was sitting on the coffee table in front of her, holding a glass of water in his hand. She brushed her red hair away from her forehead and her face felt damp and cold to her own touch. She shook her head to shake away the strange feeling. She sipped the water until the glass was nearly empty. As she drank, he watched her and said nothing.

"Is he dead?" she said.

"I don't know. No one knows."

Her sob surprised her.

She put down the glass and got up. She sobbed again, deep inside her chest, and groaned. He got up as well, put out his hand.

She went past him into the kitchen and opened the small refrigerator. He kept a bottle of Finlandia in the freezer: He did this, he did that, he had his secret ways, and in their lives together she had gradually discovered each way and treasured it as a souvenir of the times when he was not there.

"If he's not dead, he's alive someplace. Is he hurt?"

"No one knows anything. It happened less than forty-eight hours ago."

She poured the thickened chilled vodka into a glass and took the draught like medicine. And then she began to cry, holding the glass in her hand.

David Mason stepped into the kitchen and took the glass out of her hand.

She let herself cry in his arms. She cried because he was from Section and Section would always send around a man and would try to tell the woman or the child or the aged father that, well, something had happened. No, we couldn't go into it exactly, but it was a mission on behalf of the country and your son, your husband, your father showed the highest degree of duty and honor. . . .

"Is that why they sent you, to tell me that something happened but you don't know what happened?" She pushed herself away from him and tightened the belt on her robe. "That's stupid. That's really stupid." She bit her lip. "Show me something, show me who you are."

He took out his card and showed it to her. She turned it over in her hand. It was a hard piece of plastic with a color photograph of David Mason, estimator of the Field Investigation division of the Department of Agriculture of the United States of America.

"Nobody admits anything, even at the end," she said. "He said there was no Section, no Hanley, no operations division, no company . . . none of it existed if you pressed anyone on the matter. But he told me," she said. She said the last words with defiance.

"I knew him," he said, regretting the tense. "He recruited me."

"He didn't mention you. Not ever."

Perhaps the disappointment in his face pleased her. She wanted to hurt someone who could be hurt. She felt very bad.

"I'm not really supposed to tell you anything," he began.

"Then don't tell me. He never told me. Sometimes he

told me after it was over, sometimes when it couldn't be avoided—''

''—He had a train. He was taking someone across—''

''—never say anything directly. The place might be wired. Talk in washrooms with the water running—''

''It was the night before last. In Zeebrugge—''

She wasn't looking at him. ''He got the call in the middle of the night. He got dressed in the dark. I didn't ask him where he was going because he would never say. He said he didn't know what it was until they told him. He took his passport and the pistol, he took some money—''

''He was set up,'' David Mason said.

For the first time, she noticed everything about him. His voice was soft, drawling, but she couldn't catch the accent. His eyes were lazy and watching and everything about him was uncoiled, restful. His hands were very large.

''He took the passenger to Zeebrugge and that's where they disappeared. I went down there. There were machine-gun casings in the gutter and shattered glass, the kind they use in auto windows. I sent that to the desk in Brussels, they'll ship it to D.C., get a make on the car if they can.''

''So he might be dead but you don't have the body.''

He waited a moment but she didn't want to speak again.

''Well, he might be dead,'' Mason said.

''Fuck all you spooks to hell,'' she said.

''Two years ago, I was coming out of a liquor store over the Line and he was in the parking lot with a lady and an old guy, all bent up, and he was stealing my car. A 'seventy-three Rambler. It was comical. Can you imagine stealing a Rambler? I just stood there and asked him what he was doing and he said, very cool, 'Stealing your car.' Then he said he'd return it. I got it back a couple of weeks later and this guy was sent and he said he was told to offer me a job. I didn't even know what it was all about,

I didn't even know what Devereaux was. And the old man, I didn't know who he was. That's the way it works, they never tell you anything. They say it's about security but I figure that's just bullshit. But it's a job and that's something I haven't had much luck in getting.''

"He never mentioned you," she said again but now she was sorry she'd said it. His voice was easy. She felt hurt inside but his voice was easy on her. There wasn't any pressure at all.

"See, they figure he's hit and that's why they sent me. To tell you. I never did one of these things before, I didn't know what it would be like. I took the train from Brussels, changed at Geneva. I thought about what you would look like. I was trying to see what you would look like because I knew him. Actually, I just saw him that one time, stealing the Rambler. Damn. I liked him. He was about the first sonofabitch I ever met since my old man died that I figured knew what the hell he was doing. Everybody else is just faking it, but he knew what the hell he was doing.''

She felt tears again and she saw the man was not as easy as he looked, that there was something coiled inside that loose exterior after all.

"I don't figure he's hit," David said, veering the words easily the way a sailboat tacks against a light wind on Lac Leman below the town. She felt the words rushing past her and she and Devereaux were in a boat on the lake, pulling for the French side, talking about nothing except the wine and the fried perch for lunch. . . .

"If he's hit, there's no reason to remove the body. The Belgian police don't care that much and Section isn't ever going to explain what this was about. Hanley said they might have thrown him in the sea but he's never seen Zeebrugge. The sea builds in, the sea is always pounding in, you have to get out a ways to get the tow. I talked to a couple of seamen from the ferries . . . I don't think he was hit.''

Where is he? she said but there was no voice.

"They'll look into it the way they look into it. A lot of running around and then they figure they've looked enough. I'm supposed to tell you what I told you and a lot less than I told you. I'm going back to Brussels. It all started in Brussels.''

"Who was he taking across?''

"I don't know.''

"Or you won't tell me.''

"If I knew, I wouldn't tell you. But I don't know. Everything is in a compartment, you know the way it works.''

"Spies. Games. The old booga-booga. He called it the old booga-booga, a couple of kids trying to scare the hell out of each other.''

He smiled. When he smiled, he didn't look as young because the smile had sad edges. "There's someone in Brussels now, taking a look, but he was sent over from Eurodesk and they don't have their hearts in it and—''

"I don't understand.''

"Devereaux," he said, surprised. "The matter was too simple for Section to call in someone like Devereaux. So it must have been out of channels and now Section has to depend on channels to find their missing agent. No one is going to look very hard.''

"God damn them," she said. "I'll find him. To hell with Section, I'll find him.''

"I want to find him, too," he said.

She stared at him. Her eyes were fierce, and in the morning light she took on the look of some predator.

Mason thought she must be tough because she had to be a woman who could stand up to someone like Devereaux, a man who knew what he was doing. Mason saw that in her as well.

"I'm supposed to do what I can for you," he said in a flat tone. "That's always part of the instruction, I understand. Do what you can. Maybe I can do something for you."

She stared at him.

"Maybe the best thing is to take you to Brussels because you want to go there. You want to do some things in Brussels and I am going along because that's part of the instructions," he said. His voice was so laconic she almost didn't catch the implication.

She said, "Yes. Maybe that would be the best thing to do."

EIGHT

Ways of Persuasion

Stephanie Fields instructed Anna.

They sat at a bare wooden table in one of the windowless interview rooms off the main courtroom. Her hands rested on the table and Anna imitated her posture. They sat very straight and stared into each other's eyes.

"Your mother arrived from Prague a little while ago," Stephanie told her.

"She can't be my mother," Anna said.

"She has papers and documentation, but we'll have to wait and see it. The lawyers from the other side are going to arrange a stay and have a hearing next week."

"I can stay with you another week?"

"Yes," Stephanie said. She saw the leap in the large black eyes. Anna was slow to smile but there was a smile at the edge of her mouth now.

"Is she your mother?"

"No," Anna said. "I was an orphan. I can remember my mother, my real mother, a little, I think. I can remember the way she smelled. It's funny, but I can wake up sometimes and remember the way she smelled. But this woman I had to stay with, she smells different. And she drinks all the time."

"She drinks?"

"She drinks brandy and vodka even if we have little money." Anna frowned. No, that was not quite right. The role had to be more sophisticated. "But she drinks. She is drunk in the afternoon all the time. And a man comes to the apartment, but I don't know who he is. He sits with her."

"Does she have a lot of men who come to see her?"

"Sometimes," Anna said.

Stephanie stared straight at her. Anna made her bed in the spare room every morning. She brushed her teeth and combed her hair as though she did the acts consciously and took pleasure in them as individual assertions rather than as part of a routine. She seemed to want to please Stephanie. Stephanie thought she saw the little touch of strain in the child sometimes, a shadow of fear. She had seen the same look in other children, the children who were sometimes broken or beaten or abandoned or unloved, untouched, unwanted. "The abuse of neglect," someone had called it.

"Poor Anna," she said. She touched Anna's hands folded on the table.

She had taken the child into her apartment with the permission of the court. It was a bare, modern flat in a rehabilitated three-story building on the near North Side. Stephanie bought clothes for Anna, especially jeans. Anna loved jeans. Stephanie told her one night she would be a beautiful woman, and did she want to be anything besides a movie star? Anna said she wanted to be a mother someday and have children, perhaps three children. She would stop working then, she said. Stephanie had been touched by that sentiment as she was by many things about Anna; she had shared her life with Anna in the last few days like a sister. Stephanie always knew the right thing to do for Anna for the simple, uncommon reason that she was good.

The quality of goodness in Stephanie had even affected Father Frank Hogan when she had come to interview him for a deposition. Father Hogan had pried a fresh pot of coffee out of the housekeeper in the rectory and they had shared it in one of the plush, "male-club" interview rooms of the house. Father Hogan had felt warmed by Stephanie's presence that afternoon and had been unusually garrulous for someone under scrutiny by the chancery office.

Stephanie had asked about the "miracle" and Father Hogan had permitted himself a moment of silence before framing an answer. "Miracles, you might say, are in the eye of the beholder," he told her. It was a way of showing he was a man of the world. A man of faith, certainly; there was no doubt about that. But a man of the world as well. And she was a woman of the world, was she not? He noticed her legs crept right out from the lap of her blue skirt and they were long and nicely formed. That was the thing about legs, Father Hogan had once thought: Most women have pretty nice legs, all in all.

"You don't believe in this miracle?" she had asked.

"I believe in believers," he had said. He might have been making a neat point in an argument in theology class at the seminary. "I believe God moves the heart."

"Anna said that," Stephanie said. "She said 'God moved me.' It's an extraordinary thing, don't you think, for a child to say?"

"Extraordinary, and her not even all that used to speaking English," he said.

"No. She said it in Bohemian but she said it—"

"Let me put it this way, Miss Fields. Do you believe in weeping statues? I took you over to the church and what did you see?"

" 'What did you go into the desert to see? A man clothed in soft raiments?' "

"You know your Bible. Answer a question with a question."

"I saw a statue called the Infant of Prague with stains on the plaster face and a dampness on the lace collar," she said. "I saw what I saw and I can't explain it."

"So there you are," Hogan said.

"I believe in intentions," Stephanie said. "Anna is a good child and she has a good heart, but I don't think anyone has ever asked to see it. She's not so tough and she's been used by a lot of people, I think, and I don't want to be someone to use her to get a headline or be on the evening news. That isn't what this is about. If Anna had been twenty-one years old, she wouldn't have been questioned about her defection. She would have been accepted just like that. But she's fourteen and that makes everything about her suspect because children don't have rights. So she says she is an orphan and some woman is coming from Prague with a lot of papers that say she's the mother of Anna. Why do I believe those papers and not believe Anna? And if Anna sees a miracle and God moves her heart, why don't I believe it? And if Anna says she is unloved and unwanted except she was loved by her little Infant of Prague that she had in her home, why don't I believe her? Or you? Or the courts?"

"It's not really up to me—"

"She saw that statue and something in herself at that moment and it broke her heart," Stephanie said.

"We don't want the church to be used."

"You mean the Big C Church or this particular one?"

"Both," he snapped.

Her voice went soft. "I don't intend to use anyone." She hesitated. "But I intend to help Anna and this is part of it. The government is no help, they wish Anna would go home, go away. Two men came to see me yesterday, they gave me those phony ID cards. I think they were agents. I mean, spies. The government gets so weird sometimes, you actually start believing in false beards and invisible ink and all that. I'm convinced they were CIA, and they wanted to talk to Anna."

Father Hogan started. She saw it.

"Someone came here."

"No, not at all," he lied.

"They said they were State Department."

"No, not at all," he lied.

"I don't like this," she said.

"It doesn't concern me—"

"Your church, your miracle—"

Hogan said, "My connection with Anna Jelinak, whom I have not even met, does not even exist except by the coincidence of videotape. She didn't even see the statue, Miss. She saw a videotape of a statue. I can't see what I can do for you any further. Or for Anna."

And Stephanie smiled then. The smile dazzled him. He felt like he was ten years old and Sister Mary Theresa was awarding him a gold star in front of the whole class for spelling "thoroughly." He even blushed in that moment and he never blushed anymore.

"Pray," Stephanie said. "You could pray for Anna."

All that had taken place the previous afternoon and now

she was sitting with her hands folded, as though in prayer, staring at Anna and preparing to toughen her up for all that would come. It would get down to putting her on the stand at last; and a posturing lawyer from Washington, D.C., acting on behalf of Czechoslovakia and the "rights" of Anna's mother, would push words at her like weapons and it would be terrible.

Anna saw the stern, troubled look.

She smiled. "It will be good when it is over, Stephanie. Do not worry too much."

"You break my heart," Stephanie said then. She smiled and it was the same dazzling smile that had made a priest blush.

"Anna, you're going to have to meet this woman. In a room. Alone. I promise you the woman cannot take you back to Prague, but you are going to have to talk to her and I don't want you to break down or be a baby because you're not a baby. You're a woman. You listen to her and you don't have to say anything. Remember that."

"The woman was drunk all the time but she never hit me. It was just like I wasn't there sometimes," Anna said.

"If she didn't hit you, did she love you?"

Anna blinked.

"Stephanie. I don't know. Can you tell this?"

"Can't you tell when you are loved?" Stephanie asked.

Anna blinked her black liquid eyes. "The woman said I was a mistake."

"No," Stephanie said. "That's a terrible thing and it isn't true. You are intended. Everything in the world is intended. Every life. There are no mistakes. God doesn't make mistakes ever." And Stephanie touched Anna's trembling hands.

So soft, Anna thought.

Stephanie smiled.

So warm, Anna thought. Her face was flushed. So warm and there is golden all about. She realized it then, what she felt. She tried the smile on her reluctant features and it broke through. She felt covered by Stephanie's hands. Stephanie, she thought. Stephanie loves me.

"Thank you for using A T and T."

Ben Herguth jiggled his bulk in the aluminum-sided telephone booth. The phone rang three times and Julie picked it up.

"Two Langley guys been around a couple of days, they look like they don't figure what's going on either. But that doesn't explain where the fuck Miki is. Nothing from Prague except our man seems on edge, like he knows less than we know."

"Where are you?"

"Fucking Chi, where else. I don't know, Julie, I feel better if we take the direct-action approach to this and see which way Langley jumps after that."

"Is the girl protected?"

"Usual shit. A couple of cops. No big thing. She goes to bat again next Monday in court. They flew in some bag who says she's Anna's mother and the judge is not one of ours."

"That's too bad."

"Direct action, Julie," Ben Herguth said. "Snatch the kid."

"I don't like it. It's always the last option. I want Kay Davis out of this—"

"Put a hit on her."

"I told the station manager to promote her out of this story, I hope the idiot knows how to do it—"

"Or we just put the hit on her," Big Ben said. It was cold in the phone booth, cold in Chicago. He was outside a joint on Division Street owned by people in the action. He'd had a good time with two very clean and imaginative hookers sent up by Tony Lavelli, along with the comp champagne, but two days in Chi was two days in Chi. His clothes and blood were too thin for winter. Put the hit on someone, he silently screamed to Julie in New York. This was a put-the-hit-on-someone kind of town. Nobody'd notice.

All he heard was the icy caution at the other end of the line.

"I think we just keep going along the way we go along, feel our way. See what happens at the TV station, see if we can hose down the heat a little bit. Turn the heat down and then if we have to move, it doesn't look like we're doing it on the cover of *People* magazine. There's too much circus right now."

"I appreciate that. But time is money too, Julie."

"You don't have to remind me."

"We've got a lot of contracts tied up, lots of out-front dough even if the movie never gets made. We gotta be in Prague in January, fucking six weeks away, with the setup, ready to shoot. It drives me crazy thinking about it."

"I know that, Ben. I know all that." The voice was faintly weary. Ben caught the tone. Don't piss off Julie, not ever.

Ben wiped his forehead where the sun freckles were arrayed. "Whatever you say, Julie. I'm just here to back your play."

"Keep your eye on things and be in touch. Things might start moving quick."

"I'll be in touch," Ben said. He heard the click. The hookers were inside, in the bar of Lavelli's place. Division Street was filling up with Friday-night people looking for love.

Let 'em find it, Ben Herguth said to himself. He was going back to the hotel. Fuck it. He thought he was coming down with a cold. What he wanted right now was a bowl of chicken soup. He wondered if the hotel had any.

Elena Jelinak arrived in the international terminal at O'Hare Airport shortly after two P.M., and Kay Davis and the cameraman named Dick Lester waited outside the customs shed with all the other reporters.

The doors banged open—she had been rushed through the VIP line while the rest of the passengers were still sweating out their luggage—and Anton Huss was at her side, supporting her arm. She was a haggard woman in a print dress with the smell of brandy all about her. Kay sniffed, looked at Dick, smiled and plunged in.

Why had she come here?

To get my daughter.

Is your daughter devoted to the Infant of Prague?

That is propaganda, the American government has stolen my child—

"Do you believe in miracles?" Kay asked. She asked everyone that now. She had gone back to the church twice, on her own, without a cameraman and without any real reason except to see the statue again, to stand in the lines with the pilgrims who filled the street now, paying her admission at the coffee table set up in the vestibule by officers of the Holy Name Society. As the president of the Society had explained to Father Hogan: "Miracles are fine, but when it comes down to a new roof for the church before winter, the roofer isn't going to be looking for no miracle, he's going to be looking for cash." Father Hogan had given in and the admissions—called "donations"— were piling up in the rectory safe.

Kay Davis did not believe she saw a weeping statue

when she stared at it. So she wanted to find out what others saw. She somehow had a strange feeling that if she asked enough people and got enough answers, she would understand.

Anton Huss, pale and a bit shaken by all the cameras pointed at him, translated the questions for Elena Jelinak. He wanted no part of this. When it was over, he would be transferred out. Farewell Washington and all the beautiful women of the city. He would probably end up in Addis Ababa.

"What did she say?" Elena asked Anton sharply.

"She says 'Do you believe in miracles?' "

"Sure. Tell her I believe in miracles. Tell her I got fucked by a dove one day and Anna dropped out between my legs."

Anton Huss blushed. He knew that the woman was drunk but this was a disaster.

"She said she only wants to see her little girl again."

"Tell her I believe in the miracle of the workers' paradise where bread turns into stones and meat into statues of Lenin."

"Shut up," Anton said in harsh Bohemian. He smiled at Kay Davis. "Mrs. Jelinak is weary from the flight—"

"Where is Mr. Jelinak?" the bluff, red-haired reporter from Channel 7 boomed. "How come we don't hear about Mr. Jelinak?"

Anton Huss began to translate and Elena laughed. "Oh, should I tell them about Anna's father? About fucking me that night in the Stromovka park? I can tell you all about him if she wants to know that, Pan Huss."

It went like that for another minute with Anton Huss trying to save Elena from herself.

"Have you been drinking?" Channel 7 screamed. Channel 5 shouted, "What about the state of East-West relations? Are you going to see the mayor while you're here?" Channel 2, doing a standup, intoned: "The obviously distraught mother is being led away while somewhere in the city sits a lonely child, thinking of her homeland, her loved ones, the grief of her countrymen. . . ."

"And you told me nothing is worth eighty-seven seconds," Kay Davis smiled. They were in the control booth. Hal Newt had just walked in and was looking at the monitors on the panel. Cut to the crowds outside St. Margaret's; cut silently to Elena Jelinak at O'Hare, obviously drunk; cut to Stephanie Fields standing in the lobby of the Everett McKinley Dirksen Federal Building.

"*People* magazine called me," Kay said. She couldn't keep the excited tone out of her voice. "How does my book look now, Hal?"

But Hal wasn't smiling. Not that he ever smiled all that much, but he was frowning at the clips on the monitor and chewing his lip exactly as he had done at their lunch at Arnie's.

Kay didn't seem to notice. She was watching the tape, filling her head with images of the day and the day to come. The story had legs and it was going to carry her all the way to New York.

She was right in the middle of it. She had Stephanie Fields' home number, she had an in with Father Hogan and the cute priest at the chancery office and she was completely wired with everyone, right down to the head of the Holy Name Society who ran the card tables in the vestibule. She had never been as in on a story and it was the adrenaline-maker that surged in her all the time now.

"Kay, Al Buck said he wants to see you."

The words sliced right through her good feelings. Al Buck was station manager and Big Tuna had been sulking about this story, about his small role in it, and that probably meant he had leaned his $900,000 hulk on Al Buck and Al Buck was instructed to tone her down.

She did a quick frown and an even quicker smile. "Raise?"

"Yeah. Maybe that's what it is."

They went down the windowless, concrete-block corridors to Al Buck's office on the second floor at the back of the squat building. They walked right past the secretary because they were expected. Why was Hal Newt along? But then, the smart executives always kept a stooge as a witness when unpleasant things had to be said and done.

Al Buck had a big, plain office and he stood behind the desk. Pictures of the station's news stars were on the wall. Including Kay's. On the big desk was a brass plaque: The Buck Stops Here.

"Kay, Kay, glad I caught you." Big smile, pressed hands. Al led himself around the desk as if it were a maypole. They went to the leather couch and all three sat down, Kay on the couch, Al and Hal in chairs. Very informal.

"Kay, want coffee?"

Black all around and decaffeinated. The coffee came and was put on the coffee table and Al said in his big voice, "Close the door and hold my calls." All this for Kay's benefit. She understood the rules and she felt very cold in the room with the two men staring at her.

"Kay, how's the story going?" Al Buck asked.

"Great, Al," Kay said. She couldn't help the enthusiasm, she wasn't faking it this time. "No one has had a chance to talk to Anna except for that one press conference, but Stephanie Fields is going to give me a one-on-one this weekend. She wants it to break before the court hearing on Monday and—"

"Kay," Al Buck said in a voice that teachers use when they interrupt a child's nonsense monologue. "I've been talking to Hal, we've been putting our heads together, and, frankly, we think this story is getting a little carried away. Not, I want to say, that you are not doing a super job on this—"

"Did I tell you about *People* magazine?" Kay began.

"Wonderful," Al continued, as if he had interrupted himself. "But, frankly, we are getting a lot of Catholic feedback, they're offended by all this publicity. We're getting sensitive and I mean up at network level about a lot of things, but if it was up to me—"

"What are you saying, Al?"

Al Buck looked at Hal Newt.

"I think what we're saying here," said Hal, "is that it is time for you to go on to bigger and better. You know Duane Hernandez is leaving as Midwest correspondent for the network."

"I didn't."

"He's going to Nicaragua."

"That's wonderful."

"A war is always a good chance to move up," Al said.

"And there's going to be an opening coming up very fast," Hal began.

"We'd hate to lose you like the dickens but—"

"Well, it's from network, and when New York talks, Chicago listens."

"And they know the kind of job you've done," Al continued.

Midwest correspondent? Kay blinked. She saw herself in cornfields, talking to farmers. She saw herself in Kansas City, looking at beef. She saw herself in Minnesota, talking about the "flood-swollen Mississippi" or the "ice-choked Mississippi."

"You got to be kidding. I was in Iowa for four years. I mean, I got out of Iowa. I escaped the corncob jungle."

Al Buck tried a new smile that included a chuckle. Hal Newt was not smiling anymore and not trying.

"There's a lot on drugs," Al Buck said. "Duane was working on a drug distribution ring in Missouri."

"In Missouri?" Kay said in a loud voice. This was wonderland and she was talking to the Mad Hatter and March Hare.

"—step up. Network level—"

"Duane doesn't make six figures."

"We can arrange—"

"But my story—"

"—story has run out—"

"My story!" she shouted.

They were very quiet then.

Al Buck said, "Kay, forget the story. It's just a story. We are talking career here. We are talking about the brass ring."

"The Midwest slot is the brass ring? I'd rather be in Philadelphia," she said. She felt hysterical. What was this about? And then she saw it. It was the story and that didn't make any sense at all, to want to kill the story.

"Why do you want to kill the story?" she said. It was the direct, corn-fed, Iowa voice she thought she had packed away years ago along with all the other souvenirs of childhood. But it had come back to her suddenly in that moment of anger.

Al Buck blushed. He looked directly at her and his eyes went flat. "Don't be tiresome, Kay. We talk about an opportunity, we thought you would be so happy—"

"No, you didn't, Al. Don't give me that. This is about killing this story. I won't kill this story, Al. You can't make me kill it."

Hal Newt looked miserable. "Kay, this is a chance, a real golden opportunity for you."

She turned on him. Why was she ever afraid of people like this? And their stupid lunches at Arnie's?

"I've got two publishers interested. I'm going to walk away from a story like this for crop reporting in Kansas?"

Al Buck said it very flat and straight, the way an executive does when he is bottom-lining: "Three years network contract: one ten, one twenty-five and one seventy-five. To make up the difference, one bill a week in expenses and car and we pick up your rent and—"

"Last week I was on the way out."

"That was before. This is different."

"The money isn't there."

"One twenty-five, one fifty, two," Al Buck said then as though he were reciting numbers on the market wire without owning any stock. His voice was so dead, Kay thought.

"You're scaring me, Al," she said. "You think stories just disappear."

"Stories are things we make up," Hal Newt said. "The filler between the commercials. Anna Jelinak is a small story."

"My story," she said.

"We pull off," Al said. "That's the way it is." There was no shadow to his voice. None of the words carried weight.

She stared at Al Buck. She thought about it. "I've got to think," she said.

"There's nothing to think about."

In the corner of the office was the inevitable TV monitor tuned to the station. News at five, film at ten, world and national news at five-thirty P.M. Right now, however, it was the syndicated game show in which all the contestants tried to guess who their marital partners would really rather be sleeping with.

"I have to think," said the reluctant little girl who had to take piano lessons at the age of ten at Miss Groomby's house and who delayed the moment by walking very slowly down the street, hoping the time for piano lessons would pass. "I have to think."

And thought and thought.

"No. It's my story. If you don't want it, someone else will want it," she said.

"You won't work for the network ever again," Al Buck said.

"There are worse things."

Hal Newt sighed and his face was white.

"You blew it, Kay. You're yesterday," he said.

Kay said, "We'll see. You guys are strange. I mean, this is strange. You're the ones blowing it."

"Clear the building. Now," Al Buck said. "We'll send your things."

"This is crazy, Al," she said, feeling the craziness in the room. "I've got clothes in the dressing room and—"

"Dead," Al Buck said. "Dead in this town now. Clear the building now." He punched the intercom. "Send up Rollins from Security."

She couldn't believe it.

This time it was from a pay phone off the main room where the card game was going on. Ben hated cards. He felt like he was in jail, killing time. He punched in his card number and waited for the computer-voice to thank him for using AT&T and then counted the rings.

"Me," he said.

"Our man did not handle it well. Perhaps I was too . . . oblique. She quit or was fired and that doesn't resolve anything, she'll have another job tomorrow. I don't know why he blew it.''

"So what do we do now?'' Ben asked, but he knew and he felt good about it because the waiting time was over and he could throw in his cards.

"Your way,'' Julie said.

Hit her, Ben thought. He hung up the phone and went back into the card room and said he was tired and he had a cold and he was going back to the hotel. Actually, he felt better than he had in days.

NINE

Ready or Not

For a long time, there was darkness.

He could move if he crawled. The pain was constant, just at the surface, and it spread hot fingers across his body. He groaned when he moved. Because of the darkness, he could not take a measure of the pain and where it came from; the darkness intensified the feeling of pain.

He lay in the darkness and tried to isolate the pain by thinking about it as something separate from himself and, that way, to make it less. It was like being a child, shut up in a sickroom, surrounded by goblins of fever who make the world shrink and expand constantly.

He felt his left hand with his right and could feel the taut, puffy skin. When he pressed his third and fourth fingers, the pain came sharp and hard and made him sick. He vomited on the floor of the place where they had put him.

His left leg was heavy and swollen as well. He touched it with his right hand and then he tried to flex it. He could feel the place where the muscle was torn. His left leg was so heavy that when he finally tried to move, he had to crawl across the damp floor and drag the leg behind him.

How long had he been here?

There were no windows and no doors, and the damp smell of the place crept into his nostrils, his clothes, his dreams. The dreams were the worst thing because when he would start awake, the darkness and the goblins remained. The ceiling was low enough to touch when he finally pushed himself up against a stone wall and reached. He thought he must be in a basement. He could hear the rats scuttling away from him. The rats sang to each other across the darkness in high-pitched, almost crooning voices. Sometimes, when he fell asleep and could not fight against the dreams, the rats ran across his body and he felt their sudden weight and the skidding, light steps.

He thought he could go mad if it lasted long enough and if that was what they wanted.

His clothes were damp, but if he took them off he would be even colder. He huddled against a wall and against the pressing dampness of the place they held him. He tried to move his hands and arms to make heat and flex the swollen muscles.

He urinated against a wall in the corner of the dark room and the urine burned from his body while the pain made black and red flashes across his vision.

There were only three sounds in the darkness: the singing of the rats, the drip of water someplace and, once, his own voice that sounded small and flat.

"I'm alive."

* * *

Light broke painfully into the darkness.

The shaft of light illuminated the room—it was a basement, after all—and the rats froze along the walls and watched the two figures descend the wooden stairs that dropped from the floor above.

Devereaux shrank into a far corner away from the light.

The two men spoke French. The first one said he hated the rats and the second one made a mumbled joke. They carried automatic pistols that picked up the glint of light. One of them had a flashlight and searched the room along the walls.

"Fucking rats," the first one said.

"Hey, you," said the second one. "You dead? Come on, we're going upstairs."

"Maybe he is dead," said the first one, looking at the rats in the light. "Maybe the rats ate him."

"You better hope they didn't eat him," the second one said. He was a heavy man and he stood still and let his gun muzzle wave across the semi-darkness. "Hey, you, come on out. If you're not dead yet, come on out."

Devereaux said nothing. He tried to coil his body. The two of them were less than ten feet away. But the pain in his left leg let the tension out of his body and he couldn't set himself.

"Where the hell is he?" said the first one.

Devereaux pushed off but his leg fell under him. He fell heavily on the floor.

"You're there somewhere," said the second one. "Come out here now."

"Come and get me, copper," Devereaux said.

They saw him at the same time and they trained the

lights on him. The first one, who was afraid of the rats, saw he was alive and not eaten and slapped him on the side of the head with the pistol and Devereaux slumped into darkness again.

"Don't kill him," said the second one. Devereaux heard him through the fog of pain, like a voice in a fever.

"I don't see why not," said the first one.

"You saw what happened to the driver. The driver tried to kill him. You saw what happened to him."

"Jesus Christ," the first one said. Devereaux felt a hand grab his hair and felt himself being dragged across the cellar floor to the light at the stairs.

The room had a single chair.

The two men put him in the chair and cuffed him behind his back. The first one tried to cuff both legs together, but the left leg was so swollen that the cuff would not fit the ankle. The second one used a bandana to tie the left leg to the chair.

They left him. They locked the door behind them and he heard their steps go down a hall. A small, dirty window illuminated a dirty day beyond.

He tried to move the chair. He strained, levered himself and pushed. The chair nearly toppled but it skidded six inches across the wooden floor. When he pushed again, the chair toppled over and he was on the floor, his arms still fastened behind his back.

The top of the chair-back touched the bottom of his neck. For a long time, he strained forward, trying to slide his manacled arms up the back of the chair and over the top. It was like doing extreme sit-ups lying sideways on the floor with your hands behind your back.

He realized he had blacked out. Conscious again, he

lay on the floor, feeling the sweat on his lips and forehead. He licked at his sweat.

He strained this time, not to get his hands free over the top of the chair-back, but to break the chair. He felt the cuffs pulling the skin at his wrists and felt the strain in belly and arms and shoulders.

He tried this three times.

The chair cracked. The crack came like the pop of a distant pistol.

He pushed again and concentrated on pushing his body out of the chair. The crack yawned. He imagined his body free of the chair and pushed his body toward the idea in his mind. It was like hitting someone: You never aimed for the spot of contact in your mind but for a point beyond the point of contact, so that the swing was sure and followed through.

The back of the chair broke all the way through with a sigh.

He lay on the floor and tried to catch his breath and ease the strain out of his muscles. It began to rain in the world and rain fell against the single windowpane. He was so thirsty. He licked at the sweat on his upper lip.

He braced his right knee on the floor and slowly righted himself and the chair seat. The broken back lay on the floor. He half stood and slid his manacled arms down under his buttocks and the back of his thighs to the knotted bandana. By bending over, he could just touch the bandana. If he could unknot it, he might be able to drag himself to the window and smash the remains of the chair against the wall and break the window. And then what? he thought.

He closed his eyes and felt at the knot.

And the door burst open.

"What are you doing?"

The voice was full of smiles. It was the voice he'd heard in his nightmares, and it fit the grinning man he thought he had seen in that brief, blinding moment on the beach before the car hit him. He stopped his struggle and stared at the face. It was the same man, the same nightmare: For the first time, Devereaux felt the edge of fear.

TEN

In Kafka's Land

T he Ministry of Secrets believed in them. The walls of the building that contained the Ministry had few notices and even fewer names on doors. The names were not important in any case; the doors were more important because they led to the rooms that were the real symbols of authority. The bureaucrats came and went but the rooms remained and were unchanged: Men became identified with the room they occupied.

Snow fell on the narrow valley of the river Vlatava where Prague is built on the steep hills. The snow muted the clamor of the city and even the streetcars ran more silently along their tracks. It was the first snow of the long Slavic winter and Cernan felt both a child's sense of delight and an adult's sense of dread in watching the first snow.

He was summoned to the fifth floor at ten in the morning and he waited now in the anteroom for the director to see him. He stood at the window and watched the snow gild good King Wenceslas astride his horse. The pigeons huddled in the eaves of all the buildings. Cernan wondered if they dreaded the winter coming or if they only accepted each phenomenon of nature as an isolated event.

The secretary—a tall, thin man in the uniform of an Army officer—opened the director's door and nodded. Cernan sighed, turned, crossed the room and entered.

The Ministry was composed of several sections, including the divisions for internal secret police, liaison with military intelligence and foreign security. Cernan was part of the apparatus of foreign security and the director was his ultimate supervisor. He had met with the director every morning since the defection of Anna Jelinak in America.

The office was large but bare of mementos. There was a single antique desk of the Empire period and two straight chairs and a single, beautiful lamp with a polished brass base. On the left-hand wall was a modest fireplace where a little hardwood was smoldering. The director was named Gorkeho and he had been a soldier once, before he lost his leg. Everyone knew he had a wooden leg and no one knew how he had lost his real one.

Gorkeho was thin, all parchment and bones. His eyes studied Cernan's broad, frowning face as Cernan gave a little bow and crossed the room and sat down in the chair opposite.

"There is a little progress," Cernan said, grunting as he sat down on the delicate straight chair. Despite its bareness, the room was not oppressive. If there was a little edge of sadness to it, it was warmed by the fire and by the sheer presence of the man behind the desk.

"Anton Huss reports that Anna's mother was a . . . little tired . . . after the flight to America and that she is meeting with the lawyers today. In fact, the meetings should begin in about six hours Prague time. A court hearing is scheduled for Monday, and in the meantime the child has not been heard from, though the lawyers assure Huss she is perfectly all right. She will meet with her mother today as well.''

"A little progress, as you said," Gorkeho said. He tented his fingers and looked at the tips. "I have been in communication as well. On a related matter.''

Cernan stared at the older man. Gorkeho seemed absorbed by the pattern of his fingers.

"Henkin. He is in the Ministry for Tourism and Films and he is very well connected, I understand.'' Gorkeho had been a soldier and learned the soldier's trick of delivering reports with a neutral diffidence in voice and manner. But Cernan knew from the way Gorkeho framed his words that he did not like pan Henkin.

"He has his own agents, of course, and they report to him and not to the Ministry. He said that Miki has been located. It was, as we suspected, an American trick, to take him out of Brussels. He was either a willing or unwilling defector at the time.''

"He is alive.''

"He is apparently alive," Gorkeho said. He opened the tent and put his strong, thin hands flat on the beautiful desk. "Henkin said that a private contractor can locate him for us and return him for seventy-five ounces of gold. He wants one of us to arrange . . . the matter.''

"When did all of this happen?''

"Overnight, pan Cernan. While winter crept in and snow began to fall on the dear city," Gorkeho said. His voice was smooth and quiet and he was amusing himself, Cernan thought. "Henkin is to be absolutely relied upon in this, of course, and we have to do nothing but transport gold to Belgium, wait for our contact, and pick up Miki and return him to Prague. Such a simple little errand.'' Gorkeho glanced at Cernan. "It should only take you a day or two. Or three."

Cernan flushed. He glared across the desk at his superior. "Why me? I am already consumed with the matter of Anna Jelinak. I—"

"Yes. Why you? I thought. He named you, you know. How does such a great and respected servant of the Republic as Henkin know of an insignificant person such as yourself? I mean you no disrespect, of course. But Henkin is at a level so much higher than you—than me, even. We only spend money, pan Cernan, and we get little for it, and every time America receives one of our new tennis stars we are diminished that much more. Henkin produces money for the beloved Republic, pan Cernan. He brings in visitors, he brings us film companies, he presents the beauty of our great city to the outside world."

Cernan waited because Gorkeho was only amusing himself. He really hated Henkin, Cernan thought. You could tell it by the words, even if the soft voice imparted nothing.

"But where was I? I asked him how he knew of you and he said he had followed the matter of Anna Jelinak and her little miracle from the beginning because, after all, Anna was one of the coming stars of the Czech theater. And he thought the matter was very badly handled, down to the selection of Anton Huss to protect Anna from the blandishments of America or the devious plots of the FBI or the CIA. So, he had me there, although I do not blame you or Anton Huss for what has happened. Who would be able to foresee the power of the Christ Child to touch the heart of the little girl?"

Gorkeho was smiling now, Cernan thought, but there would be no change in his expression.

"So if you have failed in one assignment, why give you this assignment? That is the question I had in mind. I put it to Comrade Henkin. Why select a failure from the ranks of the Ministry for Secret Services when we have so many other agents who have not failed? Or, at least, who have not failed recently? You see, Cernan, I had your best interests at heart.''

Cernan took out his package of cigarettes. He looked at Gorkeho. Gorkeho nodded. Cernan lit the bitter-smelling cigarette with a wooden match and blew a cloud of brown smoke across the desk.

Gorkeho said, ''Henkin was impatient with me because I did not understand the world as he understood it. He said he had decided the matter of Anna Jelinak is receiving too much scrutiny. Too much 'publicity' in the American press. He said this was going to harm not only tourism but his 'complex' relationships with several companies preparing to film here. He said I did not appreciate the extreme nervousness of the 'Hollywood community,' that all creative people were sensitive to stressful situations and that Anna Jelinak's defection was a stressful situation.''

To Cernan's surprise, Gorkeho smiled. It lit the room. ''He wants you to leave the matter of Anna in abeyance for the time being. He wants the matter pursued in the courts, of course, but he wants no more extraordinary measures, such as the use of Anna's mother to appeal to the better instincts of the American public.''

''But why? Doesn't he want her to return?'' Cernan gaped.

''I ventured that question a bit more delicately than you have stated it. When he was through glaring at me, he said the matters of Miki and Anna were somehow mixed together and he had every assurance that if Miki is returned to Prague, the matter of Anna Jelinak will resolve itself quietly.''

''This is absurd,'' Cernan said.

"So much is," Gorkeho agreed. "Does he have some secret contact with the CIA that assures him of this? I do not know, I am not expected to know."

"But his Ministry is not authorized . . . to act as intelligence agents, to—"

"I can assure you, Cernan, that I was surprised as you seem to be by the extent of Henkin's influence. He educated me in one afternoon. You will go to Brussels and you will carry seventy-five ounces of gold with you and you will report to me and I shall report to Henkin until the matter is resolved. That is how influential this man is."

Cernan bit his lip. He thought of Anna Jelinak, suddenly cut off. He thought of Anna far away. He tried to think of the little girl as she had been that summer day in the shadow of Hradcany, but the image was fading.

"He chose me because he wants to leave Anna alone. Why? Is it not important to get Anna back *and* to get Miki? Both important?"

"Yes. That is logical. But there is something else at work here that has nothing to do with logic. It is Henkin's game and he has made it clear to me that it does not involve you or me."

"But what do you think?" Cernan raised his voice almost to a shout.

Gorkeho looked at him. "Too much passion, Cernan. Sit down and try to calm yourself. What I think is beside the point. What I think is that Henkin, through very unusual channels we know nothing about, has struck a delicate bargain with one or more private parties to have Miki returned to us, and it involves using you—not someone like you but you yourself—to act as the errand boy. If I probe into this, it is not profitable to me. Or you. I will probe, I assure you, Comrade Cernan, but delicately and with some grace. Not blundering ahead as you would do. We will know the truth but it will take a little while." His voice was so soft now that Cernan strained to hear him.

"Take Henkin's gold and orders and do as he said. But be careful, Cernan. Be very careful how you proceed. I do not trust Henkin, I do not trust Miki, I do not trust the Americans who arranged all this. Poke the ground with a stick before you take a step. And leave a trail so that I can follow you in everything you are doing."

"There is no danger to me," Cernan began.

"Yes. To you. The moment Henkin used your name, you were in danger. And a little danger to me but it only interests me, it makes me wary."

"And Anna."

"Yes." The old soldier sighed. "Yes. Danger to Anna Jelinak, I think, most of all."

ELEVEN

Varieties of
Religious Experience

If Henkin was worried, he didn't show it. The plane banked and descended over the fields of southern Germany and bumped rudely to a landing in the rural airport outside of Nurnberg. The taxi ride in the stately old Mercedes to the walled city took exactly nineteen minutes. In all, Henkin had traveled two hours from Prague by the time he checked into the Victoria Hotel just inside the city wall. Two minutes later, he placed the telephone call to New York. It was absurd to think about, but even a high-level government official like Henkin was subject to tapped telephone lines. Which is why he was suddenly called to make an overnight visit in Nurnberg.

The worry he had held in on the fifty-two-minute plane ride from Prague broke now in a line of perspiration across his cold, pale face. The telephone relays clicked and whirred and Henkin tapped his fingers on the desk at the side of his bed until he heard the ringing begin.

The American voice sounded distant.

"It's me," Henkin said.

The other man waited.

"Our mutual friend has been located," Henkin said. "It's all arranged. At least, I assume it is arranged."

"What does that mean?"

"He is to be handed over to my government in exchange for a certain . . . ransom. This was a very near thing. The Americans had arranged for his defection. That would have been a disaster. For you, for me. I assure you, we are allies in this matter."

"We had our doubts," said the other man. It was the same soft, sure voice that had instructed Ben Herguth seven hours earlier. It was just after dawn now in New York City, early afternoon in Germany. "I'm glad to hear that our doubts will be put to rest." Another pause. "When will you have Miki in hand?"

"I think in forty-eight hours, perhaps a little more or less. The problem is not getting Miki, it is getting a satisfactory solution . . . to our problem. Miki has shown he is not to be trusted."

"Yes. I'm afraid that's the case."

"The problem is that if he is brought back to Prague . . . well, he might be in a position to bargain his . . . knowledge to certain authorities in order to escape his punishment. You see how delicate it is."

"For both of us. For all our interests. You say the CIA double-crossed us in the first place?"

"No. Not them. The information is that it was another intelligence agency. But Americans. They had arranged Miki's defection."

"And they have Miki now?"

"No. The defection route was . . . interrupted. This is a private operator," Henkin said. His face was bathed in sweat. His shirt was soaked. He felt the grinding in his belly again, the same feeling he had had all week. "Look, there is a risk in this, but I don't want Miki's return any more than you do. Any more than your contacts at Central Intelligence do. Miki can spoil everything."

"What are you going to do?"

"Rather, what are *we* going to do." Henkin would be more assured if he could see the other man. If the other man were occupying a straight chair in Henkin's office in Prague. If Henkin could set the scene and the tone of the interview. But here he was, a worried man in a small room in an old hotel in Nurnberg, trying to make a case to another man 3,500 miles west.

"Proceed."

"Let us be honest," Henkin said. "When Miki defected, you assumed it was a double cross at worst, that we had arranged his disappearance or the CIA had. Or that Miki had made a bargain with a third party to reveal all he knew about . . . arrangements. And when that little girl in Chicago defected at nearly the same moment, you did not believe this was a coincidence."

The man in New York said nothing.

"I can get Miki but I cannot order his execution. Not in a foreign country. He is somewhere in Belgium now, the agent from the Ministry for Secret Services has been dispatched to Brussels. He will report to me when he has Miki."

"And what will I do?" the man in New York asked in the same soft voice.

"I need Anna Jelinak. I need control over her to control what must be done in the next two or three days in Belgium."

"We had intended . . . to use the child as a hostage," the man in New York said. "We arrange deals, we had twenty million riding on this next project, and suddenly Miki disappears and all the deals have holes in them. At the same time, this little girl suddenly announces her defection. She's in films, Miki's in films—what was the connection here? And we looked into it and it was a coincidence as far as we were concerned. . . . But what if we could use her to bargain with, in case it turned out you had Miki and wanted to increase the price of doing business? Or one of the agencies . . . we mule for . . . had snatched Miki for insurance reasons? My associate thought it was best to act right away, have the child under our control if she were needed. But it isn't necessary now, is it?''

"More than you understand," Henkin said. "The child is more valuable at this moment than she has ever been. When can you . . . put her under control?"

There was another pause. "Maybe in two days. Or three. We are trying to . . . dampen the publicity aspects of her defection. You people haven't helped, you've sent that hysterical woman here, her mother, and—''

"That is being taken care of," Henkin said, sounding less like a worried traveler than the director of the Ministry for Tourism and Films. "There are aspects to this you do not even understand. They are being taken care of."

"I'd like to be put in the picture," the New York man said.

Henkin sighed and thought about it, about how far he could reveal his methods and his plan to this other man. If they were partners, they were business partners only at certain times and for certain reasons of mutual benefit. Beyond those times, the New York man was a stranger, perhaps an enemy. What could Henkin reveal to him? Yet he needed the little girl in Chicago "under control" if he was to arrange the fate of Miki in a foreign land.

"Are you there?" said the soft voice from America.

"Do you think it is positive you can put her . . . under control . . . in three days?"

"Perhaps."

"Jules. This is more important than you realize—"

"We only considered her to be a hostage, a pawn if we needed one—"

"We are not speaking now of 'if.' She is needed, Jules. If I must explain, I will tell some of it and more of it as it is necessary. I am trapped by my position, I cannot run to the telephone every hour to inform you—"

"I understand," the other man said.

"All right." Another sigh, this one coming from someplace deep. He was bathed in sweat, he would have to shower when the conversation ended. He felt tired and the grinding in his belly was almost audible. What a mess. Thank God for Miki's inquisitiveness: If Miki had not known the truth about Anna Jelinak, Henkin would not have known. And if Henkin had not known, he would not have been able to arrange the assassination of Miki at all.

Anton Huss sat down at table five in the Pump Room in the Ambassador East Hotel in Chicago. Mr. Willis was waiting for him. The waiter hovered and took an order for coffee and seemed unhappy with Anton's choice of beverage. It was four in the afternoon, in that time between lunch and dinner when waiters eat and cooks gossip and the business of commercial feeding is officially in abeyance. Mr. Willis had clout.

"To start with, you know who I am and where I come from," Willis said to Anton Huss.

Anton said, "I believe I do. Nothing is very certain in the profession, is it?"

"In this case, we want to make it absolutely clear. If

you want, I can show you a card with my photograph on it.''

''We have such things as well,'' Anton Huss said.

''And you've seen pictures of the Firm,'' Willis said.

''Very nice on postcards. 'Welcome to Langley, Virginia, home of the Central Intelligence Agency,' '' Anton Huss said.

Willis smiled. ''Good. I want to tell you that we don't like this situation any better than you people do. It screws up all kinds of things you don't even know anything about.''

''I am instructed to listen.'' Anton Huss sipped his black coffee. It was bitter and matched his mood. His face was haggard. He had not been sleeping well in the week since Anna Jelinak decided to have a religious experience on live television. And now Anna's mother was on his hands as well. She was passed out in her hotel room. Each night, he had to file a lengthy verbal report with the liaison officer in the Washington embassy. He was exhausted by events and he knew that when it was over, if it ever was over, they would find some particularly nasty place to assign him. He was certain it would be an African country.

''You sure you don't want something stronger than coffee? Hell, man, the sun's over the yardarm. Loosen up.''

Anton frowned. The Americanisms jangled him.

''I'll put my cards on the table. All of them. Face up. You pick the ones you want.''

He had talked to Willis once before. The man was a fount of jargon. Anton Huss had been in America five years and yet he barely understood half of what Willis said.

''Tony,'' said Willis. ''You and I are just cogs in great big locomotives and neither of us even knows what the next town is. We just turn and the big wheel keeps on turnin'. Get it? Anna Jelinak went off her nut. Imagine what woulda happened if she'd been watching *It's a Won-derful Life* instead of what she thought she saw. Well, that's water up the creek. The thing is, we want to get her back to Prague in the worst way, same as you people do. I was telling you about locomotives. I get the buzz from high up that there are deals in deals going on right now between Prague and D.C. that you and I can't even hint at. Something like Anna Jelinak puts everyone's nose out of joint and screws up the timing. At least, that's the buzz I get. I got it official, too, Tony, you can go to the bank with it.''

"Perhaps I'll have a dry martini," Anton said suddenly. Anything to stop this torrent of words, images, clichés. What was Willis saying?

Willis signaled the reluctant waiter. The martini arrived in a large, wet glass. Anton burned his tongue on the gin and was grateful.

"We go through this the regular way, it might take months, Tony. What I am saying, what I am authorized to say, is that if you people come up with some idea, our people will be willing to help to implement it. To facilitate Anna's return."

Anton blinked. He almost thought he understood. He said nothing.

"Come on, Tone, loosen up," Willis said, his face flushed. He had the remains of a second martini in front of him and had signaled for a third. "You got Anna's mama. I can arrange that she can be alone with her, put the old home ties screws to her, you know, make her homesick. We can't fix the judge we got, but maybe we can get this transferred to a friendlier jurisdiction. You know the way it works."

Anton nodded because Willis wanted him to.

"Or maybe you people have got your own scenario."

Cernan had warned him about that. Meet with them if they want, Cernan had said. Avoid scenarios. Avoid apparent agreement. Do not argue, do not disagree, do not agree. Do nothing until we find out who is behind Anna's defection. But Cernan was not in Chicago. Cernan was not going to be sent to Addis Ababa. Huss was certain it would be Addis Ababa.

"What can be done?" Anton Huss said.

Willis smiled. It was what he wanted. That and the third martini the waiter was bringing over to table five.

"Why is she in Brussels?" Hanley asked.

David Mason stood by the side of his bed in the Amigo Hotel behind city hall and stared at the picture on the wall. He was naked except for the large bath towel wrapped around his middle. Rita Macklin was in the adjoining single room. They had been in Brussels four hours.

"Because she wants to find Devereaux," David Mason said.

"You told her too much."

"I told her a little."

"You told her too much."

"She guessed a lot of it. Devereaux told her before he went to Brussels."

"He would never have done that."

David said nothing. They let the lie alone with their silences. There was no point in Hanley reprimanding him. Hanley knew the way it was with Eurodesk. Eurodesk had its nose out of joint and still didn't know about Miki and why Section wanted him. Eurodesk was looking for a missing agent presumed dead; in fact, he was dead as far as Eurodesk was concerned. Devereaux was out of channels. Fine. Let him stay out of channels.

"She's a journalist, David." Hanley said the word as

a perjorative. "She really can't be trusted. If she had her way, she'd blow Section open. She really can't be trusted at all."

"I don't trust her," David said. He saw her in his mind's eye. They had flown from Geneva together. She was pretty, prettier than he expected. She was young. Her face was open and her eyes were bright green. She was really lovely, David had thought on the plane, and the thought mixed with pity for her because she loved Devereaux.

"What is she going to do in Brussels?"

"If I don't trust her, then she doesn't trust me," David said. "She said she had friends here. Probably other journalists." He knew the word made Hanley uncomfortable. "You can't lock her up or have her arrested, Mr. Hanley. So the next best thing is to watch her."

He saw Hanley's face in the silence. He was considering that.

"We haven't got a flutter from Eurodesk yet," Hanley admitted.

David said nothing.

"One way or the other," Hanley said. "Nothing from across the wall, either. No one has Devereaux and his body can't be found."

"And Miki?"

"Miki is in the same sad state. The other side is pulling its hair out."

"What do you think I should do?"

Hanley said, "You should have been in Lausanne, helping her buy widow's clothes. You should have been finding his life-insurance policy in a lockbox. You should not be with that woman in Brussels. She is a danger, Mason, to you and to Section."

"And herself?"

"I don't care about herself. Survival of Section, Mason.

It's the thing you have to keep in mind all the time. What we do is for Section, not for some goddamn newspaper writer.''

"If he's dead, she wants to know it,'' David said.

"Yes.''

Another silence between them.

"Yes,'' Hanley repeated. "We all want to know it.''

TWELVE

The Man
Who Limped Away

Colonel Ready smiled down at Devereaux and went to the small window and sat on the ledge. They could hear the rain on the pane and on the roof. Devereaux sat still on the broken chair with his arms manacled behind his back.

"I was the last person you ever wanted to see again," Ready said. He grinned at that but it was not pleasant. He had red hair with more gray in it than when Devereaux had last seen him three years before.

A big Belgian was in the room as well. It was the one who had tied the bandana around Devereaux's swollen leg and who had clipped Devereaux with the pistol in the cellar.

"Do you want to know all about it, Devereaux? About how I got away? I could tell you a lot of stories. You cut my leg and you thought they'd catch up with me but I got away. I still got my limp. I appreciate that reminder, Devereaux, it keeps me going. If I get lazy or comfortable in a situation, I can still limp away because I remember the souvenir you gave me.''

''Good,'' Devereaux said. He didn't smile but his voice was easy and flat. ''I hoped it would be permanent. It's better than just a scar. And you've got a scar already.''

Colonel Ready touched his cheek and grinned. The scar went from the corner of his mouth to his ear. His face was always grinning and he might have looked boyish except for the scar and the deep blue eyes. His eyes were as hard as his words.

''I had some errands to do, I had to go to Brussels, I told this idiot here to keep an eye on you, I didn't tell him to put you in the cellar, you might have died in the cellar. He's an idiot, what can I tell you. I didn't want you to die. But he wanted to go off whoring and it was easier to put you in the cellar than to keep an eye on you.'' He said it all in a measured way, giving the words no special inflection.

''I should have just killed you. The way Rita said,'' Devereaux said. ''I should have just killed you, but it didn't seem like it was enough, just to kill you.''

''But you should have,'' Ready agreed.

''How did you shake the wet contract?''

''You set me up as 'November,' so I set up another poor fool as 'November.' His name was Lars. He bought it from a Russian hitter on the Finlandia. The case on 'November' is closed as far as the Russians are concerned. They got their man.''

Devereaux did not speak. Ready had changed. The eyes showed the pain. There must be pain all the time. Devereaux had cut him across the Achilles tendon and left him there, writhing on the floor of the little house above the town of St. Michel.

They were in Nam originally, that was where they met. Ready was working for DIA and moonlighting on the side for himself. He ran dope in Nam and women and he probably shipped intelligence both ways. Devereaux kept running across him. They circled each other in Nam like knife fighters. Then Devereaux was suddenly shipped home and they would never have seen each other again except that Ready came looking for him in Switzerland that time. Ready had a scam going—he always had a scam—and this one involved a whole overpopulated and wretchedly poor Caribbean island named St. Michel. Ready had used Devereaux, leveraged him out of hiding, and then had used Rita Macklin.

The first day she saw him, she said to Devereaux: *Kill him. Kill him now.* And he had hesitated and Ready knew he had won that one, that he had bested Devereaux. And when he got a chance to take Rita Macklin, he had done it. He had raped her with particular brutal force and thrown her naked into the cells and told her how many more rapes she would endure. It had all been a way of destroying his enemy, Devereaux. And Devereaux, when he got Rita back, had thought to let the Soviets kill Ready for him, and he had cut Ready so that Ready could limp away along the trail and all the Soviet hitters had to do was follow the bloodstains and kill him.

And they had failed.

Devereaux felt the sick weakness in his bowels. He had failed twice with Ready and now he was Ready's victim.

"I'm not a man for small cruelties, Devereaux. I wouldn't have put you in the cellar. The rats might have got you."

Devereaux sat very still and did not speak.

"You weren't supposed to be killed, I told them that from the beginning. You panicked the driver I guess when you started shooting. He didn't mean to hit you. He told me that. He said he was sorry. I killed him anyway because you have to have discipline and you can't let people decide these things in panic.'' He paused. ''How's Rita? Lovely as ever?''

Devereaux pushed the words aside. ''You're working for yourself now.''

''I always was. It just took Uncle a while to catch on. Now they don't even know I exist, any more than you did until you saw me just now.''

''So what do you do next? You got it figured out?''

''The trouble with you is you've got no small talk. You never could handle the con part of it. You think this is about intelligence, about thinking about things and getting information and putting two and two together, and that's all just the bullshit part. The real part of it is the con, working the con. You got to give them small talk while you're stealing their wallets so that they feel good about themselves. Just now I was asking you about Rita, how she was, and that might have been small talk but it wasn't. I was really interested. The girl had something. I give you credit for that, Devereaux. The girl really has something. I thought about her almost as much as I thought about you the last couple of years.''

''What kind of a business are you in now? Terrorism?''

''That's right. Let's get off the subject of Rita, let's get rid of the small talk.'' Ready grinned. ''All right, we won't talk about Rita now. About the apartment you live in on the Rue de la Concorde Suisse. No, I'm not a terrorist, there's a crowded market for terrorists. Everyone is a terrorist. I think it started when anyone could get a gun. That makes it a lot easier. Like you. I think of you as a terrorist. That's your style. You cost me a lot, my friend.''

And Devereaux saw the pain at the edge of the hard blue eyes. He was glad to see the pain at least.

"If you're in business, you want money," Devereaux said. "What kind of money do you want?"

"What? For you? Or for Miki and you? I got Miki too, you see. I had to make a few calls in Brussels, see a few people, do some business. That's why this idiot put you in the cellar. I think; I have my arrangement set up."

"Our organization is interested in Miki. And me, naturally," Devereaux said.

Ready smiled. "I bet they are. And if it was just a matter of money, I would have certainly got in touch with your people. But sometimes, it just isn't all about money. You see the way it is. Everyone thinks this was about snatching Miki. I had no idea that Miki had any value. You're the goods, Devereaux. I wanted to see a way to get you, and Miki was just a bonus for me. I followed you down to Chartres, I followed you up to Brussels. So it was going to be a train, I found out. It was a pretty crude operation, using the Club Tres and depending on those boys who run it. When you want to blow up the train, just get to the engineer. I got me a driver and he didn't care which way it worked as long as he got paid. And then he went and tried to kill you. I was so fucking mad I blew his brains out right there on the beach. I was so fucking mad."

"There'll be searchers out now, Ready. You know the way it works. Someone snatched an agent and Section can't let that happen. You should have stayed in your hidey-hole and counted yourself lucky the world didn't know you were alive."

"It doesn't matter," Ready said. "The Czechs really wanted Miki back, that was clear enough. So they are willing to pay for him. And you. There's you, Dev. You're the bonus as far as I'm concerned. I thought about killing you. I hung around Lausanne, I saw you come and go, I thought about killing you. Or killing Rita Macklin and letting you know how I did it. Like you thought, it wasn't just enough to kill your enemy. You kill someone, the mind goes blank, the film ends. But what if I could kill you and keep you alive, keep you in the coffin in a way, watching your body die and yet, it never dying?"

"Booga-booga," Devereaux said.

"Sure, just the old booga-booga. But sometimes there are things in the dark that you should be scared of. There really are monsters, you know."

Devereaux smiled.

"So the Czechs are willing to pay for Miki for their own reasons. I'm not even interested in their reasons. Miki is just another way to make money as far as I'm concerned. If I was interested in what it is that Miki has that they're interested in, I might work on Miki and break him down, you know the way it's done, and then figure out who would pay the most for him. But this one is for you, Dev. So I make an arrangement through a man with another man I don't even know in Prague, and it comes down to them sending over a man and that man taking you and Miki back to Prague. You're the bonus. They'll examine you, of course, and see what you're made of and then they'll pass you along to Moscow. That's the best part. They pass you along and you go to Lubyanka through the back door and you know that Lubyanka is real, don't you, Dev? They really do have cells and the interrogation rooms where they ask you all the questions, and you better know the answers because they have goons like this idiot Damon here who likes to put himself in his work. The work is pain. That's the pleasure of it for people like Damon here. We both know there's pain, brother Devereaux. We know how to give it and take it and we know that there is no one who can stand the pain. We all break down in the end."

"Make an offer to Section. Be a rich man," Devereaux said.

Ready showed all his teeth. "You still don't get it, do you? This is endgame. With a twist, the kind you tried on me. You stay alive with your friends in Moscow and they use you, and when they really get done with you they put you out to work laying track in Siberia or they put a nine-millimeter in your head. And all the while, you tell them everything you know to make the pain go away. But it never goes away, does it?"

"Are you going to talk me to death?"

The smile faded on Ready's face. "You think it's not going to end up that way? Buddy, you don't understand. The wheel is in motion already. You'll be in Prague in less than three days. What do the Sicilians say about revenge? 'It's a dish best eaten cold.' I had two years thinking about it and it worked out better than I thought, and when you're getting the shit beaten out of you in the basement at Lubyanka, think about me."

"You talk a lot more than you used to. You must be alone a lot. You talk to remind yourself you're not dead. You must be practicing in front of mirrors."

Ready hit him then with his open hand. He hit him several times in the face and Devereaux heard a ringing in his ears.

"See, we got maybe twenty-four hours together before I turn you over. Maybe a little longer. It can be like this or we can act civilized to each other."

Devereaux spit in his face then. Damon took a step but Ready held up his hand.

"This idiot wants to kill you. He doesn't understand your psychology."

"Then why not make a sensible deal. Sell me back to Section."

Ready rubbed his palm against his trousers. "I'm going back to Lausanne after this and I'm going to see Rita. Just something else to think about in Lubyanka. She'll be looking for you and I'll lead her to you. And it'll be a little like it was in St. Michel, only I'll have more time with her, give her more instructions, show her the way it has to be between us. She's a bright girl, I think she'll understand."

Devereaux sat very still. There must be no sound, no movement, no reaction at all.

"You're already thinking about it, Devereaux. You're already seeing it, seeing Lubyanka, seeing Rita with me. It works on you, even if you try to think of something else. You'll think about it all the time when you're learning to speak Russian."

"You talk too much," Devereaux said. "You've been listening to yourself so long, you think you're making sense, but not really. Try the old booga-booga someplace else."

But Ready saw it in Devereaux's eyes. Ready saw the look and it was worth it.

THIRTEEN
The Drowning Sailor

"There's all kinds of stories about that place," Lee Reuben said. "Which one you want me to start with?"

"Well, the thing is, is it reasonable that this would be the place?"

Reuben picked up his glass of Johnny Walker Black Label on the rocks. He looked at the amber and stared through it. "Here's looking at you."

"Cheers," Rita Macklin said, meaning none of it.

She tasted the cold Stella Artois and swallowed some and put the glass down. They were in the little bar of the Amigo Hotel with its vaguely Spanish wall coverings and dark wood. She ate a salted cashew and then another and watched the face of the fat man across from her. He had been thin when she first knew him. He had gone to Brussels six years ago to report for the best but not biggest private economic newsletter in English. He was telling her about the Brussels that was not written about. He knew everything and he kept no secrets if you knew how to ask him the right questions. Now he was talking about the Club Tres, just across *Le Grand Place* from where they sat.

"There was smuggling there for a while. That was a previous owner but the same family. They're Dutch speakers, but because they're in Brussels their help is all French speaking. The place is a front but it's a public front, the kind you wink at."

"What's the kind you wink at?"

"The kind you wink at," Lee Reuben said. "Like buying votes in Chicago or kicking back to the unions on construction in New York. There are laws against that kind of thing, but that's the way it's done. Brussels is a very strange city, Rita, plunk in the middle of an even stranger country. They don't speak the same languages to each other, and they're a joke to outsiders. For the love of God, the symbol of the city is the Manniken-Pis, a statue of a little boy taking a leak. How do you explain a city like that to anyone?"

"I just want to get a handle," she said. "I've got to have some place to start."

But Lee was going into his lecture mode. Rita knew him and she tolerated it. She had known Lee a long time ago in Green Bay. Lee had been in love with her then.

"Look, Brussels is The European City. Nothing comes close. Paris is old and tired, and besides, it's full of Frogs. Berlin is broken, London is just money, Italy doesn't count. People want to do business, they do it in Brussels. Common Market, NATO headquarters, it's all here. Arms dealing, drugs, arrangements. There could have been all kinds of private contractors involved in something you are hinting at. And I wish you'd tell me more about it."

"I can't, Lee."

"Rita Macklin, girl reporter for the Green Bay *Press-Gazette*, and Lee Reuben, boy reporter for the same sheet, and here we are, drinking on expense account in the Amigo bar in Brussels."

"Lee, where do I find out?"

"What is this about really?"

"Not a story. It has nothing to do with that. If there was a story I could tell you, I would tell you. This is personal, Lee."

"Personal," he said. He looked at his drink. "OK. It's personal. You want to know about dangerous things."

"Like the place you mentioned."

"The Club Tres." He had brought up the name from the first. The Club Tres was one of a half-dozen places where matters were arranged and where you met people who could do anything. Smuggle arms or smuggle people or give you a new identity or move a hundred kilos of heroin from Marseille to New York City. Brussels was at the center of a strange world because it belonged to no one—center of a country divided by language, crunched between France, Holland and Germany, invaded first in two great wars, strangely sophisticated and provincial at the same time. Lee Reuben ladled in the history of the city he clearly loved.

"Who do you see there?" Rita Macklin said.

"A man named Philip Petty. Half-English, half-Belgian, he's the manager. About twenty-eight years old and a flaming fag and an arranger of lives. Yes. I like that. An arranger of lives. You could tell him you needed to be put in touch with Monsieur so-and-so, the prominent arms dealer, and he would ask you your name and where you are staying and he would see what he could do. And maybe, in the next twenty-four hours, Monsieur so-and-so calls you up. You might be grateful enough to give

Philip a thousand-franc tip the next time you saw him or not; he wouldn't bring it up. If your deal with the arms dealer was profitable, Philip would be taken care of somehow, by someone.''

"I see."

"No. Don't see too much. If you make your inquiry of Monsieur Petty, make certain you don't see too much. I told you, you want to know about dangerous people." He signaled for another drink.

"Why do you know them?" Rita asked. Lee Reuben had been a thin, eager reporter when they first knew each other. Now he had a weariness to match his added weight. She thought he seemed very desperate.

"Because I know Brussels." He picked up his new Scotch and drained some of it off. "Cheers," he said.

"You drink a lot," she said.

"Of course. I'm paid to drink a lot and listen to people and ask a few questions now and then. It gets to be a habit. Besides, I was never so far from home. Imagine missing Green Bay, Wisconsin."

She thought she wanted to touch him and tell him it was all right to miss home. She did nothing.

"Cheers," he said again and took another sip. He looked at her.

"It's good to see you, Rita. It's been years."

"I knew you were here. I should have come up to see you," she said. "I only came when I needed information."

"That's what I'm paid for," he said. "I'm well informed."

"You don't sound very happy."

"I'm terribly happy," he said. "Unless I drink too much and let the self-pity get to me. You're changed, Rita. I was terribly excited by you. You were so eager, such a radical, a bomb-thrower. But you aren't anymore, are you?"

"I'm just older," she said.

"You can't go there alone," he said. "Philip wouldn't talk to you. It's not a place for single women. Women get taken there. You need a man."

"I see," she said. She hoped he would not say anything.

"I could take you there," he said.

"No. I can't let you get involved."

"I can get involved. I know Brussels. You need a guide. An old friend."

"No. You can't be involved in this."

"Why not?"

"I can't tell you."

"What are you looking for?"

"Information," she said. "About a man."

"Your boyfriend," he said.

She didn't say anything.

"Did he run out on you?"

"Maybe something like that," she said.

"That's a lie," Lee said. "Nobody would walk out on you. I know that much."

"I have to find someone."

"In a dangerous place. In a dangerous trade," he said. "I was always a good guesser. I still work the crossword puzzle in ink. Your boyfriend isn't a journalist, is he? What have you gotten involved in, Rita?"

She had thought about that all the way from Lausanne. She had let David Mason get her a room here, she had accepted the fact that he was watching her, that if she got close to it, he would be right behind her. What was she getting into?

"Your boyfriend," Lee was saying. "The one you're looking for. He's in something you can't talk about."

She said nothing.

"What is he? A dealer? Arms or drugs? Is that what you got involved in?"

She stared at him with pretty green eyes and her face was very hard. It was so different from the way she had looked a long time before when they were both starting out on the newspaper in Wisconsin.

He put down the drink and kept looking at her. "I don't care, Rita. I really fell for you. You get over that but you don't either. I'd do anything for you."

"I know," she said. She had known it too. That was why she looked him up. She never intended to see him again. That's not something she would have admitted ten years ago.

"Anything," he said.

But she was getting up now. He waited for her to leave the bar. He waved a fat index finger at Pierre behind the bar and Pierre knew the signal because he knew the fat American and he came down with the bottle of Scotch and a fresh glass.

Kay Davis didn't even feel fired. It had really happened just a few hours ago but she didn't feel it as a thing yet. She took a long hot shower and made herself an indulgent cup of hot cocoa. She thought she should call her mother in Davenport, but then she thought she couldn't tell her that she had just been fired. She felt like a little girl in her terrycloth robe with the cup of hot cocoa on the coffee table. The city was spread out in stark night colors below her window wall on the twenty-ninth floor of the condominium. The view was south toward the Loop, the spires all creating an orange sky. Her view. Her town. Until 4:12 P.M. that day.

She sat on the Eurostyle white couch and propped her

bare feet up on the glass-and-chrome coffee table and took the cocoa a teaspoon at a time, the way she had done as a child when she was sick. The cocoa warmed her memory of being a little girl. She rarely thought now about being little and helpless. Maybe she was beginning to feel fired.

Why did they want to kill the story of Anna Jelinak? Why did they think they could?

She had called Stephanie Fields but got her answering machine. She had left her name. She had called the news director at Channel 7 and he was definitely interested, he definitely wanted to set up a meeting with the station manager.

So why be upset? she thought. You'll work tomorrow or the next day. This is still your town.

Hal Newt had looked at her with such sad eyes.

She put down the cup and got up. She felt a panicky sense of isolation. She went to the window and looked down at Chestnut Street below. It was narrow and there were cars clogging both sides of the street. Chicago was the next to last step up to the Big Apple and she had slipped on a banana peel.

Why did it happen to her?

And she thought of Anna Jelinak. Did Anna wonder why the statue cried? Why it moved her that minute, that very afternoon in a TV studio in a foreign city?

Kay started. She turned around because she suddenly thought she saw something reflected in the window.

It was a large man.

She felt dizzy and afraid. It was impossible for anyone to be inside her apartment. There was a doorman, there were security television cameras, there was a steel door with a peephole, and this was impossible. This building was as safe as they could make it.

The large man just stood there in the foyer and looked at her. He had a wide forehead and his eyes were set so far apart that it was hard to keep both of them in mind in a single glance. She looked from eye to eye. His face had the pebbled texture of a basketball. He stood and stared at her and said nothing.

She could not speak. When she found her voice, he was already talking.

"You're dumb, you know that?"

"How did you get in here?"

"You could be a leg up now but you were dumb. Dumb. How can you figure dumb people."

"You get out of here."

"You get a nice chance and you blow it. I could say you'll regret it the rest of your life, but what the hell is that? Ten minutes?"

He didn't move.

She picked up the letter opener. Gift from her Aunt Doris. Part of a set including desk pad, telephone book . . .

The large man walked into the room.

"Get out of here."

There was disgust on his face. "Dumb."

Oh my God, she said to herself. I don't want to die.

He took the letter opener out of her hand. He slapped her across the face and the blow sent her back into the window. The window wall shook from the force of her body hitting it.

"There was a broad once was supposed to jump through the window in an apartment in the John Hancock Building, but I don't think you can. I mean, you'd have to really hit the glass the right way, with a lot of force, to even crack it. These high-rises are built like brick shithouses."

She staggered around the desk to put it between her and the man.

The telephone rang.

Kay pushed at the desk to shove it against him. Her robe opened.

He stared right through her, the way Al Buck had stared right through her when he told her to clear the building. Her nostrils flared with the rush of adrenaline.

He was talking out loud but he was talking to himself. He was really huge, outweighing her by about 150 pounds. His fingers were large and some of them had been broken once. He wore a blue suit and an open-collar white shirt. His black hair glistened with oil.

"So how do you figure a broad throws a snit and walks out on a good job, good bucks, moving up the ladder of success? A good-looking broad, good tits, good can, and she walks out and goes to her fancy high-rise one-bedroom apartment on Chestnut Street and kills herself? I mean, what happened? She flip out or what? Yeah. She must of flipped out."

She ran across the room and he caught her by the wrist at the door of the bathroom and pushed her in. His hand was hot around her pale wrist.

"Pills," he said. "Broads do it with pills. Look at Marilyn Monroe. That was a waste. How do you figure people who got it made?"

He opened the medicine cabinet.

"Everyone's got pills," he said.

He took the bottle of sleeping pills from the glass shelf and closed the cabinet. She hit him in the face.

He looked at her. "You want me to slap you around some first?" He seemed surprised and hurt. "You make it easy, you make it hard."

"Please, for the love of—"

"Look, honey. I get no kicks out of this. Well, maybe in a way. But if it wasn't me, it's someone else. See? If it isn't today it's tomorrow, and why put it off. It's like going to the dentist to get a tooth yanked. You put it off and put it off, but you still got to do it in the long run.''

"Please, please, please," she said. He had her cornered in the small bathroom. He was twisting the cap.

"I hate these fucking childproof caps," he said.

He opened the bottle and spilled the pills out into one huge hand. She hit his open hand and knocked the pills all over and she shoved him against the toilet. She had the strength because she was so afraid; she could have lifted a car. He struck his head on the edge of the shower door. He shook his head and he was bleeding.

Kay was out of the room and running toward the front door. She opened the door and ran to the fire stairs at the end of the corridor. The place was full of electrical hums and the rush of wind against the building twenty-nine floors above the ground.

He was slow, but when he got to the hall he started to run.

She pushed open the green fire door and the door resisted a moment because of the change in pressure between the concrete stairwell and the corridor.

Her robe was open and the cord trailed behind her. She ran down the stairs on slippered feet. The stairs above her rang with the sound of his large feet. She ran down and down and down and it was like falling. The numbers of the floors were painted on the doors at each floor. Down and down, her legs without any feeling, her breath coming in great, panicked sobs.

She pushed the door that said Lobby and ran into the world. The doorman was schmoozing with the cop who came around every night because he had a girl friend in the studio condo on the nineteenth floor. The cop was big and good-looking the way young cops are before they drink too much or get too cynical about the job. He was only twenty-six but he thought he had seen it all, the crazies and weirds and winos and killers in the alleys. Now this, a crazy broad running into the lobby with her bathrobe practically falling off her so that you could see her tits.

"Someone is after me, someone coming to kill me."

The doorman turned more slowly. He hated to be interrupted when he was bullshitting the young cop.

The big man was right behind her and grabbed her as if he were merely annoyed.

"The fuck you running for?" It was as though they were the only two people in the world. "The fuck you making it hard on yourself?"

The doorman said, "Hey, man, what you doin'?" It was something he was used to saying. He acted like he owned the building sometimes. He didn't even look at the cop, who was taking a step toward the big man. The big man had a knife now and everyone saw it: Kay Davis, the doorman, the cop. The knife filled the lobby.

"Don't!" she screamed.

But he was going to stick her and he pulled the knife back so that he had room to swing it into her body. He held her by the neck, like a chicken.

The cop moved the way he moved when he was playing football. You don't even think about it, about the pain, the guy slicing off tackle toward you, the way you're going to be hit in a few seconds. You just see your body moving through spaces that open for you. That is the way he pulled the .357 Smith & Wesson Police Special, pulled it easy off his belt and aimed and fired without even thinking about it. If he had thought about it, Kay Davis would have had a knife between her breasts. That's what they all said later. The kid didn't know how easy it was going to be.

The gunshot blasted the lobby to silence. It was shocking to hear a pistol shot in the context of the lobby. A cabbie leaned on his horn on State Street to make a bus move. It didn't work.

The big man didn't really hear the sound. The bullet was between those two eyes set so wide apart. Kay saw the dirty hole in his head a moment before he keeled over.

"I want to make this absolutely clear," Hanley said in a sly voice.

Mrs. Neumann said, "Of course."

"Stowe sent a blip an hour ago and we've just ironed it out," he said.

The "blip" was a microwave signal sent in the clear from Brussels, bounced off a satellite and picked up by the Section receiving station near Indian Head, Maryland, about twenty-two miles south of Washington. Indian Head actually housed the U.S. Naval Propellant Plant, which was a top-secret base used by the four armed services for training of Explosive Ordnance Disposal experts—bomb squad people. But because the base was so vast and so secret, the government had appropriated other land near it along the Potomac River that was used for odd service needs—including the power-receiving and -transmission system used by R Section.

The "blip" had been .02 seconds in transmission and contained 623 digital sequences which were "ironed out" through a complex reverse microprocessor that elongated the signal to its normal length and then translated the code.

"There is a private contractor involved and he has made contact with the Opposition concerning the sale of certain 'damaged goods,' " Hanley said. He frowned, remembering the arch way that Stowe had put it in the "blip." Stowe was of the old school and he thought spies were better spies if they could whisper without moving their lips and if they spoke in such a roundabout way that no one—not even the person they were talking to—could understand what they really meant. He was a maddening man, Hanley thought, not for the first time. "I don't know what Stowe means by damaged goods and there's no point right now in asking for a clear signal. Time is the problem. Prague was contacted from Brussels two days ago by the private contractor. And Prague is on the move, we've monitored their embassy in Brussels constantly and it's a regular little anthill the past two days. We presume Prague—or, I should say, Stowe in Eurodesk presumes Prague—has agreed to the terms of the sale."

"What about our man?" Mrs. Neumann said. It was ten minutes to midnight in Washington. The eerie red "eyes" of the Washington Monument—aircraft-warning lights—blinked incessantly above the city. The streets were lined with painted trees and orange anti-crime lampposts. National Airport was shut down for the night and all was deep, silent, clear, save for the faraway wail of an ambulance.

Hanley got up from the chair and went to the window and looked down at the deserted quiet of Fourteenth Street.

"There is no mention of him. There is something else."

Mrs. Neumann waited.

Hanley cleared his throat. He remembered very well the matter on St. Michel of a couple of years ago. It had been a personal thing at the end and he did not approve of that. Section was impersonal, it was a tool of the government.

There was no place in Section for personal feuds. Except that time Devereaux had had the say of how the thing would be handled.

"The private contractor has a face," Hanley said. "Stowe really performed for us in the end." He said it with wonder. "He had a right to have his nose out of joint, we went out of channels with Devereaux to bring Miki out. But Stowe worked it hard and he has a face. It's one we know."

He described Colonel Ready to her. Of course, Mrs. Neumann had been in Computer Analysis then—Comp An—but she had been his confidante then and not his superior. She knew about Colonel Ready and the business on St. Michel that had nearly cost Devereaux and Rita Macklin their lives.

"We should . . ." She hesitated.

"We should watch and wait and do nothing and let him come out more into the light," Hanley said. He knew the procedure.

"But Rita Macklin. She's in Brussels. We should—"

"We should do nothing," Hanley said. "Ready is the target now. He is the private contractor and somehow he managed to penetrate security and hit our train. So he has Devereaux and Miki and he is apparently dealing Miki back to Prague. We can accept our losses."

Mrs. Neumann's hoarse whisper startled him. "Dammit, man, we're talking about our own man in there."

"He's dead," Hanley said. "If we had any doubt, we can't have any now. That's Colonel Ready whom Stowe described. Ready is dealing Miki back to Prague. Ready has him, so Ready has Devereaux. So Devereaux is dead."

"But he might be—"

"Devereaux is dead," Hanley said. "It doesn't really

matter if he's temporarily breathing. He's out of the picture, Mrs. N. We take our losses but we look for our
opportunity. Stowe identifies the man we're looking for,
the man who wrecked the train. We don't know where
he's run to ground yet or where he is keeping Miki. We
watch and wait. Stowe's a good man. Let the thing go
on the way it is. We can't interfere with fate. Warn off
Rita Macklin and what will happen? Can we trust her not
to blow up that St. Michel business and make Section
look bad? Can we trust her at all? It's not as though we
had an official secrets act to sign. She's a goddamn reporter, Mrs. N. Her loyalty is to Devereaux. And we
know there can't be a Devereaux anymore, not once Ready
got him. Tell her that and she won't have any loyalty
left, and that doesn't get us Ready and it doesn't get us
closer to cutting our losses.''

"Mason. Mason is with her. He's one of ours.'' She
said it without any tone in the whisper. The urgency
had gone out of her voice. Hanley was laying the cards
down, one at a time, and turning them over. Tarot
cards: This was the hanged man, this was the sailor torn
from the sea. This one was dead, this one was waiting
to die.

"Mason has to be careful,'' Hanley said. He said it
in such a neutral voice. He was under control and he
passed the calm across the desk to Mrs. Neumann. This
is the way it is, he was saying: This is a world of losses,
little advantages, small victories and minor defeats, gray
mixed in gray, reports filed today to be forgotten tomorrow. Agents moved in dangerous worlds because it
had always been so. "Mason is a neophyte but he's had
his training, he has to be careful.''

"If she gets on Ready's trail, Ready will get her,''
Mrs. Neumann said. She thought she was weak to say

it; she was showing a loyalty to her sex that Hanley would see as weakness.

"Perhaps Stowe will get Ready first," Hanley said, turning another card over.

Mrs. Neumann stared at the words like the face of a card. It was the card of the drowning sailor.

FOURTEEN
Train Moving East

D evereaux's mouth was thick with thirst. He felt his cracked lips with his dry tongue. The pain in his left leg throbbed gently, reminding him he was alive. He had slept and now his eyes were open and he stared into the darkness of the room. He could see light from the window.

They had taken him out of the broken chair and left him on the bare floor. Because he could not eat with his hands behind his back, they cuffed his arms in front—but they chained his right leg to a small radiator pipe that ran along the wall. He tried to pull that cuff off or render the pipe from the wall but it was no good. He had eaten the crusty bread and drunk water from a bowl. But the water was all gone now and it was dark again and the house had been empty a long time.

Devereaux slept from time to time.

He dreamed of Rita Macklin. He saw her for a moment

apart from him and then saw her beneath him, felt her body open, make its demand, insist upon him. He could hear her voice in his dream, smell her, make love to her. The last surprised him. When he made love to her in his dream, it was so good and real that when he awoke and he was still in darkness and pain, it seemed the darkness was the dream and that the lovemaking was the real side of consciousness.

In his dream, she smelled like flowers. She was innocent, thoughtful, staring away from him in a May field in the mountains above the town. The town was Lausanne in one part of the dream and it was Front Royal, Virginia, in another part, the part where they were in the cabin on the Virginia hill and it was before the time the two killers had come for them. The time before innocence ended.

He touched her and she turned to him and changed. Her open, green eyes became dark with lust. He touched her and she touched him back, she opened her mouth to taste his mouth and fell against him with her mouth working against his mouth, kissing and tasting each other with lips and tongues, and then she put her hands on his belly and he rolled with her in the field of flowers, hidden by the tall grass all around them. He opened her legs with his hands and felt her wanting to be opened, felt her hands now on his back, his buttocks, pulling him toward her.

He awoke and it was darkness and pain. He groaned, felt the familiar sickness in his bowels. Everything was the way Ready said it would be. The only thing he could do for himself was to kill himself before they squeezed everything out of him. He couldn't even save Rita Macklin when Ready came after her.

"Are you still alive then?"

Devereaux tried to speak but he had no voice left. The dryness had taken it.

"You want some water?"

He had dreamed of water. He kept his head still now. He wanted to say: Yes, please give me water. Please, please, please. He wanted to beg for water. But a strong rational part of him had thought of Lubyanka, the dread prison that was part of KGB headquarters in Moscow. A part of him thought he wanted Lubyanka less than he wanted water. Even Ready could make a miscalculation about the water. He could die in a day or two and it would be over.

"Why don't you speak? Can't you speak?"

He closed his eyes and the man came near to him in the darkness and peered at his face.

"Hey. Are you dead?"

Devereaux opened his eyes. It was the big one called Damon, the one who had hit him in the cellar with a pistol. Damon squatted down and stared at him.

"You aren't dead," Damon said. He held his hand up to Devereaux's nose to feel the breath.

Devereaux grabbed the hand with both manacled hands and twisted and the fulcrum moved the world. The big man cried out, twisted, fell to the floor on his back and Devereaux reached over his head and pulled back. The big man elbowed him in the belly. Devereaux grunted, pulled the chain taut against the big man's neck. For one moment, the big man fought with his body. In the next moment, the big man grabbed for the chain because the lifebreath was going out of him and his head was about to explode. His eyes bulged out of their sockets and his tongue protruded. He made a gagging noise over and over and his lungs pumped up and down but there was no breath.

Devereaux closed his eyes to feel better the life going out of the other man. He bunched his shoulder muscles and pulled back and the big man stopped struggling. The big man was dead.

When Devereaux opened his eyes, sweat blinded them. He reached up and released the corpse and the big man's head slammed on the floor. His eyes were open and his tongue lolled out of his mouth. Devereaux felt the pockets and found the keys. He opened the handcuffs. He found the small pistol in the right-hand pocket and opened it. It was some sort of cheap French make with five shots. He put the pistol in his pocket and tried to get up.

The left leg hurt like hell. He braced himself against the wall and rose up. When he was on his feet, he tested the left leg. He could stand on it but the pain made him wince when he lurched along the wall.

Devereaux went to the window and stared out at the night. There was a canal outside the window and all the houses were old and very beautiful. He had never been in this place and he tried to guess where it was. Below the window, the cobblestoned street was empty.

Devereaux got to the door and down the stairs slowly. No one else was in the house. When he moved, he swung his left leg out stiffly, like an old man.

Adrenaline gave him more strength than he thought he had. For the first time, he thought he had a chance. He took the pistol out of his pocket, checked the action, waited at the front door.

He pushed the door open to the darkness. The night was clear, cool and the moonlight sparkled on the canal. The old houses had stacked roofs in the Flemish style. He took one step to the street and then another and he stayed in the shadows.

The headlights flicked on at the corner and caught the shadow of the limping man. He turned, started to run, felt the pain rise up his legs into his crotch, all black and sickening. He stumbled, cursed, turned with the pistol toward the car and waited.

But two men were already out of the car.

To hell with it, he thought. This way was better than Lubyanka. He squeezed the pistol at the first shadow and the trigger stuck. The pistol was jammed. He slammed at the side of the barrel with his hand and the second man slapped him with a lead-weight sap.

He slumped but he was not unconscious. The first one took the pistol and slapped him with it. They dragged him across the cobblestones to the car. One of them went into the house and came out and said that Damon was dead. That made both of them want to hit him again. He felt the blows but he did not fall into unconsciousness.

He felt the car moving and looked hurriedly out the side window at the narrow street along the canal and the sleeping, shuttered houses with their quaint rooflines. The canal stretched out to the edge of the city and there was a tow path and barges sleeping at their piers. He saw a green sign printed in two languages:

BRUGES CENTRE VILLE
BRUGGE CENTRUM

He must have fallen unconscious then. When he opened his eyes, he was between the two men, his hands were tied again. The countryside was bright and flat under moonlight in the clear, November sky. The highway went on straight, without curves or rises. After a long time, they turned into a dirt road.

The headlights framed a weathered white house in the middle of farm fields. At the edge of the horizon, a slight gray light began to kindle dawn.

They dragged him out of the car and over to the house. One of them propped him against the wall with a pistol under his chin and Devereaux did not move. They were knocking on the door and making a lot of racket that echoed strangely in the silence of the autumn countryside.

The door opened and revealed a yellow rectangle of light. The man inside stepped back.

They pushed him inside and the place smelled stale and unused. The light came from a single lamp on a wooden table in the center of the room.

Devereaux blinked at the other man. He had a broad forehead and dark eyes. Devereaux felt the pain pulling him back to unconsciousness again. Someone said in French, "Put him in a chair, he's going to pass out again."

He felt the chair under him and opened his eyes.

He stared at the man in the chair opposite while the other men talked to each other in French.

The man in the chair on the other side of the table wore handcuffs as well and stared at Devereaux with a look of both shock and despair. His look mirrored the sick feeling in Devereaux's guts.

It was Miki.

FIFTEEN
Coincidences

Anna sat on the floor in her jeans and listened. She never wore anything but jeans unless she had to go to court with Stephanie. Those times, somewhat truculently, she agreed to dress as a little girl because Stephanie thought it best and because Stephanie had bought her the jeans in the first place. First one pair, then two and now three. She washed them by hand, with reverence.

The music was acid, full of words that expressed an unearned contempt for the world. The blocks of notes had a comforting sameness and the boy with a girl's voice on the tape lisped his contempt with ritual cant. It was like listening to the words in church.

"Can you turn it down, dear? I'm talking on the phone."

Anna sighed and turned down the tape on her boom box and went to the door and looked at Stephanie.

Stephanie was sitting at her desk in her blue terrycloth robe. From the first, she had sheltered Anna—from the press, from the representatives of the United States and the Czech governments, from the various and inevitably strange religious figures who wanted to contact the little girl who saw a miracle. She had installed Anna in her own apartment on Seminary Avenue in the quaint Victorian neighborhood around DePaul University on the north side. The rooms were not so large, but the ceilings were high and the tall windows filled the rooms with the gloomy November light during the days.

Stephanie listened for a long time and Anna Jelinak listened at the door. Something made the little girl frown. She crossed back into her room and turned the boom box off and went back to the door.

"I don't know, Kay," Stephanie said at last. "You're sure you'll be fine with—"

She broke off and listened some more.

"You really should come here."

She listened more.

"All right, then. All right. No. No. I won't. No, it's all right. Yes. I will. Yes. Yes. Yes. All right. See you in the morning. All right."

She replaced the receiver. The night scratched against the tall windows. The street side of the apartment was colored by immense sodium vapor lights with an orange glow. The trees in the parkway were bare and the wind made the panes rattle.

"Are you all right?"

Stephanie glanced up at Anna at the door as though she were startled. Then she nodded and got up. She went through the apartment to the kitchen and checked the locks on the large kitchen door. There were grates on the kitchen window that opened on a gray wooden back porch. The door had a small pane of glass. The door carried three locks. She tugged at the door with her thin arms extended.

Next to the kitchen was a maid's room with another window that opened above the gray backstairs that led down to the second floor of the three-flat building. The window was ungrated but someone would have to prop up a ladder on the stairs in order to reach the window. She checked the lock in the sash.

Stephanie went from room to room of the narrow flat, checking the locks on the tall windows that opened on narrow lightwells between the row of brick three-flats along the block.

Anna trailed behind her. Because Stephanie said nothing, Anna felt afraid.

The front door led to the common hall and the stairs that connected the three apartments in the tall building. The stairs were steep and lighted. The front door was solid oak. She checked the locks on the front door. The top lock was a chain, the second a deadbolt, the third a second deadbolt.

When she was finished, they went into the front room and sat down in front of the nonfunctioning gas fireplace that contained a television set in the hearth. They always sat in front of the television set but Stephanie rarely turned it on.

"Kay called just now," Stephanie said. Her voice sounded odd to Anna. There was a cold edge to it that did not contain life. Stephanie's voice was usually loud or angry or even gentle, but it had life in it.

"Kay said a man attacked her in her apartment. She said she was fired this afternoon when she refused to dump the story."

Anna sat on the straight chair and did not understand. She tried to smile through her puzzlement. It was the way you smiled at old people or crazy people, to make them understand you meant no harm.

"I'm sorry," Stephanie said. She shook her head. She had very white skin and small dark curls. She tried to wear her hair straight and boyish and it came out curly and too feminine for her taste.

Anna appreciated the returning smile. Stephanie talked to her like an adult. Stephanie told her the first day she really didn't believe in miracles or God but that she could appreciate people who did. They got along.

"I'm afraid because Kay is afraid and because I don't believe in coincidences."

"I don't understand."

"What about this afternoon? When your mother talked to you?"

"I told you. She talked such a lot of nonsense to me."

"Did she bring any message? From Anton or any of them?"

"No," Anna said.

"Are you sure, Anna?"

Anna made a face and didn't answer.

"Anna, are you sure?"

"Yes." Her face got tighter.

"Anna, Kay Davis got fired."

Anna blinked. What did it mean?

"Anna. Kay, our friend, Kay was fired and was told not to work on the story. On the story about you, Anna. And then she went home and a man got into her apartment and tried to kill her."

Anna understood now. It was not so uncommon. On television, women were always being threatened, attacked, even killed. A man tried to kill the woman last night. Or the night before. And the woman who was raped and beaten. Was it last night? And Stephanie told her to keep the doors locked and not to answer the doorbell if it rang and everyone around her acted so afraid all the time, as though they expected the worst to happen at any moment.

"Kay is all right," Stephanie said, answering an unspoken question.

"That is good," Anna said.

"You see why I'm upset," Stephanie said. "Why I want you to think over very carefully if your mother said anything to you."

What did she want to hear? Anna thought and frowned.

"Did she tell you anything might happen if you did not come home? Did she say that Anton Huss or someone might try to snatch you? You know, to kidnap you home? Did she say anything like that?"

Anna let her frown lighten. Was that it? "No. I don't think so. My mother threatened me the first time. I told you."

"But she threatened you like a mother."

"She said she should have beaten me some more when I was a little girl. Before I became a movie star. Well, I told her it was too late for that."

Stephanie concentrated. Her eyebrows almost met above her pretty straight nose. There was an air of intense, thin nervousness in all her gestures and facial expressions. She was pretty and men were a little afraid of her.

"I am really worried. I want to get police protection reinstalled."

Anna nodded. She liked the policemen who had guarded them. The tall, blond one was nice to look at and he taught her to play cribbage. It would be nice to have a man around, Anna thought, and let a smile creep across her serious face.

Stephanie concentrated right through the smile. "I'll get an order. I talked to Kay. She said she had a place to stay tonight, she said she would meet me in the morning at court. I am really worried about this—''

A tree branch scraped a window in the wind. The wind rattled the panes again. The night howled.

"Jesus," Stephanie said. She got up and checked the locks on the front door again. She walked through the apartment and turned on lights and checked the windows again. She said aloud, "This is stupid, I am not going to be afraid."

She made Anna afraid.

Anna went to her room and put on her robe and lay down on her bed and listened to heat clatter up through the radiator pipes. She closed her eyes and thought of the woman named Elena.

Elena Jelinak had a very pinched look to her as though she had been crying or drinking too much. Her hand shook when she talked to Anna.

"You have to stop this foolish thing," Elena had said. "You shame me, you shame yourself, to say you are an orphan in the world. You know I am your mother."

She said nothing to Elena that afternoon in the interview room. There were just Elena and Anna, two women who had lived together in four rooms in the old section of Prague down by the Charles Bridge. They had nothing to say to each other, Anna thought. She even thought Elena would agree with that.

"You did not see Jesus weep," Elena said.

Anna said, "I saw it. My Infant of Prague."

"Blasphemy," said Elena. "This is nonsense. You have gotten so famous and proud because of the films—well, you are causing no end of trouble. What if I told you that the government is very worried about this?"

The thought had not occurred to Anna. Why would it

possibly interest her what the government thought of anything?

"What do you want, Anna? You have everything."

Anna had stared at the woman. She would never understand, not any of it. How could she explain to Elena that the Child was in the statue in their rooms in Prague, that she could pray to the Child and even talk to it? You had a mother and a father and you knew love. What is it that no one can love me? And then, one day in a strange city in a strange country, the Child comes to her again, and this time the Child weeps for her, for Anna Jelinak who is not loved. In that act of love, the world opens for her. There is Stephanie with soft, kind words who shares her house and her warmth, and there is Kay Davis who listens to her, who holds her in her arms when she weeps about the miracle she has seen. There is love and she feels it as solidly as she feels warmth, as she feels the luxury of silk beneath her fingers, as she can smell the newness of the world. . . .

She opened her eyes.

Stephanie had turned on the television and was watching the local news. The windowpanes continued to rattle and the steam pipes clanged and hissed their merry sounds of warmth. Comfort in the sounds, in the wind that cannot penetrate the windowpanes.

Anna padded on bare feet out of her bedroom and down the lighted corridor that connected all the rooms. She went into the living room and curled up on the couch without a word to watch the TV and to be in Stephanie's presence. In the silence of the darkened room, they watched the images of the world on the screen and comforted each other with their presence, with the sounds of the artificial fireplace. Anna fell into a soft, drowsy sleep and Stephanie wrapped a blanket around her and she felt Stephanie's light touch and the warmth and it was so good and safe to be here, she thought. It was almost the pleasant dream of her life to be here. It was the dream she could not explain ever to Elena, to anyone else except the beautiful Child who had wept for her when He saw her loneliness.

SIXTEEN

The Price of a Spy

The third man knew what he was doing. He made a plaster cast in the morning and put it on Devereaux's left hand and it felt pretty good. The pain went away. They talked a lot in a strange language about his leg and finally wrapped it from knee to ankle in a stretch bandage. They gave him water and soup and bread.

He slept.

For the first time in his captivity, he had been fed enough to eat and he slept without restraints in a small bedroom at the back of the house. He thought of escape right away and the head man—his name was Cernan—told him that there was no real escape and that it was tedious to put a guard under his window, so they had locked the window and nailed it shut and if Devereaux wanted to break the glass, well, then they would catch him but they would have to chain him after that and his leg would never get healed that way. Cernan spoke English like a man measuring a room. The words were all very careful and exact.

He slept for a very long time. He made love to Rita in his dream again, the one that took place on the hill. After they made love, they were in Lausanne together, eating at the café below the university, and later they were talking about something in the apartment on the Rue de la Concorde Suisse when, suddenly, Colonel Ready walked into the room and he shot Devereaux without a word. Devereaux was dead and yet he was still conscious after death of what was going on. He couldn't speak. Ready took Rita in his arms and she resisted him at first and she slapped him. Then, after a while, she began to kiss Ready as passionately as she had kissed Devereaux on the hillside earlier. Her lips opened wide and she devoured him, scraping at him with her teeth bared. She made growling noises and little moans and they fell on the floor and Ready was between her legs. He could see all this and he was dead and couldn't speak.

He was bathed in sweat when he awoke. In the dim morning light, he saw he was not in chains and that his left hand was plastered. He groaned because the dream had been more real than all the other dreams. He still wore his blood-spattered, urine-soaked trousers. He limped to the window and looked out at the flat, wet landscape all around, without sign of life or other houses or cars.

The door opened and the third man stood in the frame. He nodded at Devereaux and made a "come on" motion with his finger.

Devereaux limped across the room on bare feet to the door and through to the next room. He sat down at a table in the kitchen of the house. Miki was not there. Only the first man, the one who had been waiting for him with Miki the night before. Or was it two nights before? The dreams mixed up the days and once, in dreaming, he thought he was making love to Rita in the cold bedroom of the safe apartment in Lausanne.

He picked up the bowl of coffee and drank the milky hot liquid until his mouth was scalded. He put it down and stared at the man.

The man made a motion to the third man to join the second one outside the house. There were three of them and there was Miki. This one was the leader they called Cernan.

Cernan made a face. He opened a package of Marlboro cigarettes and offered one to Devereaux. Devereaux shook his head. Cernan lit the cigarette with a silver Zippo lighter.

"You are a problem, Mr. Devereaux," Cernan said.

Devereaux waited and said nothing. Silence is always an edge if you can maintain it. The advantage might be nothing but a gram on your side of the scale, but it was just that much more.

"I came here for a defector, not an American spy. We were told nothing about you."

Devereaux picked up the bowl and sipped the coffee again. The warmth spread through him.

"Are we barbarians? We fix your hand and your leg and let you sleep. But there is not so much time and I need to know some things."

"Why are you waiting here?" Devereaux said. The question was unexpected and Devereaux watched Cernan to see if it hit the mark.

Cernan was pretty good, Devereaux thought. But the eyes betrayed him. They were flat brown eyes and sometimes they opened like traps and showed the depth on the other side.

"I will ask questions."

"I have nothing to say. Except you wait here in Belgium. If you have what you came for, why are you waiting?"

"You were not part of the equation, Mr. Devereaux."

"My name is Peter Nolan. I'm a journalist with Central Press Association, an American agency, and I'm stationed in Brussels. I was kidnapped out of my hotel room a week ago—I think it was a week ago—by men I've never seen before. This is a terrible mistake."

Cernan sighed, put out his cigarette. "You are an American intelligence agent with R Section. You arranged the defection of Emil Mikita from a party at Brussels city hall eight days ago. You are now my prisoner, a gift from the private contractor whom we have paid for the return of Emil Mikita."

"But you didn't pay for me."

"No."

"Then you should arrange to sell me."

"Who should I sell you to?"

"Whomever you think will want to pay."

Cernan almost smiled behind the ferocious mask. "Is that Central Press Association?"

"Yes. I have a number for them in Brussels. They will pay."

"I believe you," Cernan said. "Not that I do not know you are a spy. But perhaps you are very important to me. Perhaps I should make an inquiry about you."

"Why are you waiting here?"

Cernan's face was without expression and Devereaux probed a second time with the same question.

"You paid X to a man for the return of Emil Mikita. You were not instructed about me and you want to know if you have to bring me back. That would complicate matters. On the one hand, perhaps you would be rewarded, given little brownie points by the Ministry; on the other hand, no one knows about me. So what am I worth? If you paid X, perhaps someone will pay Y to you for me and you make money on the deal.''

Cernan waited, lighting another cigarette.

"Opportunities to make money in the field are not unheard of. Who would know if I am gently returned to my . . . former calling . . . and you take your money to a Swiss bank and take Miki back to Prague? A neat arrangement. The problem for you is time, isn't it? How much time do you have to arrange the deal before your masters become suspicious?''

"What if it was not about money at all? What would you say then, Mr. Devereaux?''

Devereaux hesitated.

There was a fierce certainty about Cernan in that moment.

"Not everything can be explained in terms of money,'' he said. "What if I use you to pry . . . someone else . . . to return to Prague?''

"Who?'' Devereaux said.

Cernan did let the smile fall now. "You see, an American sees everything in terms of what it will cost and what he is willing to pay. But there are matters beyond money, do you know that? But you know that, do you not? Do you know a beautiful woman—I have not seen her, but she is described to me—a beautiful woman right this moment in Brussels? A woman with red hair and green eyes and a very dangerous idea in her head? She is looking for someone and she is probably going to get killed for her troubles. Does she do this for profit? What is her motive but money? But no, she is doing this in the name of love. It is touching. Do you know anything about this woman?''

Devereaux shook his head. "I don't know what you're talking about.''

"You see, I know a lot of things," Cernan said. "I know about you, about this woman, but I do not know what can be arranged to satisfy myself. Perhaps if I can wait—a day or two days or even, perhaps, three days— I can resolve all of this and that will make me happy."

Devereaux said nothing. He stared at Cernan and the wide, flat face and flat brown eyes and then he spoke again: "Will they let you wait?"

Cernan blinked. He hardly moved at all.

"Perhaps we will talk again," he said at last.

"Will there be time?"

The question had no answer because neither man knew.

SEVENTEEN
The American Prisoners

Henkin glared at Gorkeho. It was a look to make underlings tremble. Unfortunately, Gorkeho was a soldier and was only frightened by truly frightening things. He stood at something like attention and waited for Henkin to continue.

"You have lost contact? That is an incredible admission, Gorkeho. I make the arrangement, I give you instructions that when Miki is picked up that I am to be informed and that I will take over the disposition of the matter—these are orders from the highest level—and you tell me with great casualness that you have lost contact with Cernan."

"Unfortunately, it is true. These things happen. Whatever his reasons, I am sure that Cernan is in a delicate situation, calling for absolute silence—"

"He is on a simple matter of picking up one of our

strays and returning him. I am to be informed at all times,'' Henkin raged. ''And now you admit to me that even you are not informed because Cernan chooses to not report to you.''

''If you understood our business,'' Gorkeho began, letting in his small dig without any preliminaries, ''you would understand that the agent in the field has wide discretion to meet any situation that may arise—''

Henkin said, ''There is nothing that 'may arise' in any of this. This is a simple matter of transmitting one person from one place in Europe to another. A simple matter.''

''Ah, but you are wiser than I, pan Henkin. Perhaps you understood that it needed a very experienced man like Cernan when I, too, thought it such a simple matter.'' Cernan would have understood Gorkeho's little smile. ''Perhaps it is not so simple after all, but you have done well to assign such a veteran as Cernan to it.''

Damn him, Henkin thought.

But what could he say to the grinning little one-legged martinet?

It was 1600 hours in Prague and it was snowy and already the light was failing at the end of the dreary day and they had not heard from Cernan for thirty-six hours. Was the money passed on? Was Miki in Cernan's hands? Sixteen hundred hours Prague time would be 0900 in Chicago. It was happening right now but everything that happened was of no use if Henkin could not contact Cernan and make him do what he wanted him to do.

Gorkeho was still smiling and anger bubbled inside Henkin and he wanted to tell him, he wanted to order him—

Order him to do what?

But then, he could not say, could he?

Where the hell was Cernan anyway?

* * *

Mrs. Neumann put her hands in her lap and waited for Hanley. The blip from Eurodesk had arrived at six in the morning and Hanley had rushed down to Section from his apartment on the hill near the National Cathedral on Wisconsin Avenue. The blip had been "ironed out" and the words rendered into clearspeak.

"There are only two possibilities," Hanley said.

Mrs. Neumann said, "It is true or it is not true."

Hanley frowned. "That's obvious. The motive in either case is not obvious."

"Eurodesk has received a message through the Secret section of the Czech trade mission in Brussels. Without going into all of it, there is a trade proposed. The life of an American agent for the return of a Czech citizen."

Hanley said, "Anna Jelinak. I still have an incomplete report. It seems she's the little girl who defected in Chicago more than a week ago. I don't really see any connection at all."

Mrs. Neumann glanced at the clock on her desk, next to the photograph of Leo taken two years ago at Yellowstone Park. Behind Leo was the geyser Old Faithful. The photo had amused both of them and it was her favorite of all the photos she had taken of her beloved over the years.

"It's nearly eight A.M.," she said. "When do they want an answer?"

"Twelve hours. That makes it five P.M. our time, eleven P.M. Brussels time."

"And midnight in Prague. What is behind this, Hanley? This is so bizarre."

"Coincidence, except that it is usually never coincidence," he said. "They describe November, they say he is 'damaged' but alive and they propose the trade. They don't mention Miki but we assume they have Miki as well.''

"Then the Czechs hit our train, not Colonel Ready."

Hanley had been over that ground in his mind waiting for Mrs. Neumann to show up. "Or Colonel Ready works for the Czechs," he said. "Or Colonel Ready hit the train as we assumed and sold both bodies to the Czechs. The Czechs are interested in Miki and not terribly interested in November. Or, to put it differently, more interested in obtaining Anna Jelinak."

"But that's something we can't agree to."

"Mrs. Neumann, we don't even know what the aspects of this Jelinak case are. What is the connection between Miki and Anna Jelinak? They are both in the theater world, the films—perhaps Anna is part of the puzzle picture we thought we obtained in bringing Miki across. I've only had an hour, we are cross-checking the Competition to see if they have an interest in this Anna Jelinak."

"Do they?"

Hanley pulled his lower lip. "There are inconsistencies. There is a Langley man named Willis assigned to the matter but in an observatory way. I don't know why Langley is impacted when a little girl sees weeping statues in Chicago. And I don't understand why they pick her out of the blue as the trade for Devereaux. Devereaux for Anna Jelinak, all delivered to Eurodesk by messenger from the Czech trade mission in Brussels at eleven o'clock at night."

"Is there any chance of making the trade?"

Hanley sighed. He was the operations director and Mrs. Neumann was chief of Section. Mrs. Neumann set the "guidelines" for operation but that was not what she was asking now. She was asking for all the possibilities. Did she really want to know about black-bag jobs and how they are done? Hanley frowned again. Perhaps it was time to continue Mrs. Neumann's education.

"Of course. We can simply disappear the little girl. It will take two men. The safest way is to use contractors and then flush the contractors. The next safest way is to take someone from the field—say someone like Tuesday in Ethiopia now—and bring him in, set the target, have the job finished in less than three days, and send him back to Ethiopia without really being involved in it. Then you put a negotiator of the highest level on this. I would say someone like me. You make certain the goods are as stated on the bill of lading and you make the trade. Not here, not in Brussels, some third place."

"Everything you say breaks the law," Mrs. Neumann said in her harsh whispery voice.

"Yes, Mrs. Neumann." Hanley said it with mild words. "You ask for the possibility and you shrink from the payment. You ask me if a thing can be done and then, when I say it can be done, you don't want to know it."

Mrs. Neumann put her hand on the picture frame. Leo. It is so complicated, Leo, you would be as horrified as I am. Perhaps ignorance was bliss after all and knowledge was not power because it induced a sort of weakness.

"This all began with Miki," she said. "He gave us hints and we were intrigued. Gullible. He said he knew about the Central Intelligence Agency and about dealings with arms merchants in the Middle East and how weapons were made and smuggled to the Afghans. . . . It was so intriguing, all of it. And the business about the films, about how the money was transferred back and forth between countries. . . . He lured us and suckered us and we fell for it so that we went outside our own channels and set up a senior intelligence officer and it all started collapsing after that."

"This is not a morality play," Hanley said. "This is merely real life. It is a fragmentary existence, and the scenario does not hold together because life is fragmentary and there is no scenario. The ethics are defined by the situation. We wanted Miki bad enough to do something about it and someone else wanted Miki bad enough to do something about it and our wills collided. There has been a certain amount of . . . breakage . . . as a result. Now it is at a pass where we are offered a simple trade. I think we would be foolish not to explore it."

"How . . ."

"It is eight in the morning here, seven in Chicago, and we are trying to find out the status of this matter with the Jelinak girl. I think we should be prepared to give the Czech mission an answer before their deadline. It does not necessarily have to be the final answer or even the truth. But it keeps open the possibility that Devereaux stays alive a few more hours in the event that he is alive at all. That is time that is given to Stowe and his agents to find Devereaux, find his status out."

"And Rita Macklin?"

He snapped his fingers. "An annoyance, nothing more serious. Mason follows her and she goes in circles. I leave Mason to her in the event Colonel Ready reappears. I knew that was your wish. But she's of no consequence in this, now that we know—"

"We should tell her. That he is alive."

Hanley glared at her and she blushed. Of course it was foolish.

"All right, Hanley." She hesitated. She had always been so certain and in the months since she had become chief of Section, she had learned hesitation. "We'll wait. To see what we can learn in Chicago and what Stowe can learn."

"And make them an offer before tonight?"

She nodded. "And make them an offer."

Three men walked into the foyer of the building on Seminary Avenue at three minutes after nine in the morning. It was 1603 in Prague and Henkin had finished yelling at Gorkeho.

The three men studied the mailboxes for a moment and then one of them nodded. A fourth man sat in a car at the curb. A fifth man waited in a car in the alley behind the three-flat.

Six minutes earlier, a large tow truck had careened down Seminary and smacked into four parked cars, doing severe damage to them. The policeman in the parked squad car up the block providing security for Anna Jelinak and Stephanie Fields had noticed the incident and started after the tow truck that turned west on Webster at the corner.

The three men in the foyer had sledgehammers. They walked up the steps past the unoccupied flats on the first two floors. First Floor went to work at the commodities exchange at five-thirty in the morning; Second Floor went to work at IBM at 7:55 A.M.

Anna was dressed in white and looked like a little girl. They were going to court again. Anna did not have to wear a ribbon in her hair. Stephanie said that it was too much of an effect. In fact, Stephanie knew that Anna did not want to seem to be a little girl.

Stephanie was finishing her tea in the kitchen. She wore a gray pinstriped suit and silk blouse with a small black tie. Her briefcase was worn: It was brown leather and carried her initials and it had been a gift from her brother in Cleveland when she was graduated from law school six years before.

They heard the sound at the front door and looked at

each other with fear draining all the color from their faces. Anna screamed then, one long piercing yell.

Stephanie grabbed the wall telephone. It was dead. She hit the receiver and it was still dead. She glanced out the back window and saw the man in the alley. The sledge-hammer cracked the oak door at the front of the hall. Two more whacks and the door was open and broken.

The men crowded into the narrow corridor and one went into the front room and the second man went into the first bedroom. They looked in the bathroom and the first man ran to the kitchen and saw them.

Stephanie had turned the locks and the back door was nearly open when the first man got into the kitchen.

She saw the man, saw Anna, saw she could not open the door in time. She grabbed the black sawtooth knife she had just used to cut the bread. She pushed Anna behind her to the place where the kitchen counter met the stove top.

"Get out of here," she said in a low, flat voice. She held the knife the right way, close in to her body. The real knife fighter holds it wide, but that is when the other man does not have a sledgehammer. She held it close and watched the room fill up with the others.

"Don't hurt her," Stephanie said. Her voice was calm.

"Nobody gets hurt," the first one said. "That's really up to you, though."

The voice didn't have any threat in it. The speaker had a thin face and flat nickel eyes.

"Get out right now, there's a policeman outside, he's waiting for us. You don't know who we are."

"She's gonna talk you to death, George," the second one said.

"Yeah," he said. "Put the knife down and get out of the way."

Stephanie held the knife. The first one whacked her arm with the sledge and her arm broke and the knife fell out of her hand. She blacked out and slipped to the floor, the pain all white in her head.

"Why'd you call me 'George'?" the first one said. "Now I gotta whack her."

"Don't whack her. Nobody has to get whacked."

George thought about it.

He looked at the crumpled body.

"I guess so," George said. "There's a lot of Georges."

"She saw you though," said the third one.

George thought about it.

"Yeah, you're right. And she's a lawyer. She could remember better than a lot of people."

"Yeah," said the third one.

"Well, let's get the kid out of here," said George.

They grabbed her arm. George stared at her and Anna said, in a sob, "Please do not hurt Stephanie. I love Stephanie."

"I won't hurt her, she'll be all right," George said. "You've got to go downstairs now."

The other two men led Anna through the apartment, past the shattered front door and down the stairs. George bent down over Stephanie's crumpled form and shot her then, very clean, once through the base of the skull. The sound was small, even in the quiet apartment, because of the silencer screwed onto the .22 automatic. Anna never heard a thing.

EIGHTEEN

One Morning in Brussels

Philip Petty the manager spoke to Jans: "The woman who came in alone tonight?"

"Who else would I mean?"

"Well, the problem with what you're talking about is that she might be connected with some agency we're not aware of."

"I've looked into that."

"You have pretty good sources," Philip agreed. They were drinking coffee and brandy in the tavern of the Club Tres. It was a little past dawn and they had not locked the front door although the last customer had left two hours ago. They stood on each side of the wide oak bar with their shirt collars open.

"She's a very highly paid freelance journalist. Everyone is a freelance journalist but not a lot of them make any money."

"Who pays her?"

"Legitimate sources. American magazines. She has a contract with one of the weekly magazines."

"But this place is not news."

"Well, you're being coy again, Philip. You don't want me to speak plainly."

"I do want you to speak plainly, Jans. I just don't like to jump into something if there's some way to avoid it. You know that being cautious is—"

"I know. So I haven't proposed anything yet."

"You've talked about killing her."

"I've talked about having her killed. I'm not talking about you and me killing her. I've talked about talking about her to someone."

"That guy with the scar. I wouldn't like to cross him. You know what he did with the driver? I guess the driver didn't obey some instruction or something. I wouldn't cross someone like him. You think he would be interested in that woman?"

"Maybe he would be. She's talking about the man, the one we didn't like. The American. He was a fag-basher if you ask me. I didn't like him at all."

"You're right."

Philip poured the brandy.

"She might not even be interested in the operation the other night."

"Come on, Philip. It is not a coincidence she comes here. Not so soon after what happened."

"Nothing happened, I remind you. We're the go-between. I didn't like him at all. He ordered me around as though I were a servant. As if I didn't exist."

"Oh, you didn't like him? That's a good one. You liked him well enough. I saw the way you looked at him."

"He ordered me around. And he didn't trust anyone."

"Well, Philip, he was right about that, wasn't he?"

"The trouble is, I don't really want to know any more about what happened than we know now."

"We don't know anything. We provided a car and a driver."

"Well, I don't want to go beyond that."

"Are you going to call him or should I call him?"

"I'll call him. I just want to finish my coffee."

"Don't get drunk before you call him."

"I never get drunk."

"Sometimes when you're like this you get drunk."

"I never get drunk," Philip repeated. "I'll call the man with the scar and I'll tell him about the woman with the red hair who is asking all the questions, pumping old Reiter at the bar last night. He was enjoying himself, Reiter was. The woman might interest our friend; maybe we can make a little more money, set something up for her to make it easy for the man."

David Mason turned over in bed and reached for the telephone.

"Yes."

His voice was dull. He squinted at his watch. It was seven.

"She telephoned the concierge from her room for a taxi."

"All right," he said.

He replaced the receiver and got up quickly in the darkness of the hotel room. He pulled on his trousers and buttoned his shirt. He slipped into his shoes and grabbed a raincoat. He had come to Brussels without a raincoat and he'd bought one the first day. It wasn't raining at the moment. The dawn was full of edgy clouds.

The last thing of all, he slipped the pistol into the pocket of the raincoat. The pistol was small, a Walther PPK automatic, and he almost carried it now as a matter of habit, the way he was taught.

He took the stairs to the lobby and saw Rita Macklin at the concierge's desk. He waited at the edge of the lobby until she crossed to the entrance of the hotel and stepped outside. He crossed the lobby after her and saw the concierge catch his eye. He nodded once, almost imperceptibly. He felt the pistol in his pocket.

She was waiting on the curb in front of the Amigo Hotel. The sky was wet with clouds.

She smiled at David Mason. "You never sleep."

He grinned. "They teach you that at the Acme Spy School. One of the first lessons."

"I just wanted to make sure."

"We can do it two ways. I can follow you in another cab, but that's expensive and I don't speak French very well. *Cherchez la femme*. Well, I suppose that would be good enough."

"I can't decide about you."

"They teach you that as well."

"You must be a good student."

"Not particularly. But when the alternative is cleaning out toilet bowls with a toothbrush, I get motivated."

"The youth of America."

"You're about my age."

"Years older. Centuries older, David." But it was not said with unkindness. She took his arm. "Get a taxi."

The Peugeot crept to the entrance and they slid into the backseat. "Gare Central," she said.

"Where are we going?"

"Bruges."

"What's in Bruges?"

"A man who can be bought and who says he knows about him."

David Mason was silent. He frowned. What were his orders exactly? Hanley chewed him out pretty well the last time, considering it was a coded message and might be on file somewhere. He had lied to Hanley, not for the first time. Why was he letting her have such a free rein anyway? To find out what she could find out? Or because he was in love with her?

He thought about that.

She was Devereaux's girl, he had decided, and that might be part of the reason he was in love with her. They were chasing a ghost if he was dead and he was . . . what exactly? The heroic younger brother? He had read the book when he was fourteen and it had filled him with warm pleasure—it was *How Green Was My Valley*. When his brother dies, young Owen goes to live in the house of his brother's widow and acts as surrogate husband for her. Not to sleep with her but to do the manly things. It was a child's dream. He did not want him dead, of course.

She had taken his arm and asked him to call a cab. Owen Morgan, a man you are. He smelled her presence. She smelled of wildflowers and milk. She wore no perfume and he felt embarrassed at his thoughts and blushed and the Peugeot made a sweeping curve in front of the central station up the hill above the center of Brussels.

To hell with Hanley. He knew he had to see this thing out the way he had started.

"He talked to a friend of a friend of mine."

"Section should hire you for Eurodesk."

"There is no Section." She turned to him and her utterly green eyes were deep and cold. "You forgot."

"I never forget." He felt stung by his brother's widow, as though he had become a little boy again. "I just don't believe in all the bullshit."

"The booga-booga," she said.

"Yes."

"He called it the booga-booga." She had said it before to him but didn't remember. She kept recalling him, saying secret thoughts out loud as though to make his presence in her mind stronger. Would she forget him? Would she remember him so clearly in twenty or thirty years? She still made him part of the past tense. It made her strong enough to sleep at night. The grief was always there, yawning and sore like a throat that has been abused by sobs. It hurt too much but it had to keep hurting during the day. Only at night did she have to be numb. She had to have a drink and not think about him being around. Not see him in the corner of her room. Not hear his voice. Not smell him next to her in bed. That was past; that was gone. Except she kept looking for him because she had to know what really happened. But keep him part of the past tense to make it easier when she found out. Don't make him alive in mind or she would break into a thousand pieces, knowing he was alive and that she couldn't find him.

"The old black magic," Mason said. "We get so careful being careful about the small shit, we forget about the big shit."

She took his arm and her hand was strong.

"I can't shake you. Not yet. I can shake you when I want to shake you, but I don't want you running all over Belgium screwing it up for me. I don't forget about the big stuff either. You're Section, you're another goddamn spook and I don't care if he got you a job or if you're his long-lost son or what you are. I don't give a damn about you or the spooks. I have to find out about him. There's some connection with those two fags at the Club Tres and what happened. Whatever happened. You won't say but I get the idea now."

"I don't know."

"That's a good trick, David. You say that so honestly that anyone could believe it. But I don't."

"We live in an age of unbelief," he said.

The driver said something about the meter in French. Mason paid and they slid out of the cab and walked into the grimy depth of the central station. The place was full of people, some of whom had slept the night. The walls were dirty. Everything about Brussels struck him as shabby and a little grand, like royalty fallen on hard times. He liked the city because it had so few pretensions, even when it was quite beautiful.

He took her arm again to stop her. She turned to look at him and waited.

"The man in Bruges," Mason said.

"He said a man like Devereaux was in a house there four days ago," Rita said.

"What else?"

"The 'what else' is when I meet him in Bruges. You stay away from me in Bruges, David, I mean it."

"All right."

"I'll get a room there for tonight, when I meet him. There are steps to the meeting, and if he sees you he won't go through with it."

"I see," Mason said.

They bought tickets and waited for the train on the platform beneath the station concourse.

"Devereaux is alive," David Mason said. He said it for himself and for her and he didn't see the tears in her eyes.

She thought her heart would break.

NINETEEN

The Infant of Prague

Cernan took out the weapon. It was the very good Czech remake of the original Israeli Uzi submachine gun which was the weapon of choice for bodyguards and terrorists. He clicked the action and pointed it at Devereaux's bare chest.

"Well, I receive a message and then another message."

They were alone in the kitchen. The two big Czechs were outside as usual. Miki spent all his time in his room at the back of the house, reading and smoking as though he did not have a care in the world. He made it clear that he resented Devereaux for screwing up his perfectly good defection and that when he returned to Prague, he might register a complaint about it with someone, perhaps Henkin. He mentioned Henkin to Cernan several times, as though he might have to do something about Cernan as well if he were not treated with more respect. Cernan frowned whenever Miki mentioned Henkin's name. Once,

Miki told Devereaux that Henkin was his mentor and that Henkin would do anything to have him returned, which is probably why he had sent Cernan, because the mission was so important.

And yet, a curious lethargy had come over the operation. They had been in the farmhouse for two days, fretful days of Cernan waiting for something. Perhaps now it had come.

"Good news?" Devereaux said.

"No," Cernan said.

"I see."

"Perhaps you are not so valuable to them after all," Cernan said. The eyes revealed nothing. The face was set. Perhaps a little too hard.

"No. Perhaps not."

"You pretend not to be afraid?"

"Yes. I pretend."

"Good. Because you understand my choice now?"

"No," Devereaux said. "I didn't understand at the beginning."

"There is no interest in you. Not in Prague, not in your own country it seems."

"You were going to trade me."

Cernan grunted.

"You offered me in a trade and there were no takers? I don't believe that."

"They make two crosses," Cernan said.

"Double cross. How did they double-cross?"

"It is of no importance now." Again, he made a sound that might have been a sigh, and he brought up the Uzi and checked the action to make certain the first round was seated in the firing chamber.

Devereaux did not speak. He saw the way it was. The distance between the two seated men was seven feet. The table could be overturned. Cernan would get off a few rounds and that would bring the Czechs in from outside, but at least it would be a fighting chance. Only lambs went to the slaughter with meekness.

"I do not understand you," Cernan said in a very soft voice. Again, he seemed to hesitate. He brought the barrel of the automatic weapon down. He stared at Devereaux. "Why do they not want you to be returned?"

"What did you want? Whom did you want? Whom did you contact?"

Cernan smiled. "We contact the right people. They know you. They agree to this . . . trade. Then, in less than six hours, they double the cross, they—"

He stopped, shut his eyes fiercely for a moment and then opened them.

Devereaux saw his eyes were wet.

What was this about? Why were they waiting in a farmhouse in the middle of Belgium for two days? What the hell was this about?

"You are not authorized," Devereaux said suddenly.

Cernan waited.

Devereaux smiled.

"What do you mean?"

"You are not authorized. What are you making a trade for when you are not authorized?"

"I won't argue with you. You're a prisoner. You have limited importance."

"Important enough for you to do something for which you are not authorized. Two days we wait here. Is it so hard to get back to Prague? Don't the East German freighters still use Zeebrugge? Or Antwerp? Or any of a dozen places up and down the coast? Is it so hard to bring me back to Prague and make your deals from there? You came to get Miki; you have Miki. Why wait, Cernan?"

The tone was mocking, almost teasing, certainly with the edge of an insult to it. Cernan caught the tone all right. He pointed the barrel at Devereaux's chest.

"Are you so brave? Or are you crazy?"

"You don't want to kill me. You want something else and you want me to tell you how to get it."

Cernan said nothing. The Uzi created the mood for the room.

"What do you want?"

Cernan looked at the Uzi. He waved the barrel toward the stove. "Make coffee. No, do not make it too easy for me. You make coffee and throw it in my face? That is a nice trick, I think of that trick on the first day when you look at me with the bowl on the table. We both do not fool each other."

"We do not."

Devereaux moved to the stove and lit it with a kitchen match. The gas burned bright and filled the room with gas smells. He was clean, for the first time. He washed in the mornings and his pants were clean, if torn and a little tattered at the knees. The smell of urine was gone and he felt almost well. His leg was not as stiff and the swelling was almost gone. There was a long and ugly bruise on the shin and another from the knee to the buttocks. The water boiled and he dropped coffee grounds into it and watched the grounds stain the water. He cut a piece of bread from the loaf and buttered it. He put the coffee in the bowl and poured in milk. He put the bowl on the table and dipped the bread in the bowl and chewed off the end.

Cernan was on the far side of the kitchen now, watching Devereaux eat. He held the Uzi but now it was not pointed at Devereaux.

"Do you know about Anna Jelinak?" Cernan's voice

was almost shy. The tone surprised Devereaux but he said nothing. He kept his eyes down and ate. After a moment, he shook his head.

"On the same day that you take Miki, Anna Jelinak is in Chicago. In the United States."

"I've heard of it," Devereaux said.

"It is my duty to see to her protection on the tour of the United States. I assure you, the visitor to Prague has every protection, every courtesy. But it is not the same in the United States. There is a very violent country, very brutal, very hard for people."

"It builds character," Devereaux said.

Cernan did not bother to frown. The American agent had intrigued him from the beginning. He had represented a way out of a twin dilemma for Cernan. Now, perhaps, he was about to die and it wasn't even his fault.

"Nearly ten days ago, she is in Chicago and a very strange thing. I cannot explain it. She is in a television place, what do you say it is?"

"A studio?"

"A studio. She is in the studio and they are showing a film of some 'miracle' in a church in that city. It is something you hear about, usually in Spain or Italy where the people have nothing else to do but make themselves crazy with talk about blood on statues or paintings. On this film is the Infant of Prague, which is an icon in my country, a religious relic. It is a statue of Christ as a child, as a King, from when people believed in kings and such things."

"I know what it is," Devereaux said. He had stopped eating. The monologue was getting very strange, he thought. He stared at Cernan's eyes and they were looking beyond this room.

"They say she sees a miracle in this statue, that it is crying for Anna Jelinak who has never even been in Paris, not to say Chicago. Now they hold Anna because they say she wishes to defect. I do not believe this. This is a girl who is in the film in Prague, who is very well loved in my country. She has everything. She wishes to defect? No sir, I do not believe it, sir. And since it is my duty to find her and to bring her home, I send her mother to her. Now, what happens? This other duty intrudes upon me and it is completed and what do I think?"

Devereaux stared at Cernan.

Cernan sighed, broke the spell. "It does not matter. I expect to sell you back to your side, but the cross is double. They say one thing, they do another thing. There is nothing to be done with such people. I do not hate you, Devereaux, but I cannot bring you back to Prague. It is too . . . well, I cannot tell you. But I cannot let you go, perhaps then my superiors would question me. So what can I do but kill you?"

Devereaux saw the apology was genuine.

"You can tell me about the trade. What was the message?"

"I want Anna returned to Prague. And you will be returned to your countrymen."

"What did they say?"

"I use one of my old runners. One of my trusted runners, he is in Brussels now, he puts the message to your Section. No, don't deny all this. There is Section and you are part of Section R. So they answer: Yes, but it will take several days to arrange. All right. But what do I learn now from my runner?"

"What do you learn now?"

The room was bleak with silence. Cernan stared at Devereaux with sadness, the look reserved for people we know are dying.

"Anna is kidnapped. It is the way it is in your violent

country. A woman is killed, and Anna is gone. What a mad place is your country. I meet Americans and they all look mad to me. Is it the madness you all share that is destroying you? Madness. One minute I can talk to rational people and the next minute. . . .''

Devereaux saw tears. He did not expect tears. He felt suddenly shaken to see the tears. Why was this strong man crying?

Devereaux saw the hand tighten around the trigger of the very good copy of an Uzi.

"Let me ask you: Why were you assigned to this matter when you already were working to get Anna returned?"

Cernan blinked, the tears stopped, the eyes were wet. He stared at Devereaux as though trying to understand the question. And then he realized it was the same question he had been asked by Gorkeho in Prague. Why was Cernan so important to the matter of getting Miki back? Twelve hours ago, he had made a secret contact with Gorkeho and told him everything and Gorkeho, who had not approved the trade in advance, said he could proceed for as long as it was "useful." It was Gorkeho who told him how frantic Henkin was to make contact with him. It was Gorkeho who told him not to contact Henkin under any circumstances. Intrigue was haunting Prague as well as this farmhouse in wet, cold Belgium.

"There is no connection."

"You have made the connection," Devereaux said.

"That is a way out for me. To get rid of you and get Anna returned."

"No, Cernan."

Cernan waited.

Devereaux stared at him, saw it almost as a shape. "You're a senior man in your service. Is this the job of a senior man?"

"What do you mean?"

"To get Miki."

"It might be."

"Why was it you?"

"Because it was me."

"Was this Anna Jelinak matter . . . was it ongoing?"

"I do not understand."

"What were you doing about Anna when you were told to get Miki?"

"I do not see any connection."

Devereaux felt sweat like fear on his lip. He wiped his hand across his mouth. He had to make Cernan see the same shape he saw.

"Miki is in film, Anna is in film, I never heard of Anna until a moment ago," Devereaux said. "But the connection is obvious, isn't it?"

"I ask Miki this about Anna Jelinak. Believe me, he does not understand this matter."

"There has to be a connection and you have to be the connection, otherwise there's no sense in why you're involved in both of these matters."

Cernan started. It was perfectly true and he did not understand it at all.

"If a man sees an accident one morning and then sees another, very similar accident in the afternoon, would you believe he had any connection to both accidents? Other than merely seeing them?"

"Yes," Cernan agreed. "It is too much coincidence."

Devereaux nodded. "But perhaps the first accident was merely an accident and the witness saw it. But maybe then he planned the second accident."

And Cernan thought of Henkin. Cernan saw the shape of Henkin's arrogant face and saw that everything had come from Henkin—the assignment to pick up Miki, the fact that Miki was for sale at all, the security arrangements for Anna, the urgent advice of Gorkeho twelve hours ago not to make contact with Henkin. . . . What was happening in Prague at this very moment?

"But Miki and Anna, they are . . . defectors . . . at practically the same time."

"So they are accidents," Devereaux said. "But at a late stage, you are called in to take part in both matters."

"I was assigned the matter of Anna from the first. It was my security that had failed."

"And Miki?"

"I had nothing to do with Miki."

"Until when?"

Cernan thought about it.

"There is no connection."

"You are the connection, Cernan." Almost gently. "Who is Anna Jelinak? Why is she important?"

"She is important to the film of Czechoslo—"

"Let me interrupt. She is no more important than a tennis star defecting. Perhaps less important. Why are you willing to offer an American agent for the return of a little girl?"

"Because *you* are of no importance," Cernan said.

"Why did you cry?"

Cernan did not deny it. He said nothing and thought of Henkin and thought of Anna kidnapped somewhere in the vast, hideous interior of the United States.

"Who is Anna?"

"A little girl."

"She is more than that."

Cernan looked at the American with heavy eyes. "It should be enough to be a child."

Devereaux frowned.

Cernan stared at him and the gun felt heavy for the first time.

Devereaux understood and it brought no pleasure to him to solve the riddle.

"Anna is yours," he said.

Cernan said nothing.

"Your child," Devereaux said.

The countryside still pervaded the room. Outside the window, the single oak tree shed its last leaf of autumn.

"You guess this thing. You make a guess to everything."

"And no one knows," Devereaux said.

"Do you read hearts?"

"I read your eyes. You sit in Belgium with a prisoner and a returning defector and you sit here for two days, making a private deal that falls through. Anna is not that important."

Cernan said, "Go to hell."

"She never was that important. You arranged her security and it broke down. Suddenly, you're assigned like a junior officer to pick up baggage in Belgium. Come on, Cernan. If you're going to kill me now, tell me the truth."

But Cernan pursed his lips like a child who would not speak, no matter how dire the threats made against him.

"Your child," Devereaux said. And saw it was true.

Cernan stared at him without tears because he did not cry at all. Just for one moment and the American understood.

"It does not matter," Cernan said.

"You make a trade for me and they accept. Then Anna is made to disappear. You know and I know that it wasn't the same people in both cases. There is more here than Anna. And if it involves you, it must have to do with Miki."

Cernan slowly put the Uzi on his lap. He was staring at Devereaux but only seeing his own thoughts. It was Henkin, he saw. If he was the connection at one level, Henkin was the connection at another level.

And Gorkeho understood. That's what was going on in Prague. That's why he was permitted to stay in the field a little longer. This was between Gorkeho and Henkin, and Anna was just a little puppet who didn't understand anything at all.

And Cernan's eyes filled with tears again.

TWENTY
Life for a Life

The merchants of Bruges built the money houses in a time when there were kings and when faithful people in other parts of Europe built cathedrals. The very first money exchange was in Bruges and was called The Bourse because that was the name of the owner of the house. He engraved his family coat of arms on his house and it is still there. His coat of arms consisted of three money purses. Bruges was made of commerce and the sea. When the sea retreated, it left Bruges the fine old buildings of the first merchants and the canals and the great public squares and the lingering holiness of commerce past.

Rita Macklin registered at the Hotel Adornes in the oldest part of the city. The hotel huddled on one of the canals less than a mile from the central square of the town. The hotel was specified, the time of the meeting was specified. She scarcely had time to wash up before the meeting.

The man came to see her in the lobby of the hotel at one. He nodded to her sitting on the couch in the little lobby and he went to the front desk and ordered a bottle of Jupiler beer from the woman behind the desk. She went into the kitchen and got the beer and a cold glass. It was that kind of a place. He went to the couch and sat down next to her and poured the strong beer steadily in the glass.

"You weren't followed," he said.

"Not here. You know I was followed from Brussels, but I made him go to the Holiday Inn and I came here. I wasn't followed here."

"We watched you. We saw him at the train station. Who is he?"

"You know all about him," she said. "If you don't know about him, you don't know anything about this business and I'm wasting my time."

The man, who wore a seaman's outfit with pea coat and stocking cap, smiled at that. He had a red beard and merry eyes. "We know about him."

She sat with her hands on her jeans. She wore jeans and a sweater and she had no baggage with her, other than the inevitable raincoat. The lobby was small and plain and the furniture was comfortable on the wooden floors. The woman who owned the hotel was in the breakfast room, tending the fire.

It was raining now but no one noticed. It rains in Belgium and then stops and then rains again and then stops and no one notices after a while.

"The man had gray hair and gray eyes. He was hurt, I know that. His hand was swollen, this one, and he moved with a limp. He looked pretty banged up. I think he was hit by a car. That's what I heard about it."

"But alive," she said. Very small voice.

"The last I heard."

"When was that?"

"Three days ago. He left the house where they kept him. He went away in a big car, maybe a Mercedes-Benz."

"Where is he now?"

"What about the money?"

She gave him the money. He counted it. The woman who owned the hotel glanced at them from the breakfast room, but she could not leave it because she had the fire going strong. The good smell of the burning dried wood filled the hotel and made it seem very warm.

"It might be harder," the seaman said with a smile.

"How hard?"

"Two thousand dollars."

"All right," she said.

"That was easy. I should have asked for more."

She stared at him. "Don't get cute."

"Tough girl, huh?"

"Tough," she said.

"Well, he was pretty banged up, like I said."

"You said. He's alive though."

"I didn't say that."

"You said it. You want two grand for it."

"Yes. Well. I'm not sure. But it's a good bet. The problem is your keeper. How do we get rid of him?"

"I told you I could shake him. I told you and I did it. Now leave that up to me."

"If he queers the deal, that's it. No more contact. We're in enough trouble now."

"Who's we?"

"Me and my partners, you might say."

The voice was light, the accent was English learned the English way.

"I can shake him."

"You have to. We don't want any trouble and we don't want nothing to do with agents."

"How do you come by all this information?"

"Bruges is small, very small. You're a sailor, you understand how small it is and any fiddle that goes on, you learn about it right off. Sailors talk to sailors and now and then they have something worth talking about."

"So you know where he is? You take me there."

"I don't take nobody no place. You get your money and you go get yourself a bicycle over at the train station. You get a map and you go out of Bruges and you go out along the canal that goes down to Damme. It's the old town. You do that about four this afternoon, when there's still light."

"And what happens when I get there?"

"You'll see. See, if you shake your friend, it'll show up when you go for your bicycle ride. I think—"

"I haven't ridden a bicycle since I was fourteen years old."

The merry eyes smiled even more. "Learn." His voice was abrupt. "Two thousand dollars, girl. You bring it along and you learn to ride a bicycle."

The sailor put down his beer and got up and walked out of the front door without another word. He walked along the canal a way and past a Citroen parked at the curb. He walked along the canal until the Citroen came up and he got into the back without a word.

"It'll work. She'll be alone."

"Good," the other man in back said. And they both looked out their side windows at the rain as the car splashed along the cobblestones, out toward the edge of the old city.

* * *

She remembered how to ride a bicycle almost right away.

The baggage handler in the station had been surprised to have a customer for the rental bicycles in November but he didn't say so. He had very good English and she was an American and pretty. He said she would get wet riding a bicycle. It was a poor little joke but he always used it. It meant he was friendly.

She rode the circular route through the park that goes around the south end of the town and up to the west, where she could pick up the straight canal that goes right to the sea at Zeebrugge. The parkway along the canal outside the town was marked by a long straight bicycle path and a long straight road separated from the path by a row of trees. The branches were bare and the grass was turning brown. Farm fields fell away in straight dimensions to the flat horizon. She wore a red beret she'd bought in town and the rain came down on her face and made it shine. She pumped hard against the pedals and there was no one on the path. The gloaming light was almost gone.

She had told David she was going back to Brussels and would meet him in the bar at the Amigo at seven. She called him from the train station where she bought a ticket for Brussels and made a fuss about buying a copy of the *Herald-Tribune* and asking everyone where she could catch the train for Brussels. She went to the platform and got on the train at the last minute and got off the train just as the doors closed. She went back around the platform and over a small knoll into the grass and picked up her bicycle and rode through the parkway around the south end of Bruges to the canal path.

The car lights picked her up on the path. The car was coming from Damme and parked about four hundred feet west of her and waited for her. She knew the car was for her.

She slowed as she approached. She saw it was a gray

Mercedes. She felt her body becoming very warm and her eyes were wide and a sense of fear replaced the tentative sense that it was all hopeless. She was really going to see him. The adrenaline surged in her. She was close. She was this close. She was terribly afraid and the fear made a sick knot in her belly but she knew she would go through with it, right to the bad final moment.

She got off the bicycle and walked it up the grassy slope to the road and leaned it against a tree. She locked the rear wheel with the automatic lock from the seat.

She got in the car without a word.

The other man was dressed in black and the driver did not turn his head. They swung around in the empty roadway and headed west again, toward the sea. No one spoke. The second man in the backseat next to her lit a cigarette and blew the smoke against the side window. He seemed bored.

"Where are we going?" she asked.

"Shut up," he said.

She put her hands on her knees. The bottoms of her jeans were wet. The rain had lasted all day. The fields were matted by the constant rain and the black earth was opened here and there where a farmer had finally turned the field for spring to come.

She held the knife open in the pocket of her raincoat. It was just a Swiss Army knife, the kind with a red handle that is not a real Army knife at all but the kind that all the tourists buy. The blade was two and a half inches. If she had planned it out, she would have bought a real knife in Brussels but it had only come to her at the last moment, when she talked to the seaman in the Hotel Adornes, when she knew what she had to do.

So when Colonel Ready came to her, she would shove the knife into his throat.

She was certain Colonel Ready was waiting for her at the other end of the ride. Devereaux was dead; Rita was dead; at least Colonel Ready would be dead as well and David Mason would get the note at the Hotel Adornes and understand what Rita knew and why she had to go alone and kill Colonel Ready.

She had known it for certain from the moment in the Club Tres when the old man—Reiter—told her about the man with the interesting scar on his cheek that went from his ear to the corner of his mouth. The interesting man who had talked business with the two fag waiters.

Colonel Ready had Devereaux and that meant he was dead. In a little while, Rita would be dead too. It was stupid and pointless, but it was the way it had to be because she loved Devereaux more than her life. It was the only way she could love.

The car pulled up at a little house at the end of a road in the middle of fields. There was a gray Citroen there as well, in a small shed behind the house. She got out of the car and let the second man lead her up the single stone step to the door. She felt the knife in her hand in the coat.

The door opened.

The light was small in the wooden kitchen.

She had the knife and felt the blade and waited to see better. Then she saw the hulking shape at the door on the far side of the kitchen.

She stared and dared not speak.

"Rita," he said.

It was the voice she thought was dead. She thought she might be dreaming the voice.

Devereaux said her name again.

TWENTY-ONE
Looking for Anna

She opened the red thermos and poured out a little chicken soup. Chicken soup. Mrs. Neumann smiled for the first time. Dear Leo. Leo had driven down to Fourteenth Street from Bethesda, where they lived in a house off the Old Georgetown Road near Wisconsin Avenue. Leo had delivered a thermos full of homemade chicken soup.

"You're not gonna never come home, home is gonna come to you," he said to her in the visitors' lobby where he had to wait for her.

"Leo, my love," she rasped and hugged him and kissed him on the lips. They were married so long that no one believed they could still love each other. Chicken soup was like flowers.

"You sound terrible."

"The same old cold," she said.

"The same on the phone. I made the soup. You ever coming home?"

"Things are . . . things are confused."

"You got people work for you, you can't do everything yourself."

"Leo. I want to come home, with all my heart. I want to put on that nightgown and have you make love to me and be all warm with you in the bed. I want to sleep a week."

"You don't get away with sleeping right off the bat, honey."

She tasted the soup and thought of Leo and let the thought warm her. Then the door opened and Leo was gone and the soup lost its taste.

Hanley sat down. He had not gone home in two days either and he looked it. He had no one waiting for him in the old apartment on Massachusetts Avenue.

There was unspoken intimacy between them. The matters were grave and they spoke in a kind of shorthand.

"Mason found a note she left him. She said she had a rendezvous with Colonel Ready and she was going to kill him and he was supposed to follow after her. He found a bicycle she rented on a path outside Bruges."

"Belgium police."

"Yes. He made the notification. Just a tourist, met this girl, was supposed to meet her for dinner in some suburb and she didn't show and he found her bicycle. He's a correspondent for Central News Associates."

"They know that cover if they check with their own intelligence people."

"It's the best we can do for now. Besides, it's mostly true. Straight police case."

"Poor girl. She knew he was dead and it wasn't true at

the time at all and now she's dead. The whole thing is blown.''

"Our Pennsylvania cousins keep in touch." Hanley meant the FBI. It was the newest jargon, fitted for the FBI building on Pennsylvania Avenue. "They're absolutely bonkers about the mess in Chicago. I think it's genuine. No trace of the girl. Not a trace. And Langley?'' She had not spoken but Hanley was talking as fast as his thoughts were processed. "Langley is uncomfortable. They make little probes in Brussels, here, Chicago. They made contact with the Czechs a couple of days before Anna disappeared in Chicago. The backgrounder is Langley wants the girl sent back home. Or did. Why is Langley involved at all? Because we had suspicions from the beginning. And Miki gave us a hint. This is bigger than a defection and we knew it all along and we didn't tell Devereaux.'' The last remark was the closest Hanley was willing to come to express regret.

"Finding the little girl really is up to the cousins. This is their business," Mrs. Neumann rasped again.

"But we can't get back our agent until she is found. And we don't even know if the Czech contact in Brussels is interested in trading anymore.'' The thought crossed both of their minds.

"Someone walks into a house and snatches a little girl and murders a woman and that is just possible, isn't it?'' Mrs. Neumann was not speaking to Hanley. "Why? Why, for God's sake?''

"Why tie Devereaux's return to getting Anna back to Prague?'' Hanley said. "I don't understand any of it. We messaged back through the couriers to whoever has Devereaux, but there hasn't been a reply.''

"Did you try again?''

"Yes."

"What about the woman in Chicago? The television person?" Mrs. Neumann asked. She was so tired. Her life had become confined to this room in the corner of this vast, dreadful building. The smell of the bureaucracy filled the corridors. It was musty and mean. She spent her life now asking questions and never getting the full answers.

"The cousins are on that. Working it to death, but Kay Davis doesn't know any more than they do. The dead man was someone who apparently knew someone on the janitorial staff, some sort of juice loan or something, and that was how he gained access to her—to Kay Davis'—apartment. That's all anyone knows."

"All anyone knows is nothing. We have lost an agent, we have botched a simple defection, now we're probably responsible for the death of that woman."

"The one in Chicago—"

"Rita Macklin," she said. "Is this all some attack on Section? Is this part of—"

Hanley felt the same shiver of paranoia. The trouble with paranoia in intelligence is that it is often truth disguised lightly by neurotic delusions.

"Stowe and Eurodesk in Brussels pinpoint the wreck of the train to the driver. His name was Klaus Beng and he was freelance. He was vetted by Club Tres. His body was found washed up in the harbor at Zeebrugge four hours ago. Chaser is pursuing the Ready connection."

Mrs. Neumann closed her eyes. She thought of Leo and she thought of sleeping in Leo's bed. She opened her eyes and there was chicken soup in a thermos. And Hanley across the desk from her.

"Continue," Mrs. Neumann said and unscrewed the

top of the thermos of soup. Continue questions, continue answers. At least the smell of the chicken soup blotted out the mean, musty smell of the bureaucracy all around her.

Ben Herguth said, "I don't understand it."

The man called Julie sighed. "It isn't so complicated. You botched killing Kay Davis."

"I admit it. Who would think a guy could fuck up something that simple?"

"So what can we do? So Al Buck gets her the job back, with a raise, and we go on from there. You got the little girl—"

"Stashed tight, Julie," Ben Herguth said.

"But you killed this lawyer—"

"Don't lay that on me, Julie. That was someone else. One of the buttons did it, doesn't have a brain in his head. You think three guys could handle one broad and one little girl without making a mess."

"So the FBI is making it uncomfortable, even the cops are putting heat on this, they look bad. . . . I don't know. I'm only doing this for Henkin. Henkin wants the girl. It's complicated but it has to do with Miki. Henkin says it's the only way he can push the button on Miki. He doesn't want Miki back in Prague and we don't want Miki loose in the States. Miki has to be a dead man."

"You told me," Ben said again. "I still don't see it. If Henkin is a big shot, hell, he's in a fucking Communist country, he can whack anyone he wants."

"It doesn't work that way," Julie said.

Ben Herguth listened. He sometimes felt he was spending his life in phone booths. He wanted to be back in L.A., he wanted to be out of this terrible environment. Julie was feeling sorry for himself but at least he was in a big office, sitting in his own environment. Big Ben was getting too old to be on the streets, working out of phone booths. It was cold in Chi.

"Henkin wants to arrange something for Miki," Jules said in his vague way. "He doesn't give me the details, but we have to have the girl for . . . leverage. All right. We have no choice right now. We've got contracts signed, we have to 'mule' for Uncle, all this is going down in January, and here it is the middle of November. This whole thing keeps falling apart and we keep propping it up." Jules, at the other end of the telephone in a warm corner office in New York, felt sorry for himself and it was a luxury.

He said, "Ben, the more you deal with government people, the more you realize one thing."

Ben waited. He had heard this before.

"You realize the only people on earth who know what they're doing are people like us."

Ben shivered because it was so damned cold in the phone booth.

TWENTY-TWO
Bargain

D evereaux held her. They stood in the kitchen and he held her for a long time and felt her strong body beneath his fingers. He inhaled her scent, he pressed into her curves. She clung to him and she was crying a little, more from a sense of relief than anything else. He was alive! They might have been survivors of some tragedy who suddenly realize they are still alive when all around them are dead.

The kitchen was growing dark. The light of the brief November day moved from gray to gloaming purple, colored by a distant setting sun that dropped into the clear from the clouds.

"Why?" he said at last.

"I had to come after you. I thought you were alive. And then I thought Colonel Ready had you and I had to kill him. I had to come after you."

She told him about Club Tres on *Le Grand, Place* in

Brussels and about the man named Reiter who described Colonel Ready to her. She had come after Colonel Ready to kill him. She took out the opened knife in her raincoat and he smiled. He held it a moment.

"It's a little knife," he said. He closed the blade and put it in his pocket like a souvenir.

It was. She saw it. It was absurd. It was as though she had reasoned everything out but it had only been a dream and when she awoke—now—she realized how absurd the dream had been.

"My God, where are we? Can we go? Is it over?" she said.

He held her and looked at her in the fading light. Her eyes were so bright. He touched her lips with his fingers and she opened her mouth. He kissed her. It was a deep kiss and it went on for a long time, with hunger and hurt at both ends of the kiss. She strained against him so that he could feel her breasts and the warmth in her belly.

Night came heavily around the house and pressed against the windows. The men had gone, Miki had gone, they were alone in the world.

"Can we leave now?"

Devereaux shook his head.

"Everyone is gone," she said.

Devereaux shook his head again. He felt the sense of the others still around the house. Perhaps they were in the shed where they had taken Miki. Perhaps one or both of the big Czechs were outside now, having a cigarette.

"Who are they?"

"Cernan knew about you. Cernan knew you were coming after me."

She was a little angry now. "Dammit. I thought you were dead."

"Maybe I am," he said.

"Damn you," she said. "Colonel Ready—"

"Had me," he finished. "Sold me. Sold the defector I was carrying across. To these men. Who have been sitting here a couple of days, waiting for something. And then you came along. So I think we're going to know pretty soon."

"Who are they?"

"Czech Secret Service. Come to take Miki back to Prague. He was the defector. The one I went after. The night I left you. And didn't tell you."

"And what are they going to do with you?"

"I thought they were going to kill me," he said. He stared at her and touched her cheek with his hand. His touch was so gentle that she scarcely felt it. "I never thought I would see you again." His words were as clumsy as his touch was sure. He could never tell her things because all the words sounded false to him, as though they had been used too many times by other people who did not mean them.

"Dev." Her voice caught. She wanted to crawl inside him, to wear his skin, to be so completely part of him that when he died, she died.

They heard a sound on the porch outside the kitchen. Devereaux dropped his hands. He limped to the window. She made a sound and put her hand to her mouth.

"They're out there talking," he said.

"You limp like Ready. Like that terrible day in Lausanne he came to kill you."

"He hasn't killed me yet." The voice was flat and cold and the words didn't comfort her.

Cernan came into the dim room. He did not carry a gun. He looked at Rita, then at Devereaux.

"You see?" Cernan said to Devereaux.

Devereaux inclined his head. He understood.

"I cannot stay in Belgium forever. If I go back to Prague, it is without you. If I go back to Prague, it is without this woman."

Devereaux said nothing. Rita crossed the room, reached for him. But now his body was set, cold, apart. She could not cling to him.

"She loves you," Cernan said.

"And what do I do?" Devereaux said.

"You understand?" Cernan said.

"I think so."

"I have maybe two days. Maybe three days. Anna must be delivered safe, delivered by you here."

"I understand."

"If you cannot—"

Devereaux said nothing.

"I wish you no harm," he said to both of them. "It is a way a matter must be done."

"Why does Henkin want contact with you?"

Cernan stared, thought about it. He shrugged. "I think it is to kill Miki. That is what I think. That is why I think about Anna. I talk to Miki today."

"You were a long time in the shed," Devereaux said.

"It is not that Miki enjoys pain. He does not believe that I am authorized to inflict pain. It takes him a long time to understand this."

"What does he know?"

Cernan grinned in the almost darkness. "Miki knows everything."

"And Anna. He knows about Anna."

"Yes. He told me that at last, about Anna and that Anna was my child. It was the last thing he told me. Could Henkin be aware of this as well? It has to be. It was why I was chosen to bring Miki back to Prague. Except I was not to bring Miki back at all. How do you order a murder?

You hold out something that the murderer wants and you offer to give it to him if only he will kill. So the killer does the bidding of the man who has a prize. My child is the prize. I feel it in my bones. Henkin will want me to see that Miki does not return to Prague.''

Rita broke in. ''I'm a journalist, you can't—''

''Shut up. Please, I mean, shut up,'' Cernan said. ''You make the bargain for me and now I will buy the bargain.''

And Rita shivered, touched Devereaux, felt the cold and unyielding body. ''What bargain did you make?''

''Your life for Anna's freedom,'' Devereaux said.

Rita gasped. And then she hit him very hard in the face. Blood came to his lips. He looked at her and she hit him again with her fist. He didn't move.

Cernan said, ''Do not do this, woman.''

''I would have died for you,'' she said.

Devereaux said nothing to her. He stared at her and there was blood on his mouth. He didn't wipe it away.

''We watch you,'' Cernan said. ''From Brussels. And then you come to Bruges. I do not care about you, how close can you come to me? I tell him this. I say, 'It does not matter to me. Colonel Ready will come after her, he inquires about her from the gentlemen in Club Tres, in a little while Colonel Ready takes her and that is nothing to me.' I tell your man this thing to see what he will say, because everything is true, Rita Macklin. Colonel Ready knows you are in Bruges. In a little while, he has you. What does he want with you? But maybe you know. I think Devereaux knows.''

And Cernan was smiling. Her fist was poised for another blow. She stared wildly at Devereaux's impassive face and the trickle of blood on his lips, dripping down his chin.

''That's why you made the bargain with this man,'' she said.

Devereaux said nothing because all words lied or were misunderstood. He had wanted her to understand him when he held her a moment before and let his body flow into her body in a dirty farmhouse kitchen in the middle of this lost world. If she didn't understand him then, he could never make it more plain to her.

"There are clothes, your passport, the tickets," Cernan said abruptly. "The night plane from London—"

"All right," Devereaux said, breaking his silence. He stepped away from Rita. "I don't have a choice. Let me go, let her go. I will get Anna."

"Is that your word? Will you swear before the saints?"

"On the Infant of Prague if you want," Devereaux said.

"No, I do not believe in saints or miracles or oaths."

Devereaux said nothing.

"You signal the runner in Brussels and he will tell me the truth. You must have Anna and she must be alive."

"If she is dead—"

"Then Rita is dead."

"She was never—"

"She is dead in any case. Colonel Ready wants her as he wanted you. He is this close behind her. Only I am a little more quick than he is. After you give me reason to be quick." Cernan smiled and it was not pleasant. "You must bring me Anna and I will give you your life. And the life of this woman. It is more than a fair bargain."

Rita saw then the way it had been. She was going to be killed by Ready—or worse. And Devereaux would be dead as well and there was no hope for either of them. Unless he had made this bargain, this terrible understanding to trade a life for a life.

"Dev."

He did not speak to her. He felt her reach for his hand

and it was enough. He said to Cernan, "There can't be a misunderstanding. A life for a life."

Cernan nodded.

"No. No misunderstanding at all. I will find Anna and then you will show me that Rita is safe and alive and then we can complete . . . the bargain. But if you hurt her, I will hurt your daughter in the same way. If you kill her, I will kill Anna. Just so there is no misunderstanding."

Cernan shook his head slowly. "No. I have no illusions, American. You are brutal, a brutal people you come from. To kill is nothing to you, even an innocent child. You—"

"Save it for your masters, Cernan," Devereaux said. "I want you to understand because there's no turning back. I will kill her if you harm Rita, and if you harm her, after your daughter is dead, I'll come after you. I'll kill you in the same way. I want you to understand there is no turning back once you do harm."

The words were finished and the silence was all that was left. Rita touched his hand again and this time he opened his hand and covered her hand in his palm and closed his hand. To keep her safe for a little while longer.

TWENTY-THREE
Methods

"We are preparing to close, sir."

"Really? What time is it?"

"It is six in the morning, sir. It will be light in a few minutes. We close in the morning, sir. Can I call you a taxi? Would you like me to drive you back to your hotel, sir?"

"I'm only staying at the Amigo, it's just across the square."

"Perhaps we will see you in the evening?"

"Do you always close about now, Philip? You and Jans?"

"Yes, sir. Club Tres is for the night only." He smiled. A nice-looking boy.

"Where is Jans?"

"We are not too busy on Monday night, so Jans leaves early. We take turns."

"I see," David Mason said. He put down his drink along with a 1,000-franc Belgian note. "Is this enough?"

"It is generous, sir, whatever you wish to leave."

"No, I meant for another drink."

"Well, sir, we are closing."

"I need another drink," Mason said.

"Well, let me lock the door." Philip smiled at him. "Let me lock the door and then we can see about that drink." He moved around the wide oak bar to the big door and pulled the lock across. "There. We won't be disturbed then," Philip said. He wondered what the American boy had in mind.

Mason stood up when Philip came back to the bar and hit him very hard in the stomach. Philip bent over and felt the waves of nausea and Mason hit him very hard in the face. He broke Philip's nose. Philip sank to his knees and Mason kicked him in the stomach and Philip gagged. His nose was bleeding. Mason hit him a second time in the nose and then picked him up by his shirt and slammed him against the bar, so that the edge of the bar smacked Philip sharply in the kidneys.

Mason took him by the shirt and slammed him against the wall that held the picture of the naked woman and the naked woman fell on the floor.

Mason slammed Philip against the bar again and Philip could not scream with the pain because he didn't have any breath in his body. He heaved for breath. It came at last and he moaned. Mason sat down on the bar stool and Philip hung onto the bar to remain upright.

Mason said, "Tell me about Colonel Ready. The man with the scar on his face."

His voice was good, calm, almost sweet. There was a natural softness that did not carry any inflection.

"You broke it. You broke my nose."

Mason hit him in the stomach again.

Philip groaned and retched but he had nothing in his stomach. He held his stomach and reached for a chair and collapsed into it. He groaned over and over and rocked back and forth.

"Tell me about Colonel Ready," Mason said.

"You are killing me," Philip said.

"That's not the answer, Philip," Mason said. He broke the bottle of Stella Artois beer across the edge of the bar and grabbed Philip by his hair. He held the jagged edge of the bottle to his face.

"I know how to contact him," Philip said.

"Why did you sell out the train?"

"Who are you?"

"The last person in the world you ever wanted to see, Philip. Maybe the last person you ever will see. How old are you, Philip?"

"Thirty."

"That's awfully young, Philip."

"There was a lot of money. We only supply the driver. And the car. We picked a driver. All he wanted to know was the name of the driver."

"He got to the driver. You picked out the driver for him. When you picked the wrong driver, you wrecked the train. When you wrecked the train, we lost a man. When we lose a man, we get upset. You upset us, Philip. Terribly. So what can you say to me to stop me?"

"My God, my God," Philip said.

"No. That won't do it."

He pushed the jagged edge into Philip's right cheek. Philip didn't even feel the pain for a moment, until he saw the blood on the edge of the bottle. He put his hand on his cheek and felt the pain and screamed in a very high-pitched voice. He screamed and screamed and then Mason said, "Shut up. The next time, I cut your eye out. So just shut up. I want you to concentrate."

"My God, my God."

Mason lifted the bottle. Philip felt the blood on his palm. He said, "I'll tell you everything, everything."

"I know," Mason said. He put the bottle down on the wide oak bar. He waited.

"Colonel Ready. Except he said his name was Driver. He had all kinds of names. That woman that came here to ask about him called him that. He was interested in her."

"Yes. I know. I know all about it. He killed her. He was after her, he must have followed her to Bruges." He paused, staring at the bleeding man. "She's dead. We lost a man and we lost her, so someone has to pay for the damages. We have to reduce our losses."

"I called him. Jans called him. You want Jans."

"I'll take care of Jans, Philip. I want you now. Does it hurt, Philip?"

"Yes."

"Good. Now tell me about Colonel Ready and how you contacted him."

He told him about the contact. There was a dead letter drop at the stamp shop near the statue of the Mannekin Pis. You dropped the message one day in such a way and you got a reply the next day. In this case, he had got Colonel Ready in person at Club Tres. He was a mercenary contractor and he had a lot of money. He gave some of it to Philip and Jans. After all, they weren't involved in anything. They just provided the stationhouse for the trains and the driver and the car.

"We were not involved," Philip said. His voice was a moan. The blood was dried on his cheek but the scar would be very bad.

"You were involved," Mason said. He stared at Philip. "You fucked with the United States government, Philip." He said the verb softly, almost with a child's wonder. His voice was even more soft than it had been at the beginning. "But you might survive yet if you do everything right. I want you to get hold of Colonel Ready. I want you to call Jans and tell him to drop a message this morning and then to come over here. I want you to tell Jans that you got visited by a man who was the conductor of that train. The man in black. The man you set up."

"But Mr. Driver killed him."

"No. He did worse than that. I think he did worse than that. I think I know what Mr. Driver did and I think the man in black is alive but wishing he wasn't alive. So if I figured it right, then Mr. Driver or Colonel Ready is going to wonder what the hell is going on with you. So I figure he'll come over to talk to you about it."

"He's a bad man."

"Yes, Philip. But better the devil you know. I'm here, Philip, and I just beat you up a little bit. Just a little body slamming. I can beat you up for a long time. I wasn't in Nam or anything like that, but I did grow up on streets. You learn a lot of things. So I can beat you up until everything hurts and you piss blood and all that stuff and you still won't be dead. I'm going to get Colonel Ready and kill him. And maybe I won't kill you and Jans because, like you said, you were not involved. I make myself clear to you, Philip?"

Philip stared at the calm-eyed madman and nodded. When he found his voice, he dialed the black telephone behind the bar. It rang for a long time because Jans was sleeping. Mason poured himself another beer and sat on the stool at the American-style bar and waited while Philip talked to Jans.

TWENTY-FOUR

The California Message

The driver was a sandy-haired kid who chewed gum. Mr. Willis was sweating by the time he stepped to the curb at Los Angeles International Airport. The sun was pale above the smog in the bowl of the city and Willis was dressed for November in Chicago. He let the kid open the back door of the stretch Cadillac and got inside. There was a television set. He turned it on and then off, just to see if it worked. There was a glass divider between the driver and the big rear compartment.

- The kid rolled the divider down. The radio was full of jungle sounds.

"Roll the divider up," Willis said.

The kid said, "No sweat." He pushed the button that sealed the rear compartment. He crawled through the lanes that led away from the airport on the ocean and drove north toward the city.

Los Angeles had charm but you had to look for it. The

center city was full of big buildings without character or pattern. There still were no pedestrians and some of the streets had not even bothered with sidewalks. All the cars seemed exotic and Willis stared out his side window at the cars and the drivers. The limousine was cool and Willis felt dry and tired. The address was a stunted, whitewashed two-story building on Sunset, below the hills. He told the kid to wait and crossed to the entrance and went up the carpeted cement stairs to the second floor. Suite 201 was right off the stairs. He went through the door and the girl at the reception desk wore a white silk blouse that was open enough for Willis to stare at. He said his name. The girl went to a door and opened it. Willis saw a plastic penis sitting on the floor of the second office. A plastic penis, he thought. He filed the image.

The big man was smoking a big cigar and wore a camel's-hair sport coat that made him look even bigger than he was.

He looked at Willis and didn't say a thing. Willis nodded toward the door. Ben Herguth shrugged and followed him into the corridor and down the stairs. They both had an aversion to talking in a place where walls might have ears.

The limousine roared down Sunset toward the ocean. The destination was a fish restaurant in Beverly Hills, off Rodeo, but the driver was instructed to go by way of the beach and take his time making a big circle through Santa Monica and Westwood.

"We want to know about her." Willis made his voice flat, almost uninterested.

"Her? Who her?"

"Cute," Willis said.

"Hey, fuck you, G man. You fuck this up from Jump Street, so you got nothing to say about where it's going."

Willis said, "You know how much trouble you can be in?"

"Fuck you, G man. I'm shitting in my boots, you got me so scared."

Willis tried it a different way. "Look. We were caught flat-footed by Miki. When Miki pulled a defect. We don't know where the hell he is, we don't even know if he's alive."

"He's alive," Herguth said. He liked the look of surprise. "Temporarily."

"We need smooth relations," Willis said. "First that little girl pulls a religious defection in Chicago. We got heat from the Czech ambassador, the White House got a personal note from the Czech President. It would be just our luck that Prague closes its borders for a few months. That'd be just what we need."

Herguth said, "You need? I sympathize with you and what you fuckheads need. What about me? I got a production company ready to shoot a twenty-eight-part miniseries, I got a hundred and thirty-five contracts inked in with time, dates and termination periods, and what the fuck do I do with all of it if Prague closes down? It's too late to shoot it in Spain. Besides, Spain doesn't have snow. This is supposed to be the life of Napoleon and Napoleon needs snow. You know. Russia. That kind of stuff."

"And we've smoothed the way for you, haven't we?" Willis said.

"For a price."

"For a bit of patriotism. So tell me, Ben: Where is Anna Jelinak?"

"Beats the shit out of me."

"You aren't gonna tell me. I come all the way out here to see you."

"I'm touched."

"Look. The heat is real. Emil Mikita disappears in the West. We had nothing to do with that, I can assure you. Fucking Miki didn't know which way from Sunday about how to come across. Then, the exact same day, Anna Jelinak defects. Prague looks like a prize sap, Uncle's punching bag. Countries get pissed off just like people when you start cuffing them around. We didn't have anything to do with Anna. We didn't have anything to do with Miki. But it looks like we did. I got a rocket for you, Ben. It came down this morning before I left. The rocket says that certain people in Prague are so pissed off about Miki and now Anna disappearing that something better shake loose soon or you can kiss your mini-series on the tokas good-bye."

Ben Herguth smiled.

It wasn't what Willis was looking for.

The smile got wider as the limo pulled into Rodeo Drive.

"See, Willis, you guys at Langley ain't got a clue. Everything you touch turns to sugar maple shit. Anna is all tied to Miki after all but not the way you think. Give it forty-eight hours tops and Miki's problem is solved and Anna's problem is solved and Prague gets happy again. What you don't know, you can't fuck up. So let's eat lunch in peace."

"What kind of message is that for me to bring back?"

"I give a fuck what kind of message you bring back. I'm just telling you the way it is. Everything is taken care of because we aren't waiting around now for you to do something. Don't worry, Willis. You're in California, nobody worries in California. It's warm, Willis, even in November. Don't worry about a thing."

"I am trying to impress on you that the Czechs are upset—"

"Fuck 'em. They live in a cold climate. If they lived

in California, they wouldn't even want to be Communists. You ever think about it. The only place Communism works is in cold climates."

"Like Cuba."

"So, one exception. Count Nicaragua, maybe two. But it still proves the rule. People worry when it's cold. I'm not cold, I'm not worried. Two days, Anna wakes up in Prague and that's all over and you guys can take the credit for it if you want, I give a fuck. Two days, Miki is buttoned up permanent and we can go ahead with our fun and games and not worry about anyone being a snitch. And when January comes, Napoleon goes back to Russia to get the shit kicked out of him, except it won't be Russia, it'll be Prague with a few onion domes thrown in. A forty-five-million-dollar extravaganza, we sell a hundred eighty mill in commercials on first and second run, world-wide distribs, videotape, tie-ins. Plus a full three-hour movie in six foreign languages, particularly French since we got the leading frog lady of the day to play Josephine. What a tush she's got on her."

The limo pulled up at the curb and Sandy jumped out of the driver's seat and opened the back door.

Ben Herguth slid out, stood up, patted his clothes and waited.

But Willis was rubbing his stomach.

"You ain't hungry?" Ben said with a smile.

Willis shook his head. He wondered if he would ever be hungry again.

TWENTY-FIVE

Devereaux Goes Home

Brit
ritish Airways was nearly forty-five minutes late arriving at Kennedy because of traffic, and the helicopter across Long Island to LaGuardia was late, and the United flight to Chicago was late taking off because of traffic at O'Hare.

Devereaux felt the ache of travel and the ache in his stiff left leg and all the pains of spending nearly eleven hours in the air or trying to get in the air. The shuffle through customs at Kennedy was routine; the Swiss passport was Devereaux's own, given to Cernan by Colonel Ready. The passport number would show up in twelve hours on the computer at Section because it was a creation of Section; it would be the signal that Devereaux—or someone using Devereaux's passport—had entered the United States.

O'Hare was bright on this November afternoon and there were souvenirs celebrating Christmas or the Chicago Bears in the newsstands. Devereaux walked the long corridor from gate F12 to the main concourse at Terminal Two and then pushed through the people to the street. Traffic was standing still. A black cab driver in a yellow car was screaming insults at a white man in a black limousine and a paunchy Chicago policeman was yelling at both of them. The street was narrowed by construction barriers and filled with private cars, cabs, limousines, police cars, rental vans, suburban buses and airport service trucks. Devereaux stared at it all for a moment, his head filling with the noises of his native land and native city. Each time he came back to the States now, the brutal vitality of it—the colors, the openness, the obscene grace—startled him. He was a stranger now. His exile had no roots.

He reentered the terminal and found the entrance to the subway by asking directions from three different policemen. The car was waiting in the station and he fell into a seat and closed his eyes. His single bag—packed by one of Cernan's men—was between his legs.

The doors clicked closed and the train picked up speed, emerging suddenly into the light and climbing to an elevated trestle at River Road. The day was bright with bright gray clouds and there was the smell of snow in the air. The train screamed along the tracks heading south and east toward the Loop. Devereaux stared at the pitched roofs of the bungalows and the dense traffic clogging the Kennedy Expressway. He was tired and drained and it was more than the two airplane trips. It was the thought of Rita held hostage mixed with the thought of coming home.

He detested nostalgia and the memories of a past life.

What had he been all his life but the outsider? First on city streets, outside the law and protection of home, then inside a secret agency so buried in the government that its very name was snatched from deep within the funding bill that created it. Subparagraph R became Section R. And Devereaux became a pawn named November and lost his right to ever come inside.

He accepted that. He could stand the silence, the cold, the aloneness and being apart. And then, by accident, he would suddenly be thrust into a reminder of all the past he had lost and the waste of it. Now he was on a Chicago El train, screeching along above the low bungalows down to the heart of the high-rise city, and he might have been ten years old again, starting out on the streets with his knife and his guts and his savage sense of self.

There was too much pain in nostalgia. Yet the past kept thrusting itself at him. It hurt him more now to be in Chicago than to have endured all the real pains of the past week.

He closed his eyes to shut out the city.

But when he closed his eyes, Rita was near. He could smell her and touch her.

"I've told the police that."

Kay Davis picked up her glass of white wine, studied it, put it down. She had done that a half dozen times. The man across from her did not touch his vodka.

"Yes. Is it secret?"

"No, Mr. Devereaux. But Al Buck was really generous, really a prince about it. I mean that. In this business, you never get a second chance. He had been calling me, he said. He said it was wrong, his way of handling it was wrong. He took the blame, he said he wanted me back at the station and that I could go after the story any way I saw fit. He was really terrific. He took the blame for everything and he gave me a three-year contract and he said he must have been crazy to want to jump off a good story like this one and would I come back. So I came back.

The story was kind of petering out anyway because the statue stopped crying and this court thing could have gone on and on. . . . My God, I think about Stephanie. I talked to her that night, the night I was attacked. I mean, it's so coincidental the way things work."

"Yes. Almost like a miracle in itself. I mean, a miracle for you. Not for Stephanie."

"You're all the way here from Zurich because of the miracle."

"Yes. There's interest. Particularly in Switzerland."

"Why?"

"It's a country without faith, divided by a number of religions. It has to believe in something."

Kay Davis smiled at him. He was a good-looking man, she thought. Not television, of course. Devereaux had showed her his Swiss passport and the all-purpose little plastic card that identified him as a correspondent for Central News Associates, Zurich. In fact, if you looked in the Zurich telephone directory, you would find a number for the news service, as well as an address. If you went to the building off the Paradplatz in Zurich and went to the right floor, you would find a news agency office, filled with clippings for scores of papers, dust and dirt, and an old man trying to make a living by providing news items for parsimonious newspapers in a half dozen countries. Yes, Monsieur Devereaux was a correspondent, he would answer.

"Are you going to be in Chicago long?" she said.

"Perhaps."

She gave him a smile from her eyes to her mouth. She turned toward him in a certain way. Her knee bumped his knee and he saw what it was. He smiled at her. "You're a good-looking girl," he said.

"Woman."

"Of course."

"Would you like to go out to dinner some night? After the ten o'clock show?"

"Yes," he said.

"Aren't you offended that I asked you?"

"Flattered," he said.

"You should be," she said.

He smiled again. "Tell me," he said. "Tell me about your part in this. Weren't the police interested in the co-incidence? Your getting fired and that man attacking you?"

"The police were interested in my getting fired and that man . . . that man . . . knowing I was fired. But it was in the early edition of the papers, someone in PR had dropped it into one of the gossip columns."

"Really?"

"I was hot news myself for a few days. The police think it was just one of those crazy things. They still don't have a name for the guy."

"That's odd, isn't it?"

Kay Davis shivered. It was the cold of the cocktail lounge and it was something else, something in his voice. That was it. He was cold, his eyes were cold; he feigned interest in her but it was all cold.

"Odd," she said.

"And the little girl was kidnapped. What did the police say about that?"

"They said it might have been connected. The detective said there was a connection, he was sure of it, but he couldn't figure out what the connection was. And there was the FBI then, after the kidnapping and Stephanie's . . . death. It's so horrible, all of it, and I feel . . ."

"Responsible," he said.

"Yes."

He said nothing. Did she expect him to say something?

She waited for some note of comfort in his voice but there was none.

"Did it happen? Actually?"

"What?" she said.

"Did the statue of the Infant cry?"

Kay Davis stared at him with wide eyes. She almost had forgotten. She saw the statue, not as it was but through the television eye. Through the lens. On the monitor. The tape for her voiceover. The reason for everything that happened, that had seemed to happen.

"I don't know," she said. "I saw it. I mean, I was there in St. Margaret's. But I don't know. I can show you the tape." She was making her voice smile. "I've got a VCR at home. We could watch it. Other things."

"Yes." His voice was absent. "Sometime I would like to see the tape. But the child believed it."

"Anna saw the tears."

"What about her mother?"

"Her mother? She didn't believe it. I showed her the tape and she said it was a trick. She didn't believe it."

"Where is she?"

"She's living in the Czech embassy in Washington. She's waiting for word. The FBI said it would be best to wait to see if she were contacted by the kidnappers."

"I wonder what the FBI thinks."

"It's a kidnapping for ransom. Except. There's been no word for all this time. And they think—well, I know they don't say it outright, but they think the little girl was killed. That something went wrong and the kidnappers have just dumped her body somewhere. It's a matter of time."

"Yes." He stared suddenly into Kay. She felt startled and even afraid and she shivered again. "What do you think, Miss Davis?"

"Is this all connected to the story of the weeping statue?"

"Perhaps." He picked up his drink and tasted it. The lounge was dark, there was background music, and the peanuts on the bar were roasted in honey. "Perhaps the statue wept for all that would follow. Both the cause and the effect."

Kay Davis finished her glass of white wine.

"Another?"

"No. I've still got a ten o'clock show. Where are you staying?"

"The Drake," he said.

"That's such an old-fashioned place."

"I know but I don't know Chicago. You ask at American Express in Zurich and they give you a name and that's it. We only know the clichés of other cities." He smiled. It was a sad little smile, she thought, and she felt touched by it. The coldness of his face, she thought, was earned and had turned inward. It was not directed at her. She felt an instinct about him.

"You don't think she's dead," Kay Davis said.

"No."

"Why?"

"Because there must be miracles."

"Do you believe in statues that weep?"

"Yes. I believe what I see. If I stop believing what I see, then there's no point to having sight."

"Who took her?" She asked as though he might know. He might know everything.

He shook his head. "*Why* is more important. The FBI says it was for ransom and no one asks for ransom. Was it for perversion? That seems unlikely. The pervert doesn't go to so much trouble when it is easier to take children off the streets. Perhaps a religious dispute? It couldn't be a jealous sect. Religion doesn't have much zeal left in it, does it? So what is the reason?"

She stared at him and felt a strange warmth grow in her that suppressed the shivers.

"Why?"

"To use in a bargain. To make a deal," he said. His voice was so quiet that the background music almost overwhelmed it.

"By whom? For what?"

Devereaux shook his head. His eyes were staring at something beyond her. She turned and looked and there was nothing in the darkness. She looked back at him.

"What do you see?"

"Something," he said. "Are you all right now, then? Do you have protection? The police?"

"For a while. But I'm all right. No one understands how he got into my apartment. The security staff was given lie-detector tests and a couple of them were fired and everyone in the building is really upset. But I'm all right. I really am."

"Good," he said. There was the cold thing in his voice again.

"What's wrong?"

"I think you should take a few days off," he said.

"Who are you?"

"The name on the passport."

"Should I report you to the police?"

"If you want," he said. His eyes were sad, she thought. Maybe he pitied her. The warmth she had felt a moment before began to wane. She got up from the bar stool.

"It doesn't matter about the police," he said. "I could tell you a story about myself and it would be good enough to convince you. I could even tell you the truth and it would just frustrate you because no one could believe it. So I'll tell you this: In a little while, you are going to face some danger and then, if it turns out all right, you'll be all right.''

"Danger? Are you threatening me?"

"No. But I'm guessing and I'm a good guesser."

"What are you guessing?"

He couldn't tell her now. He gave her a telephone number instead. In case she needed it.

TWENTY-SIX
Damme

The bicyclist could be seen for a long time, pedaling down the bike path that ran between the road and the canal. He crossed the canal at the edge of Bruges and the busy auto route and then started down the long, straight path that led to Damme and beyond. But he was going to Damme.

Damme was old and small, just a crossroads village with a few overpriced restaurants that suggested a Flemish painting of the last century. The people in Bruges went to Damme on the weekend to dine and pretend they were from a great metropolis. The bicyclist bent his head as he rode the upright three-speed. It was raining a light mist and the morning light was gray and reflected the color of the North Sea fifteen kilometers away.

The bicyclist reached the crossroads of Damme and put his bicycle against a tree and waited. He was dressed in black and wore a black sailor's cap on his head. He wore a black pea jacket and black trousers and a black sweater. His face was flushed with exertion and there was a long scar that ran from the corner of his mouth to his ear. His eyes were blue and cold and they saw everything.

David Mason stepped from the doorway of the shuttered restaurant across the road and stood on the sidewalk. The man with the scar grinned at him and walked across the road to him.

"The pistol is wrapped in the newspaper and I shoot well. Not the highest rating but good enough to kill you," Mason said.

"I'll certainly remember that," Colonel Ready said. He smiled at Mason. "Have you killed anyone yet? Or will this be the first time?"

"Not the first time."

"You enjoy fag bashing? You did a nice job on Philip. I think you've almost convinced him to get out of the business. You didn't have to beat him up to get my attention," Ready said.

"It was a matter of getting Philip's attention."

"So what are you?"

"Section."

"You coming after me?"

"If I have to."

"I see." The grin faded a moment and then reappeared. "It's out of my hands now in any case."

"Is it?"

"Sold them both. A matching pair, you might say."

"Who?"

"Miki. And Devereaux."

"What about Rita Macklin? What about a red-haired woman?"

The older man looked puzzled. "I haven't gotten around to her."

"She disappeared. She came down that path you were on and disappeared."

"I don't know about that." He looked at Mason. "You want to know about Devereaux? It worked nicely with him. He didn't know what hit him. The only screwup was the driver. He panicked at the last minute, almost killed my brother. Brother Devereaux, brother in arms." He smiled. "Old Miki wanted to go west, put out his feelers and couldn't get any bites. Until Section came along. I think there must be parts to Miki but I'm not interested. I wanted Devereaux. Maybe that's why they used him, because they knew Miki had parts and they wanted an old hand. We were in Asia together, going back, you know that?"

Mason stared at him and didn't let the gun hand waver. Ready was talking fast, like a salesman edging around him.

"That's right, turn when I move, keep the piece pointed right at me."

"You sold Devereaux East?"

"Now you've got it," Ready said.

"Where is he?"

"I don't have a clue."

The smile was infuriating. He thought he could get away with it. He pulled the trigger. The silencer thumped and the bullet whistled past his face.

Ready blinked.

"You might have hit me."

"I might have," Mason agreed.

"Well, maybe I could figure out how to get in touch. With his new keeper, I mean."

"They're in the country."

"There's every possibility," Ready agreed. He had flinched after the fact, when he heard the thump. Now he was smiling again. Happens every day, somebody shoots off a piece in your ear.

"Stop fucking around," David Mason said.

"The problem is, you want to shoot me but there's the chance that I can arrange you an introduction with Devereaux's keeper. That's a problem all right. On the other hand, my problem is you: I was curious about you. You banged up Philip pretty good. Maybe you'd just as soon shoot me."

"Maybe," Mason said.

"But Section teaches patience. Like the chaser in Brussels, sniffing around like a bloodhound. What's he going to do with all his clues? Paper shufflers. You were direct, lad, I like that. You went to the source and beat the shit out of him. That's the way to do it." He grinned. "You were right behind Rita Macklin, weren't you? How'd she give you the slip then?"

Mason said nothing.

"Come on, lad, cheer up. If she got lost and I didn't get her, then it must be the party who already has Devereaux. Maybe he wants to put them in a glass cage together and watch them fuck."

"I could put it in your gut."

"No." Ready was still grinning. "You got the gun and I got you by the balls. You pull the trigger, lad, and I'm liable to snap your balls right off."

"So what do we do?" Mason said.

"Well, I was thinking of killing you. Right here. The more I think about it, I think I won't right now."

"I've got the gun."

"I've got the balls," Ready said. "No. I think the thing to do is find out where little Rita went. I had plans for her. Maybe Devereaux's buyer has plans, too. We could find out together."

"What plans?"

"I've got to break her, lad." Ready smiled as if he were describing a prized possession. "I like her, I like the way she feels, I like the way she looks. I'm going to break her down and when she's really broken, then everything will be just fine."

Mason said, "I really do want to kill you."

"I know, lad. I've been an inspiration to you, haven't I? But learn a little patience and we'll see what we can see."

Ready turned then and began to limp across the street to his bicycle standing against the tree.

"Where are you going?"

"Back to Bruges," he said over his shoulder. "Drop a dime and call a number."

"All right," he said. "We'll go back together."

"You going to ride on the handlebars?"

"We'll walk," Mason said.

"You walk out here?"

"Yes."

"Why?"

"Looking for Rita."

"You must be in love," Ready said. "That's really something, that girl turns on a lot of men."

"Shut up."

"I'm riding my bike, I'm afraid. My leg," Ready said.

"We'll walk," Mason said again.

For a moment, the lips turned into a snarl. He stared hard at Mason and Mason saw how death could be done so easily. He held the gun steady in the face of it. He tried his own smile. "It'll hurt to walk all that way back," Mason said.

"He gave me the limp; I got him. Maybe I'll get you."

Mason kept smiling.

TWENTY-SEVEN
Out of Control

The President had the flu and was in Bethesda Naval Hospital northwest of the District. He appeared at the window of his suite of rooms in the morning and waved at reporters below and shouted encouraging words to them in a hoarse voice. All for the evening news.

Mrs. Neumann watched the President wave from three monitors set on three different channels in her office credenza.

There was no sound in the room save the steady "on" hum from the computer terminal in the corner. The terminal screen was blank. Ten minutes before, it had flashed the "eyes only" message to the director of operations and the Section chief that a certain Swiss passport with a certain number invented by R Section had been used seven hours earlier by someone passing through customs at Kennedy Airport.

"Is he alive?"

"If he is," Hanley said, "why doesn't he contact us?"

"And assume it is him," Mrs. Neumann said. She watched the mesmerizing monitors but saw nothing. "Assume it is and you have to assume what else?"

"He was captured and escaped."

"He didn't come back here because he had escaped," she said.

"Yes. But what could the reason be?"

Mrs. Neumann looked very tired. She closed her eyes a moment to get rid of the television images. She rubbed a finger over her eyelids. She opened her eyes and the world remained. Hanley looked as tired as she did.

"He was a captive. Somehow, Miki or his masters double-crossed the train. They took in Devereaux and then offered him as a trade for that girl in Chicago who sees weeping miracles," Hanley said. His mouth was curled in Midwestern Protestant distaste, for Catholics and their icons. "Now the child has disappeared. And now Devereaux has reappeared. The conclusion—at least in logic —is that Devereaux has been let go. For only one reason."

"He wouldn't work for them," she said. She stared at the three monitors. There was war in Nicaragua on one and a fire on a train on another and a starved-looking African child with bloated belly on the third.

Hanley tented his fingers and stared over them at her.

"He hasn't gone to work for them," she said. She said the words in a very plain and sure way, to make Hanley understand she believed them.

"He has come into this country and he has not made contact with Section," Hanley said. His voice was soft, exceptionally so; it was nearly a whisper. "He is here and he was held by the Czechs."

"We don't know it was them."

"No. There was a person described in this business by

Chaser in Brussels whom we assume was Colonel Ready. Perhaps Devereaux was held by Ready. Perhaps this is a repeat of all that happened in St. Michel. Ready did get the girl and got Devereaux to do his bidding for a time. I know the agent." He closed his eyes and saw Devereaux clearly, heard his voice, saw the arctic calm in his face. "I know the agent. He draws the line. He came in through regular customs when he could have gone through the Canadian or Mexican doors. So he knew the passport number would flash back to us in time. He doesn't mind letting us know he's out and that he's here. He just hasn't gotten around to giving us a jingle."

"Is that sarcasm?"

"Of course," Hanley said. "Whatever he is doing, we would not wish him to do. And perhaps he feels a bit misused. We never told him all the implications of conducting Miki to our station."

"We misused him. We should have told him all the implications of the train."

"There was no need for him to know," Hanley said.

"There was, in retrospect."

"I told him to be careful."

"Mothers tell their children to watch at street corners and not to talk to strangers. There are specifics in warnings and there are generalities."

"Mrs. Neumann, I—"

"The world knew that Miki wanted to come out. And no one wanted to touch him because it smelled. It was too easy. And what could Miki do for us? He hinted and hinted and we thought he was worth a small risk, out of channels, to get him on our side, to hear what he had to say about our competition at Langley. To give us leverage today for the next budget battle tomorrow or the day after tomorrow. Was it all worth it? We always put a price on things, don't we, even when we don't know what they are really going to be worth.''

She said it the way she had said it before, almost in the same words. She said it like a dull child repeating a lesson she does not understand. She said it like an incantation, as though the words might change the result.

Hanley waited for the words to end. The result was the same.

"If he isn't alive, then someone is very stupid using his passport," he said.

"Or smart. Perhaps it's an illusion. Perhaps it's a way of cocking a snook at us."

"Colonel Ready?" Hanley said.

"Perhaps. He was the heart of the deal. At least, according to the description we got from Chaser about the man at Club Tres. And Mason—"

"Yes. He's kicked the traces. Chaser said he bollixed things up. Just brutality. He knew the rules, he knew the regs. But he was young," Hanley said.

"It's no excuse," she said. "Let the CIA fight their secret wars. We are in the business of intelligence. We are in the business of putting two and two together in all the combinations. We are not thugs, enforcers, hit men."

Hanley said nothing; Lydia Neumann came from order and computers and pure intelligence. She was not of this world, he thought. She would have to learn that sometimes they broke the rules because there are no rules when it comes down to it.

"Perhaps he had no choice," Hanley said.

"What does Devereaux want here?"

Hanley waited a moment for Mrs. Neumann to see the obvious. She did.

"The girl," she said.

"Our little infant of Prague," Hanley said. He was the

prairie Protestant again. "And we don't know where to find her. So we're of no use to him. Or, perhaps, he might think we arranged the kidnapping ourselves. In any case, he doesn't want to consult us for advice."

"We don't have private operators," she said.

"That isn't true, Mrs. Neumann." Gently. "You think of this as a vast army because you are an orderly person with an orderly mind. You can speak to computers; it is your background and your genius. There is no order out there, Mrs. Neumann, only chaos. We sort through the billions of bits of chaos hurled at us and we try to understand a billionth part of it."

She said, "You are becoming a philosopher. There still have to be rules of procedure."

"There are no rules. Rather, there are rules that are always broken."

"He can't do this. He's making a run for the Czechoslovakian Secret Service."

"Yes," Hanley said. Mrs. Neumann finally understood what Hanley had realized the moment he saw the passport number flash on his computer terminal screen two hours ago. It had been intuitive for him; Mrs. Neumann proceeded by logic. Hanley was the man who held the lamp until she could become accustomed to seeing in the dark.

"I will not permit this," she said. "I want him in. I want to notify the other agencies."

Hanley said, "This is our thing."

"No. Section comes before the man." She stared at him. "The good of Section."

"Does the position change you?" Hanley said.

"Yes."

"All right," he said. "I still make my protest."

"Noted. The problem is too much secrecy. Agencies get in trouble because they get too clever. Devereaux is trouble for us out there. Bring him in and proceed with logic.''

"How do we do it?"

"Straight. We have reason to believe a man working for the Czechoslovakian Secret Service has entered the United States with the intention of tracking Anna Jelinak,'' she said. The hoarse whispery voice was as neutral now as a government report. "Description. The usual. No. He is not with Section. We have an agent carried on the Mexico City morning report with Section named November. We keep this clear of Section."

"And that is a deception," Hanley said. "He could point this out."

"Every person ever arrested claims he works for the CIA," she said. There was a sadness to her voice he had not noticed before. Did the position of director really change you all that much? Or was it the prospect of facing chaos that changed you when you really longed to believe in the rule of logic, order, sanity?

"I'll send out the notification."

"Priority," she said.

"I'll do it myself," he said softly. The room was darkened and only the lights of the television monitors and a small lamp at the corner of the desk softened the darkness. The litany of disasters was repeated silently on the three monitors as the evening news unfolded in three gospels. Was there one truth at the heart of the three readings?

Hanley sent the message to the agencies within twenty minutes. The alert was top secret but it was general so that all the agencies got the message in clearspeak.

Which is why, shortly before midnight, people in Los Angeles and New York—and Chicago—knew Devereaux was coming.

TWENTY-EIGHT
This Little Fishy

Al Buck kissed wife number two good-bye and smiled at Nana, who was six, and frowned at Jeremiah, who was thirteen, and opened the door of Apartment 19H and walked into his world. The elevator hurtled down eighteen floors to the lobby, there being no thirteenth floor in the square glass-walled building at 1345 N. Lake Shore Drive. He crossed the lobby, picked up the *Tribune* waiting at the security desk and let the doorman do his job. He stepped into the back of the stretch Lincoln and settled into the black leather. The television set was not on.

The fucking television set was not on.

He threw the paper down on the seat and leaned forward and knelt across the rear-facing seats and knocked at the divider glass.

The driver turned and opened the window.

It wasn't the regular driver.

"I've got a standing order. The television is supposed to be on. You know who I am? You know where you're taking me?" His face was a little red. It was a lousy way to start out the day.

Then he saw the gun.

The driver had the gun.

"What's this?" Al Buck said.

"This is a gun," the driver said.

"Is this a joke?"

"No. It's a nine-millimeter Smith and Wesson with a thirteen-shot double-action automatic. You kneel on the seat and keep your face close to the window and we're going on a little drive."

"Where are you taking me?"

"Shut up."

Al Buck held onto the back of the seat and the driver turned right at Division Street and Michigan Avenue. He went down Division past the shuttered nightclubs that looked shabby in bright daylight. He turned into an alley before they got to Rush Street and the car stopped. The driver said:

"Get in the front seat. With me."

Al Buck got out of the car and the pistol was on him. He had never had a gun pointed at him. He thought of some situation like this. He could remember just about every television program he'd ever watched. There had been something similar in "Mike Hammer," he thought. What did Stacy Keach do? Wasn't it about rolling under the car? He shut the rear door and opened the front door. He slid onto the leather and slammed the door.

The driver wore a black hat and a black jacket and a white shirt and tie. He pushed the stick into "D" and rolled heavily down the alley to the corner, turned left and headed back toward Michigan Avenue. The day was so bright and warm for November that the men and women surging up and down the avenue seemed to have light steps, as though it was spring after a long winter. Miss Humphrey would be waiting for him. In a half hour, she would call his home. His wife would tell her the driver picked him up a half hour ago. Then they would dawdle some. It might be an hour more before they called the police.

The driver held the pistol in his lap. In "Remington Steele"—no, wasn't it in "The Enforcer"?—Edward Woodward reached across and hit the driver hard in the kidney and dropped to the piece in one motion.

Al Buck sat very still. The limousine reached Lake Shore Drive and surged into the six-lane highway that runs along the lake. The lake was shrouded in fog because the water was still warmer than the air. There were clouds on the horizon like a line of sailing ships.

They went south, skimming the Loop and Grant Park. The driver turned off at 31st Street on the South Side and meandered down side streets to an area of abandoned factories south of the Prairie Avenue historic district. Then they were bumping across open ground, south of Soldier's Field and below the pilings that held up the roadway of the Drive. This was an abandoned place, Al Buck thought. And he knew he was going to die.

The driver stopped the car.

He turned to look at Al Buck and picked up the automatic pistol. He put the pistol in Al Buck's face. "Open your mouth," the driver said in a soft voice.

Al Buck opened his mouth.

The driver put the pistol on his tongue.

"I'll ask you questions and you'll tell me answers. If you get all the answers right, you go back to the office and say you were delayed. If you get the answers wrong, I kill you and put you in the trunk and drop the car at Lot

C at O'Hare. Those are the only two scenarios today, Mr. Buck. You understand?''

Al Buck made a sound around the pistol barrel.

"Answer this one: Who told you to pull Kay Davis off the story about the Infant of Prague?''

Al Buck's eyes went wide.

The driver took the pistol out of his mouth.

"What is this about? This is about some story? All this is about some story?'' He licked his lips.

"Are you that naive?'' the driver asked.

"Easy. It's just—well, it was Jules Bergen. He gave me a call the day we had our . . . misunderstanding . . . with Kay. He said he was getting hell from the Archbishop of New York about the story. You know the story was networked. He said the Archbishop said there were outbreaks of weeping statues in Queens. He said we should downplay the story, he said the Archbishop was a friend of his. That isn't a secret. I told the FBI, they checked with the Archbishop, I think. I mean, that's all there was to it.''

The driver said, "Who is Jules Bergen?''

"Are you kidding?'' Al Buck smiled. "President of the network is who.''

"So you fired Kay Davis.''

"Are you a friend of hers? Look—''

"And why did you hire her back?''

"What is this?''

Devereaux shoved the barrel against his cheek and Al Buck's eyes went down, trying to see the barrel below the level of vision. His eyes were wide again.

"You keep forgetting about the pistol,'' Devereaux said.

"I won't forget.''

"Why did you hire her back?''

"Because. Because Jules called me at home. He said he got my message that Kay was terminated and he said he didn't want that, he said he didn't want anyone to lose his job because of a private favor, and besides, it would make the network look bad if it came out. He said I was to make sure that she got her job back. So I got her job back. I thought that was really decent of Jules. He's that kind of a guy. A decent guy. He's on all the committees in New York. His wife has been very sick for years but he still takes her out."

"Swell," Devereaux said.

"Can you take the gun—"

"Does Jules call you up a lot? Asking you to change stories, drop stories, add stories?"

"He does not," Al Buck said. "He's a busy man. He runs the network, he's got production to run, he's always between Los Angeles and New York, he doesn't have time."

"But he made time," Devereaux said, not to Al Buck.

"What is this about?"

"Who was the man who tried to kill Kay Davis after you fired her?"

"We didn't fire her. It was a misunderstanding." And he felt the barrel push into his cheek. "I don't know who he was, swear to God, no one does, the police don't. I offered a reward. The station offered a reward, I mean. We stand behind Kay a thousand percent."

"Swell," Devereaux said.

"Who are you?"

"Someone interested in weeping statues," he said. "When did Jules call you? The second time?"

"It was late. Late at night. Real late. I don't know how late."

"What did he say?"

"I told you. He said he got the message from me and he felt terrible about Kay and he said to get her back."

"What did he say exactly?"

"How do I remember what anyone said exactly two weeks ago?"

"What did he say?"

"He said he got the message. He said to get Kay back."

"What did he say about the statue or about the story?"

Al Buck blinked. He stared at the driver.

"Now, that's funny. I forgot about that."

"About what?"

"He said not to worry about the story."

"He said that?"

"He said it's silly making a fuss over something like that. Something about let it run, let it die a natural death."

"Let it die?"

"He said the story would take care of itself."

"What did that mean?"

"He was saying maybe we shouldn't get so excited after all."

Devereaux waited and stared at the sweating man and then removed the pistol from his cheek. Al Buck rubbed his cheek with his left hand. He kept his eyes on the driver.

"All right, Al," Devereaux said. "You did good."

"What is this about?"

"You don't really want to know, do you?"

"No," he said.

"We've been at this about thirty minutes. You figure you can explain thirty minutes at the office?"

"Yes," Al Buck said. He shivered. It wasn't going to go bad. He was going to stay alive.

"I'll drop you off," Devereaux said. "You tell them what you want. But you don't mess with Kay Davis ever again. Ever. In fact, the best thing would be to get her promoted out of Chicago to New York. Do you think that would be the best thing?''

"Yes."

"Good. That would be the best thing. And the other best thing would be not to talk about this. You call up your friend Jules and Jules will wonder about you. He'll wonder if you are a person who should stay alive.''

"What do you mean?''

"You get in your office, you shut the door and sit down and turn off the television set and you just think. Think about someone who is up here talking to someone who is down here and telling him to do a little thing that would make the network look like shit if it came out. You think about that and think about some gorilla coming around to Kay Davis' apartment and trying to kill her. And you think about Jules calling you up in the middle of the night and telling you to retract the thing he told you to do less than eight hours before. Then, if you can connect the dots, Al, you think what it would mean to you if you called up Jules and said you got a visit from a man with a gun who wants to know about Kay Davis and Al Buck and good old Jules. Then you think of Jules connecting the dots and maybe deciding that you think too much. Do you get it, Al?''

Al Buck wasn't dumb. He was merciless and he had been in television a long time and he did things he didn't like to do, but he wasn't dumb. He saw it. His eyes got big and his face went white.

Devereaux saw that he saw it. And it would be all right for Al because he wouldn't tell anyone anything.

Devereaux put the pistol on the dash and almost sighed.

It would be all right.

And he wouldn't have to kill Al Buck after all.

TWENTY-NINE
Competition

They sat in the old tavern on the great square in Bruges in the afternoon. The tavern had tall, mournful windows and no bar, except a serving counter where the large women made their orders and carried them to the long, wooden tables. The walls were the color of spoiled mustard and there was a dampness in the place that reeked of age. Mason and Ready ate large sandwiches made on rough local bread and drank liters of Jupiler beer. The beer was cold and the cheese sandwiches were tart with strong mustard. The two men did not talk to each other because they were both waiting.

Cernan came into the tavern alone.

It was just after four and the rain had stopped. The square was full of shoppers again. There were restaurants and shops on two sides of the square. The third side was occupied by an ancient city hall and the fourth side was dominated by the ancient battlements and the great clock tower. Because this was Flemish Belgium and not French Belgium, the clock worked, even though it was centuries old.

Cernan sat down in the wooden chair across from them. His face was flat and his eyes looked sewn on. "Who is this one?"

"An American agent," Ready said. "I had no choice." He smiled. "He wants to know what happened to his friend."

"It is of no business to him," said Cernan. The words were flat, careful, polished to serve the greatest amount of meaning with the fewest sounds.

"It is my business that you have not returned to Prague," Ready said.

"No. You are in a mistake," Cernan said. "You have no more business with me."

"But you came."

"I came," Cernan agreed.

Colonel Ready stared at him. "That is extraordinary enough for me to ask you why."

"I will ask: Why do you signal me?"

"To show Mr. Mason that you have Devereaux and the girl. You have the girl, don't you?"

"Yes," Cernan said.

"Where?" Mason said.

They ignored him. They glanced at him because he had made a sound but they ignored him. Ready was smiling.

Cernan said, "What do you want?"

"I want to buy her."

Cernan blinked. It was the only sign he made. He said, "Why do you want her?"

"That is my business. I can offer a fair price."

"No. Not at the moment. Perhaps never."

"But you came here."

"I am always curious," Cernan said.

"You have her, though she could not have tracked you down. I was on her trail, Cernan, I was this far behind her. Give me a day more and I would have had her. How did you get her, Cernan? You weren't linked to the train, so you must've lured her to you."

Then Ready grinned because he understood: "She thought it was me. She would do that, she was good enough for that. Even brave enough."

Cernan nodded his head. His brown eyes glittered again in the soft Flemish light, which was diffused and yellowed and reminiscent of a dim Vermeer painting. Mason sat apart from them and listened. He held the pistol in his coat pocket with the safety off.

Cernan listened. When Ready paused, he did not volunteer a sound.

"Devereaux is loose," Ready said. He said it without inflection. He said it with a sort of wonder and then grinned. "The bastard got away. You let him loose."

"He is employed."

The word was curious. Mason felt he was losing ground. "Where is he? Where is Rita?"

Cernan finally noticed him. "Are you so foolish to be with this man? This man would kill you like a fly. You are young, which is a reason at least for your foolishness."

David Mason did not blush. He felt the weight of the pistol in his hand.

"I have a piece," he said.

"Good," Cernan said. "Hold on to it. Are you going to shoot me in this public tavern? Are you going to shoot both of us? Pah." It was a sound of dismissal. He turned back to Ready.

"Where is he?" Ready asked.

"Why must I tell you anything? You are not yet of the Secret Service, are you, Colonel? You had something to sell and you were paid your price. That is all the concern you are to me."

"What can he do for you that I can't do for you?"

"You have no . . ." Cernan hesitated, looking for the word.

"The girl. I want the girl. What do you want me to do for the girl?"

"Do you have friends in America?"

"Many," Ready said.

Cernan considered. He looked at David Mason, as though seeing him for the first time. "You. What are you? CIA."

Mason said nothing.

Ready grinned. "Tell him, son. We're all professionals here. He's with Section."

"So if my agent fails, I can take him back to Prague with me."

"No problem," said Colonel Ready.

Mason did not feel fear or even anger. He felt a curious sense of being apart, of stumbling into something so deep and wide that he would have to fall for a long time before touching anything or striking the bottom.

"If a child disappears, who takes her?"

"In the States, you mean?" Ready said. "Kidnappers."

"Agencies of government?"

"Unlikely. How was it done?"

"They kill her keeper, break into her house, take her. They ask nothing for her."

"Then they want to signal someone or make a bargain with someone. A trade. Tit for tat, Cernan."

"That is what I think," he said. His voice was very soft. "He told me: Ask Miki, Ask Miki. So I ask Miki and now Miki is persuaded to tell me. Miki say: Perhaps it is these people because he knows what these people do. So: Do you know these people?''

"Who are these people?" Colonel Ready said.

"People in America. Certain people."

"I understand," Ready said. "Yes. That makes sense."

"What are you talking about?" David Mason said.

Cernan sighed and looked at Colonel Ready. "You want to see Miss Macklin? Then come with me. Perhaps if you succeed where the American agent fails, you can win your prize, Colonel."

"You're not going anywhere," Mason said.

"What are you going to do, sir, shoot me?" Cernan said. He got up and scraped his chair across the tile floor.

Mason got up. He thought about it. Could he shoot someone in a tavern in the middle of a Belgian city? And he realized he could not. He followed Cernan and Ready out the door. The sun broke through and dazzled the rain on the cobblestones. Buses and cars and bicycles poured into the square from the spiderweb of narrow streets beyond. A large Mercedes-Benz was parked in the square. They walked to the car and the rear door opened. He decided.

He pushed Colonel Ready into Cernan's back and the two men tumbled into the car and David Mason had the piece out. He had decided to join the party by force but it was a little clumsy. He didn't even feel the policeman's club land on his head, behind his left ear.

THIRTY
Illusions of Faith

Big Ben Herguth felt cold. New York always made him feel that way. In fact, every place except Southern California made him feel that way.

The day was bright but deep shadows painted all the crosstown streets, and it was chilled in the shade. Every time he had to go to New York, there was more shade. He wore the houndstooth jacket that made him look even bigger than he was. His shirt collar was open and he wore a chain around his size-22 neck.

The limo dumped him—it felt like getting dumped—in front of the seventy-three-story smoked-glass and pre-rusted steel building that served as network headquarters. The noise of New York was all around him, a pounding noise that would give him a headache after a couple of hours and would only be soothed by a pitcher of martinis and a twenty-two-year-old piece of ass. He hated New York: People didn't walk, they loped. And New York was where Julie was. Herguth felt cold and a little afraid every time Julie summoned him.

There were two outer offices, and when he got to the inner sanctum on the forty-ninth floor he felt out of breath, as though he had walked up all those stairs. The room was completely silent save for the occasional interruption of a *wa-wa-wa* ambulance sound.

Jules Bergen was sitting on a couch and he was studying photographs.

"Hello, Ben," he said. He did not look up from the photographs. Ben Herguth kept his distance, remained on the other side of the immense room.

"Get yourself a drink," Jules Bergen said. The voice was distracted. "This is really good work, this last batch."

"Is that Anna?"

"Yes. I said I wanted her naked this time. She is terribly developed for someone fourteen. Did I mention I had a ten-year-old in here last week, she was sent over by one of the agencies? She was very professional, she spoke well. She wanted to sit on my lap after a while. Sometimes I'm tempted. But right in the office . . . How would it look?"

"It wouldn't look good," Ben Herguth said. He made a double Beefeater on the rocks. He drank it down like medicine. He made another. Jules Bergen only drank Perrier.

"You seen these?"

"Sure," Ben said. He had collected them. He was Julie's collector, among other things. Make a run down to Mexico now and then, get a bunch of spic kids, take the stills and sometimes the videotapes. He wasn't really interested in the little boys though. He made that clear. He liked the girls without body hair.

"How is Anna?" Jules asked.

"I talked to the keepers, she's learning the rules. She

keeps quiet, she doesn't pull no shit like that screaming shit she was doing."

"They aren't molesting her?"

"No. Just the pictures you wanted."

"Yes." Jules had a dreamy look in his vacant, blue eyes. He was the second most powerful man in television. He owned production companies, was a movie producer by proxy, owned stars and their contracts, owned twenty-three percent of the stock of the network, owned fine paintings. Owned as much as a man can own. He liked little girls just on the lip of puberty. It was a discreet passion —almost a hobby—for a man as powerful as Jules Bergen.

Ben prowled the room. The carpet was gray and deep enough to sleep on. Books on the walls, respectable titles. Television monitors. The trappings of power. A photograph of the President with his arm around Jules.

Ben Herguth stood in front of Jules and looked down and saw the photograph of Anna standing naked in the middle of a dim little room with her sex organ exposed and her hands at her sides. She looked sad. Maybe even frightened.

"Skoal," Ben said and took another swig. Being with Julie made him want to drink.

"What is happening?" Jules said, staring at the second picture of Anna.

"Willis from Langley drops a dime, says some guy from this fucking R Section is in the country. Just a word to the wise. I told the keepers to watch themselves. I got four guys in that house on the kid, they got no trouble. Willis is still telling me he's trying to find out where the fuck Miki is. Miki is not in Prague, definitely, but no one is making a deal for him right now. Fucking CIA, these guys are like spies in comic books."

"And Al. Did you look into Al?"

"Al Buck had a visitor. He doesn't say he did but he did. He was fifty minutes late going into the station. Someone had a talk with him. He don't want to talk about it, so I figure it has to do with this business."

"Kay Davis?"

"Yeah, I figure the certain someone had a talk with her too. I figure that Kay has got to come to no good end, you know?"

"Be careful this time, Ben." Jules looked up, a small sharp look of annoyance on his face. "I don't want that mistake repeated. I had to call Al twice in one day, once to promote her which that idiot didn't understand, once to rehire her. It annoys me to have to repeat myself, Ben, to cover my tracks. You're supposed to cover tracks."

"I'm sorry, Julie, I swear to God it won't happen again."

Ben was almost white in the face. The tan didn't help and the martinis didn't help.

Jules had small hands and a precise way of speaking. He pursed his lips and stared at Ben standing before him. Then his look softened. "When this is over, I want you to go to Mexico again."

"You got it, Julie, you tell me when. You tell me, you got it."

Jules nodded. "I know, Ben." He studied Anna's nakedness. "Fix Kay when you can."

"I'll fix her."

"The problem, the central problem, remains. Miki knows. Miki knows us and about CIA and everything. No one should know that much."

"No."

"A man was sent out to pick Miki up. He went and he's not been heard from for nearly five days. Henkin hasn't made contact with me since he told me to take in the little girl. The girl was the illegitimate daughter of the agent he sent. I don't presume to understand how these things work in Prague; Henkin has every incentive to get rid of Miki, perhaps more than we do. Miki knows and Miki has to carry what he knows to a shallow grave. If Henkin is indecisive in this, we are going to have to decide for him. I want Miki dead before November is over."

"What do you want me to do?"

"Contact Willis. I want the name of an absolutely reliable contractor. Money is no object, of course. If Henkin can't act, we will have to act. At least Henkin knows where Miki is supposed to be, which is more than Willis or the Langley Firm know."

Ben licked his lips to get rid of the dry, sour taste.

"What about the little girl?" he said at last.

"We took her for leverage. Obviously, if we find Miki—or if Henkin can act in time—the need for leverage is over."

Ben thought it was going to be that way from the beginning. It didn't affect him one way or another. He shrugged inside his big sports coat.

"Willis said in L.A. that Langley is putting fifteen million dollars on *Life*," Herguth said.

"That's a substantial sum. How can we mule for them this time?"

"The laundry is coming out of Credit Suisse in Zurich as well as two suitcases we mule direct into Prague. The arrangements are all made. The big assault on Moscow has room for every extra we could lay our hands on and we got a lot of Czech Army volunteers. The money is substantial for them, for doing what they like to do anyway, which is run around shooting their guns off. It's going to be a nice film, Julie."

"It's going to be another overpriced piece of shit," Jules Bergen said. "I like your enthusiasm, Ben. It comes from living in California. But I can afford to see things as they are. *Life of Napoleon* is a preordained piece of shit, crammed together by burned-out, sold-out people between coke breaks, starring a substantial cast of people without a wit of talent, mouthing meaningless lines. It'll make us richer than we already are. I like the action, Ben, don't get me wrong. It's like looking at these pictures. They interest me, seeing her naked like this. But I wouldn't want to see her. Not as she really is. I like the illusion of action. You give me that, Ben. You are the supreme fixer, the ultimate wired man. Your talent is in your enthusiasm.''

Ben felt put down but that was the way Julie was. He was not used to it exactly, but it had happened often enough not to put Ben in a sulk for days.

Jules was enjoying himself. ''Because I'm a patriot, my country permits me to steal. Because I'm the president of a great television network, my lies are made into gospels. I am as fake as . . . as that miracle in Chicago, but if I said tomorrow that I was not a patriot and not a great man, no one would believe me because their religion is already in place, Ben.''

''Yeah, Julie,'' Ben said because Julie was getting wound up.

Jules smiled at him. His eyes were mellow and kind. ''I really like you, Ben. I like what we're doing. I like everything except that Miki is still alive and not dead. How long will it take to make him dead, Ben?''

''I don't know. I'll do it as fast as I can.''

''Do it fast, Ben,'' Jules said.

''You know I will.''

Jules sighed. He touched one of the photographs. ''Poor little girl with her weeping statues and miracles. Do you suppose she still believes in miracles, Ben? Do you suppose she is praying right now to the statue to rescue her? Do you think she knows she is going to die?"

Ben said, "I don't know, Julie."

"Find out, will you?" He looked at the photographs and touched them with his fingertips. "Find out for me. I like to know how long the illusion lasts. I mean, when you are naked and afraid and you know that nothing is going to save you ever again, do you finally give up on the illusion?" He paused, thinking of it. "Or maybe it just becomes so much stronger."

THIRTY-ONE

The Slavic Soul

He was a large man with the eyes of a saint. He came off the plane through the connecting tube to the terminal, looked left and right, and then started down the concourse. He saw the man waiting for him on the other side of the security barrier. The other man was as he always had been: gray, pale, cold. Denisov shivered and went to meet him.

Denisov said, "You are too much the stranger to your own country."

"I'm glad the country treats you well."

"It is well," Denisov said. He didn't smile. His eyes stared at Devereaux through the rimless spectacles. The spectacles were his last link with his own past. They reminded him of Moscow and the dark winter nights and the old wife and the lumpy bed and the clamor in the kitchen and the smell of vodka and the music of Tchaikovsky in the park. That had been his past and it had no link to the present except for the man who walked with him down the main concourse to the cocktail lounge between two terminals.

They did not speak to each other as they walked. They walked as old friends but they were old enemies. Denisov had become the reluctant defector one night in Florida when he had lost the last game to Devereaux. He had grown accustomed to his exile. He had money, even friends, but the Moscow nights haunted him in winter and remembered scenes of his past made him hurt and made him recall the pain Devereaux had inflicted upon him by forcing his defection.

"What about the information?"

"To business? Then. So. I am accustomed to American manners." He opened his briefcase and put it down on the bar.

They were in the Crossroads Lounge that connected the departure floors of Terminals One and Two at O'Hare. Beyond the window wall, planes boomed and struggled aloft and came down at a frightening pace—one every fifteen seconds. The afternoon sky was still brilliant with sunlight and the air beyond the lounge carried the sweet, nostalgic smell of diesel fuel. They were two business travelers who met for a moment and shared a drink at the most anonymous bar in the world.

Denisov spoke: "Jules Bergen is a wealthy man and he runs a wealthy conglomerate. There is no other kind, I think. It is a large company with extensive assets including the license to five television stations, agreements with a hundred and ninety-four affiliates, radio stations, a record company, two casino hotels in Atlantic City—"

"What about Prague?"

Denisov blinked. He almost smiled. He reached for his glass of iced vodka and drank a little. "I am a man of business."

"Filthy capitalist pig," Devereaux said.

Denisov studied him for a moment.

"Should I sell my shares in this company?"

"You have shares?"

"I have a portfolio that is divested."

"Diversified."

Denisov frowned. "I talked to my brokers."

"You have more than one?"

"One in Los Angeles, one in New York. Of course. And one in Switzerland."

"Of course," Devereaux said. He smiled. He put down the money.

"This is only part," Denisov said.

"The rest in ten days, after I get back to Lausanne."

"If you get back, eh?"

"I have great expectations."

"Every man alive has them. But some die anyway."

"The stage Russian is heard from again. You're affected too much by the Slavic soul; you begin by making aphorisms and end up by believing them. Tell me about Prague."

"The network owns sixty percent of Trans-Global Films. This is a cinema company. It makes international arrangements. I think it is a laundry, only two films in five years it makes itself. They are middlemen for many others."

"How?"

"They arrange movies. They work with governments from the top to the bottom, to the local commissar. If you film in Poland, they arrange for you."

"A Communist front?"

"You are too suspicious, my friend. No. They are American firm, owned by the network and forty percent by BH Productions. That is Ben Herguth, who does not produce anything."

"Your broker knew all this."

"And other sources. I have lived in California six years now. As you know, as you arranged." Denisov looked at him.

Devereaux tasted the icy vodka. "Is exile so terrible?"

"Existence is to remember. You separate me from my past."

Devereaux said nothing. He was in the city of his childhood. He was surrounded by brick and steel reminders of his past. He closed his eyes to them; he refused to see them for fear of creating pain.

"Information," Denisov said. "I am still the old spy. The trade is the same, inside or outside. Information is always available. You call me because I know some things. Because I am in California. This is about film and television."

"So Ben Herguth is a shell company?"

"Yes. But this is what you ask: What is Prague to any of this? Well, they make a film there. They make six films there in four years. They do not make themselves, you understand: They arrange. They get permits, they smooth the way, they bribe officials, they arrange transport and storage and accommodations. Now they make a new film about Napoleon. They will film in Prague."

"Was Napoleon in Prague?"

"No," Denisov said. "I ask why they film in Prague. They say that Prague looks like Paris from the inside and like Vienna the way it was from outside. And it is a hundred percent cheaper than using Paris. They use Prague also for Moscow when Napoleon attacks my country."

Devereaux had stopped listening. He put his large hand around his drink and stared at it. He had been in the States for just twenty-four hours and the tiredness was gone. He had taken the plaster cast off his hand. He felt very close to the end. One way or the other.

"Is the company on the square?"

"Do you mean honest? Of course not," Denisov said. "This is the cinema business. They steal, same as everyone steals."

"You've lost your sense of morality."

"Yes. It is the decadence of the West. I am diseased by it."

"But rich enough to indulge the symptoms."

"Alas," Denisov said. He shrugged in his black cashmere overcoat. He had a large head and his eyes were crystal blue, like mountain lakes. They had known each other in the trade. They had come against each other one too many times and Devereaux had conducted Denisov to his side. They had been old enemies and were still; but in a world without friends, they had become accustomed to each other.

"Then they deal in Prague, they have contacts. Who would the contacts be?"

"You only asked last night," Denisov said. "But there is Emil Mikita. I spring a name out of my glove. This is surprise to you?"

"Out of your hat," Devereaux said. "Emil Mikita. How did you get the name?"

"He is called Miki," Denisov said.

"I know."

"I asked and everyone said he was the man to know in Prague. In the cinema. It is surprise to me that you know his name as well. But then, that is what they tell me."

"What?"

"Everyone knows Miki."

"I need a little more than information," Devereaux said. He looked at his drink and then at the Russian. The Russian had put on weight and he had not started out small to begin with. Denisov was not the best he could do, but he couldn't call on Section. He had the feeling Section would not like the game.

"So," Denisov said. "I shipped through a bag." He had understood from the beginning, Devereaux saw. The checked-in bag contained a gun and check-ins were never X-rayed.

"There might be problems."

"Ah, well. My life is dull. Perhaps we need a problem." He paused. "How many?"

"I don't know. Perhaps a half dozen, perhaps less."

"Will you say this is five thousand dollars?"

Devereaux nodded. "Ten days after Lausanne."

"Is this your account or your agency?"

"At the moment, I pick up the bill."

Denisov grinned and displayed the fierce square teeth set evenly in his wide mouth. "Good. It is pleasure more for me that you pay."

"You knew that when I called."

"Yes. You are running outside the fence again." The image was more striking because Denisov had a wide but faulty command of the language. At language school in Kiev he had learned English with pain and without pleasure until one afternoon a colleague introduced him to a recording from *The Mikado* of Gilbert and Sullivan. He became a Savoyard overnight; he could not get enough of the music of the two eccentric Englishmen. He learned all the words to all the songs before he fully understood them.

"I'm just trying to find the gate," Devereaux said. "To lock myself back in."

"You are the exile, comrade," Denisov said. "I am exile too. We are all without country in the trade, is not so? We are both out of our countries and we have no place in them."

"Russian self-pity."

"Perhaps," Denisov said and smiled to mock the other man. "What matters to you?"

"A little girl. She was kidnapped a week ago. We get her back and we return her to her own country."

"What is?"

"Czechoslovakia."

"Ah. That girl who saw the statue weep."

"Yes."

"Tell me: Is truth?"

"What?"

"The statue. Does it weep?"

"There are no miracles," Devereaux said.

"Yes. So I believe also. But if there is one miracle, then I do not have to believe this anymore. So: Is truth?"

"I don't know. She thought so. And now I think I understand. About Miki, about her. About why she was taken. They couldn't stop the miracle show at St. Margaret's Church and they couldn't stop the news and they couldn't let Miki come across for some reason. So they want to leverage the Czechs: Get Miki and we give you the girl. Except the Czechs don't know they have Miki already. There's a man who wants her and he's putting his neck out for her."

"And you? You know this and where she is?"

"Yes," Devereaux said. He put down a ten-dollar bill to cover the two drinks. The planes catapulted with nothing to spare into the crowded sky. The huge bar was filled with strangers staring out the windows at the planes.

"What do we do?"

"Kill people," Devereaux said. He stood up at the bar and waited for Denisov.

THIRTY-TWO
Night Call

Hanley rode in the back of the Diamond cab as it crossed the Fourteenth Street Bridge and followed the signs around to National Airport. What would Mrs. Neumann say to this? Hanley pulled his overcoat tight. She would be told in time and it would be made clear. If Devereaux wasn't lying. He didn't want to think about Devereaux lying.

He had not heard from Mason for forty-eight hours. The Eurodesk people in Brussels used the current Central American slang to describe the situation: Mason "was disappeared." Devereaux, Macklin, Mason. The other side had everything going for it, whoever the other side really was.

The plane was a Boeing 707, really more plane than anyone needed for a short trip to Chicago. The side of the plane was painted with the familiar colors of one of the three biggest airlines in the country. The plane, however, was on permanent lease to the United States government. Specifically, to an agency called International Land Management and Evaluation, a subsection of the Department of Agriculture in the budget but, in fact, a part of Section.

Hanley was the only passenger. The interior of the plane was vast and spartan. The rear section was partitioned by wood and held the freight area. The front section had ten seats. The pilot and navigator invited Hanley to sit in the cockpit. Hanley accepted.

"What's the cargo?" the pilot said, casually flicking switches and reading dials.

"I'm not sure," he said. "Are you fueled for a long flight?"

"Chicago? Hardly nudge the gauge."

"Then Lakenheath. In England."

"Jesus H. Christ," the pilot said. He wore a turtleneck sweater and a nondescript leather jacket, just like pilots in movies. Hanley thought he seemed very young and he wondered if he really wanted to watch this.

The plane took its turn in line and rumbled across the tarmac of National and lifted off at the last moment before it would have crashed into the Potomac River. Washington spun off to the right at a dizzy angle, the Washington Monument blinking its ugly red eyes at the plane, with the White House glowing and tiny below. The plane veered across Virginia and the Maryland panhandle, climbing over the Appalachians before leveling out at 35,000 feet. Hanley noticed he was gripping the chair arms tightly and he did not remove his seat belt. The navigator belched. The pilot flipped three switches, turned and stuck out his feet. The plane flew on above the clouds. The night was very clear from here, beneath the moon and stars. It was a

Nebraska night for a boy, Hanley thought, remembering himself as he wanted to have been. Dream on the stars, the old man said to the boy of himself.

He thought of Devereaux.

I need a plane and a Europe landing site, not far from Belgium. The west of Belgium. I need medical supplies, just in case.

Hanley had held the receiver of the red phone calmly and listened. The cold voice at the other end was simple and direct, pronouncing each word carefully.

I can't do this, Hanley said at last.

If you won't, then I won't play for your team.

You are trying to blackmail me.

You set me up, Hanley, you and Mrs. Neumann, and you didn't tell me what this was about. This was no simple defection train, was it? If I have to take her out myself, I'll do it, but it will cost you more than you'll want to pay.

Each word in memory is cold, precise, each syllable is pronounced. The words are cut and dried, without texture or emotion. The words have no feelings left in them.

Are you threatening?

Of course he was. He had no time left. He had already sent the signal to Cernan. ANNA. One word. It cost him four hundred dollars. The woman was absolutely reliable. She sat at the phone and dialed the number in Belgium once every fifteen minutes. The phone rang precisely nine times. Then the woman in Chicago hung up. Fifteen minutes later she dialed again. She dialed and dialed for two hours and thirty minutes. On the first ring of the eleventh dial someone completed the connection in Europe. There was no sound, just the ether. The woman in Chicago said: "Anna." The connection was broken. The message was complete.

But Devereaux did not have Anna. Not yet.

Devereaux said the plane should be ready to go at eleven, precisely, from gate F12. Section could arrange this with O'Hare. If no one showed at eleven, then they weren't coming. It was that simple.

Hanley sat in the cockpit as the night became clear and Indianapolis glowed orange and white in the middle of the Indiana prairie blackness. The pilot was reading a paperback novel by Ed McBain. The navigator was still busy before a green scope, looking at the world through electronic eyes.

Hanley stared out at the reality of the earth from the cockpit windows. The earth glowed at the horizon and the land was black below, beneath stars and moon. Now and then there would be a city and all would be light and then it would fade again and the night took over the earth. The earth was unchanged at night in all the centuries of man, except for the glow of cities. Hanley thought suddenly of the Cathedral at Chartres.

"You've flown to Europe," he said to the pilot.

"Sure." The pilot turned the page and marked it by bending the page at the corner. He put the book away and stretched and yawned. He looked at his watch. "Long flight across. Need some grub. I'll fetch us some good old ORD cooking when we get into O'Hare. When we going to Europe?"

"At eleven. Gateway F12," Hanley said.

"Gotta go with my trusty navigator to plot a route. Hey, Randy, you want to send out for pizza?"

"Sure, I'll go for some pizza," said the navigator.

"You like pizza?" said the pilot to Hanley.

Hanley saw the immense brightness of Chicago loom at the horizon. The brightness was exactly cut off at the lake and defined the shoreline around the south end of Lake Michigan. He noticed then that the plane had been descending.

The pilot was back to business now, flipping switches, talking to O'Hare.

The earth came up slowly and the stars were lost in the redness of the sky above the city. Hanley felt the strap of the seat belt locked around his waist. He watched the sprawling city fill the windows of the plane. He closed his eyes and was surprised to think he might have uttered a prayer.

THIRTY-THREE

Operation

"Do you trust this man?" Denisov said in French to Devereaux. They sat in the back of the rental Ford that had been stolen from the shuttered Avis dealership on Western Avenue.

"He knows how to drive."

"He provided the information."

"That was another man."

"How can they be certain?"

"There are only five or six operators who can pull something like this off. You use logic. If it was in Chicago, they have to be out of Chicago. There are two operators in Chicago. They do snatches, assassinations, the major anti-personnel stuff. It is one or the other. The source checks and pinpoints it. Then he fixes the focus by putting money out. Everyone is for sale."

"Yes," Denisov said. He had checked his bag through because it contained a nine-millimeter automatic with three cartridge packs that would not have made it through the X-ray machine at Los Angeles International Airport. The weapon was in the right-hand pocket of his dark blue raincoat. He sat behind the driver.

"You guys talking French?" said Anthony Riolli.

"He is certainly a genius," Denisov said in good French.

"Twenty-two hundred," Devereaux said in English. "You know."

"I know."

They got out of the car. They were in a deserted stretch of West Adams Street in the heart of the black ghetto on the West Side.

"Why can't the FBI find her?"

"Because they don't know how to look for people," Devereaux said. He took the weapon out of his pocket. A black face appeared at a window across the street and stared at the two white men with guns.

"They talk to police," Denisov grunted.

"They're always the last to know. You want to know about bad people, you talk to bad people. You explain it as business. There are always enough snitches and a few of them actually know something."

"Why do you think she was kept here?"

"Why not? They going to take her all over the country?"

"What do we do?"

Devereaux stared at the Russian. The night was breathless and dead cold. The streets were lined with sticks of trees. The old houses seemed to lean against each other for support. The black face disappeared at the window and a light went out. It was a wooden house and there was no point in going through the alley because there was a huge Doberman Pinscher in the backyard. All the backyards in the poor neighborhoods had dogs. They were an alarm signal and they were hard to get through. Devereaux had thought about the backyard but they would have had to shoot the dogs and waste ammunition.

Denisov checked the safety and tried the action. He and Devereaux stood in front of the wooden door.

"Steel plate?" Denisov said.

"I hope not," Devereaux said. He tried the handle. The door was locked. He looked at the lock. He ran his hand along the seam of the door.

"These guys have confidence," he said. "One dead-bolt. A Lawson. Not more than an inch and a half. One kick," he said.

And kicked.

The rotted wood splintered with the blow and the door blew in and Devereaux threw the stun grenade into the hall. The grenade shook the ancient house and windows blew out. He and Denisov went in crouching, guns extended.

The first man was on the stairs.

Denisov shot him twice. They didn't use silencers. There was no point to it really.

Devereaux shot the tall man with white hair who came out of the back door beneath the staircase. The bullet hit his shoulder. Devereaux kept firing.

Denisov was on the stairs and shot the man at the top of the stairs. The man fell and dropped his Uzi and the gun went off, spraying a round of bullets into the plaster of the stairwell.

Devereaux finished White Hair with a bullet in the face and went into the back room. Anna Jelinak was sitting at a table with cards in her hand. Other cards were face up on the table. She stared at Devereaux.

Devereaux swept the room with his gun hand, crouching at the door. The dog in the backyard barked and hurtled itself against the back door. The back door had two bolts and a chain on it because it was the preferred point of entry for burglars.

The shot came behind him. He turned and the black man was staring right at him with a red smudge on his white shirt. Devereaux fired point blank but he was already dead. He fell forward.

Denisov came down to the landing. His face was white and his eyes glittered. "Everyone is dead," he said in Russian.

Devereaux looked at Anna.

"Come on."

The girl got up. She held the cards in her hand: a King, an Ace of Spades, a seven. He walked around the table and saw the hallway cluttered with bodies. There was the smell of cordite mixed with the instant, putrid smell of death, of urine and feces and warm blood flowing. They were all deaf from the shock of the grenade and gunfire.

"Come on," Devereaux said again and grabbed her arm and dragged her over the bodies.

She screamed once and he slapped her as hard as he could and the blow dazed her. They brought her outside and pushed her into the back of the car. Denisov sat next to her, Devereaux next to the driver.

Tony was listening to the portable police radio he had mounted on the dashboard. "They haven't even made a call yet. You know what that is? Good old 911. You call 911, it'll take hours to get a cop out there. Especially this neighborhood."

"Change cars," he said.

"This is good for hours."

"Change cars," Devereaux said.

The next one was a bright red Pontiac Bonneville with a white interior. They picked it up on Irving Park Road, near Shulian's Tavern on the north side.

The girl said nothing because she had felt the sting of the slap and she could not hear very well.

Tony knew his driving. He wheeled the Pontiac like an MG.

"Not fancy, Tony," Devereaux said. "Be slow. This isn't a bank job and they aren't in hot pursuit."

The radio squawked on: "Reports of gunfire at 2218 West Adams. A neighbor calling . . ."

"See?" said Tony.

Denisov said, "I expect to receive payment in my box by the end of December."

"You'll have to report it then on this year's tax," Devereaux said.

"Yes. That is my concern." The departure level at O'Hare was nearly empty and the planes were taking two or three minutes between takeoffs now.

"Let him off at American," Devereaux said. "We get out here."

He pushed open the door and reached for the seat lever and pulled it. Anna climbed out. She had no coat and the night air plucked at her bare arms. She wore a dirty blouse and jeans. She held the three Bicycle playing cards in her hand and stared at the large man with gray hair and gray eyes.

"I don't have time to play with you, Anna," he said in a soft voice. "We walk to the plane and if you shout or attract any attention, I kill you just like I killed those men. Do you understand?"

Anna stared at him.

The car was already pulling away.

"Do you understand?"

The planes bombed the air overhead.

"Yes," she said in a small voice.

"Do you see the gun?" He slipped it a little out of his pocket.

"Oh, please, sir, I will not—"

"All right. We go now."

All the clocks in Terminal Two read nine minutes to eleven.

They walked by a kiosk and he touched her arm. "Buy that jacket." She picked up the navy and orange Bears football jacket and slipped it on over her blouse. Devereaux gave the woman behind the register a fifty-dollar bill. The terminal had the insomniac look of an updated Edward Hopper painting. Fluorescent lights made everything daytime bright; only the faces were gray.

Devereaux slipped the pistol into the white metal wastebasket by the washroom entrances when Anna turned to stare at a bag lady curling up for the night on one of the vinyl chairs.

They crossed the terminal and passed through the metal detectors and Anna did not seem to notice anything. Her face was blank with shock and her eyes were tired. A Chicago policeman stared at Devereaux as though he knew him from someplace.

"Keep going, Anna," he said, and the voice was not meant to be friendly.

They walked down the wide, bright corridor all the way to F12 near the end. The terminal was quiet down here. The nearest passenger boarding area in use was F6. The clock read 10:59.

The boarding area had a red rug, fake mahogany check-in desk and no destination listed on the board. Hanley stood at the desk.

"I forgot my ticket, can I pay on the plane?" Devereaux said.

"This is not a joke."

"No." Devereaux held Anna by the arm.

"How did you arrange it?" Hanley said.

"Are you going along?"

"No. You're cleared out of here. I'll go back commercial and face the music at midnight." Hanley looked glum.

"It shouldn't be too bad," Devereaux said.

"Aiding and abetting a kidnapping? This girl has rights."

"She has the right to live," Devereaux said. The smile faded. "So do I. You forfeited a lot of your rights back in Chartres. You should have told me."

"I cannot tell you what I do not know. Miki is valuable but I don't know why."

"I do," Devereaux said.

"What do you know?" Hanley said.

"The tip of the iceberg. Are we ready to go?"

"Yes."

"You have the supplies?"

"Money and a weapon. Where is the other weapon?"

"In the trash bin right by the men's urinal just as you get out of this corridor."

"All right. I have to return it."

"Yes. See to the details, Hanley, and let the big things take care of themselves."

"Sarcasm doesn't help your case."

"But Miki will."

"He's not going to return him, you know."

"Yes. I know. That's what he thinks now."

They stared at each other. "I wish this had never happened," Hanley said. His face looked gray beneath the lights.

"Yes," Devereaux said. "But beggars still walk, don't they?"

And he led the child by her arm into the umbilical cord

that linked the building with the plane beyond. The pilot had gotten two kinds of pizza from the delivery service in Rosemont—pepperoni and cheese and sausage. There were cans of Coca-Cola as well, but they were not very cold.

THIRTY-FOUR
Cernan's Game

They were in a car and it was raining.

Rita huddled in her jacket and held her arms across her breast. She stared at the rain. There is a way to be a prisoner and this is one of the ways: You sleep, even when you're awake. You hold yourself in. You don't scream in your mind about the constrictions or the injustices. You hold yourself in and endure this moment and the next moment. The rain beat down on the steel roof, and the car was intimate with breaths, smells, body heat. The motor was running and it growled very low, very steadily. If she listened hard to it, it made a voice and was saying the same thing over and over. She realized she could imagine any number of combinations of words. She closed her eyes.

Cernan was in the house at the end of the drive. When he came out, they would go to another place and wait. He had received the signal from Brussels just before dawn. He had gone into the bedroom where she slept huddled in her clothes under a blanket. He had touched her shoulder and she started awake. "He arrived in England. He has Anna. In a little while it will be over."

It will be over, she thought. She opened her eyes because they were bringing Miki to the car from the shed where they had kept him. Miki staggered a little between the two men who held him up. They shoved him into the backseat next to Rita. His hands were manacled.

"I need a cigarette," Miki said in very good English. "This is absolutely disgusting." He put on a brave front. Cernan had hurt him over a long period of time until he told Cernan everything and then it had been all right. He had told Cernan about Henkin and about the American companies. Cernan had been satisfied then and Miki had regained a little of his old self-confidence, even if one eye was blackened. He had even flirted with Rita over the past two days. She had to hit him finally and he pouted. Some men were worse than women.

At that moment, it was clear and calm in Prague. Henkin sat at his famous desk in the corner office of the Ministry and waited for Cernan to be put on the line. When he heard Cernan's voice at last, he felt such relief that he scarcely was able to speak at all.

"You have Miki."

"At last, I have Miki," Cernan said. Why had the secret call to Gorkeho been transferred to Henkin's office? What had happened in the last twenty-four hours in Prague?

"And why does this take so much time?"

"Because it was a difficult matter. I can tell you when I bring Miki back."

"No," Henkin said. "We have different orders. I have orders for you now. Is Miki safe?"

"Yes, Director."

"Cernan, you are authorized as a member of the Secret Service to execute Emil Mikita now and to return immediately to Prague."

Cernan said nothing.

"Are you there, pan Cernan?"

"Yes, Director. I am not authorized to—"

Henkin raised his voice. "Do you hear me? I am Conrad Henkin, I have ordered you—"

"I am not authorized," Cernan began again. It was the weary, nagging voice of the eternal bureaucrat.

"Cernan. I am speaking to you man to man. I have learned many things. I have learned things about Miki that would make you sick and you are a man of the world, yet I want to tell you—"

"Director," Cernan began.

"Be quiet, Cernan. Miki has arranged the kidnapping of Anna Jelinak. That is your daughter. No, don't deny it. I know this; more, Miki knows this thing and it was arranged by him and his American conspirators. That is why Anna 'defected' in Chicago despite your excellent security arrangements. Everyone was in it. I suspect even Gorkeho. I know that the man you trusted, Anton Huss, he was an agent for Miki. It was no coincidence that Anna defected on the day Miki defected. It was arranged as insurance. So that if Miki . . . if Miki did not defect, then you would lose your daughter. Don't deny it again, Cernan; I know she is your daughter. Miki told me this thing."

Cernan said nothing. Henkin nearly smiled.

"I have made my own . . . contacts. I want to get to the bottom of this, Cernan. That is why I trusted you with this assignment. I have located Anna and I can arrange her release. It is in the process of happening. But if Miki comes back to Prague to work with his old gang—and I mean with your superior, Gorkeho—then, I am afraid, they will make me powerless.

"You must do as I order you. I am your superior. Miki must be dead and you must see to it at once and then return to Prague. Anna will be safe and we will confront this gang of conspirators."

Cernan said, "I do not understand."

"It is enough that I understand. You must believe me in this and trust me," Henkin said. "I love Anna as you do, as a daughter. She is a bright star on the Czech stage. I am her mentor, she is my protégée. I wish her every good thing, you know this."

"Yes, Director," Cernan said. The voice was soft, almost in awe.

"Eliminate Miki now. Eliminate the problem and return to Prague and we shall see about cleaning up this corruption," Henkin said.

Another long pause.

"Cernan. I know you were to call Gorkeho." Softly, with just the hint of menace. "I have arranged for Gorkeho's calls to be transferred. I have issued a warrant for the arrest of Gorkeho. He is part of a conspiracy against the state. Against me. Against our precarious position in international commerce."

So there it was, Cernan thought. Gorkeho had played for time, played against Henkin from the beginning. Everything Cernan had learned from Miki—about Henkin's corruption, his involvement with the American interests— somehow, in the much more intricate and ruthless world of internal politics in Prague, Henkin had beaten Cernan's man. And Henkin was explaining that to Cernan.

In that moment, standing alone in the farmhouse, Cernan saw the way it was. Henkin had arranged the kidnapping of Anna to use her as leverage against Cernan, to force Cernan to kill the one man who had all the secrets about Henkin and the corruption in Prague. It was dirty and cynical and Henkin had used his daughter and . . . it had worked. That was the worst part of all.

"Yes, Director. I am confused, merely. I do not understand. But I am a soldier of the Republic and we must follow our orders."

Henkin wiped his lip dry.

"Yes," Henkin said.

"As you say," Cernan said. "So it must be done."

"Yes."

"Miki must die," Cernan said.

"Yes. That is my order," Henkin said. "His finger," Henkin added, thinking of Jules Bergen. Jules Bergen had wanted proof. Let it be Miki's finger with the beautiful ring on it. Cernan only grunted an agreement, then he broke the connection.

For a long moment, Henkin waited and then put down the receiver.

Four buildings south, Gorkeho stopped the tape machine. It was little enough but it was enough, he thought. The game with Henkin was not over yet.

Rita saw Cernan stand in the doorway of the farmhouse a moment and then walk out to the car. He opened the door and motioned to Miki.

Miki climbed out. He stood in the rain that fell on his bare head and he was afraid.

Cernan took out his Uzi and pointed it at Miki.

"You are someone who knows too much," Cernan said. "I have spoken to Henkin. He wants me to kill you. And then he wants me to cut off your ring finger, the one with the big ruby on it, and bring it to him in Prague. What do you think of that, Miki?''

Miki began to plead.

Rita stared out the window of the car. She could not understand the two men speaking in the strange language, but she saw the pale horror on Miki's face and she thought Cernan meant to kill him and was telling him that he was going to die.

"Please do not kill me," Miki said.

"What will you say when we get back to Prague? You will say it is all lies, that I tortured you and made you say fantastic things. You will run back to Henkin and ask his protection and Henkin will give it to you. For a little time. Until he can take you out one day and put a bullet in your head and dump you in the Vltava River. What good are you to me?''

"No, no, I will tell them the truth," Miki said. "Please, let me live."

"But I have my order now. I am told you must die and I am a soldier of the Republic. I am the servant of the state."

Miki said, "Then for God's sake do not kill me."

"You told Henkin that Anna was my daughter. Why did you tell him this? Who told you this thing?"

"Elena."

Cernan looked strange, as though he were puzzled. "Why would she say this thing?"

"I don't know. It was just gossip. Just a rumor. Anna . . . Anna had no father. You were in the Party. Elena's brother and cousin were part of the hateful Dubczek regime in 1968, they were unrehabilitated in 1968—"

"They were taken to the Soviet Union when the tanks came into Prague and they were never heard from again," Cernan said. "So Elena, who was not part of them, had to share their ignominy. She was a woman. She had no place to turn.''

"I never told—''

"You told everyone everything, Miki. You knew everything and you lived on gossip. The only thing you never told was about Henkin and the American companies and how he was bribed and bribed very handsomely to arrange matters. Arms. Arms, Miki. Theft of arms from the Czech people! For what? For money, Miki. Money for you and for Henkin and for a few others, and because of our brilliant bureaucracy, we would never know of the theft. Where did the arms go?''

Miki was trembling, tears ran down his face.

"I should kill you," Cernan said. "You are loathsome, you are a disease. You steal from your country for what reason? For money? You had enough. You had too much. You have the American disease. You need everything. I should kill you, Emil Mikita." Cernan spit on Miki in the rain. The spittle washed down Miki's handsome face and the rain obliterated it.

Miki knelt in the mud by the gray car. Rita put her hand to her mouth. She saw he was crying.

"Please, I beg you, do not kill me.''

"Get up, Miki. You are not even a man—''

"Oh, God, let me live!" he cried. "Mother of God, let me live.''

"Get up," Cernan said.

Miki was gripped by hysteria. He shook and screamed. His eyes were large and out of control.

One of the men came around the car and pulled him up and pushed him against the fender of the Mercedes.

Cernan said something to the man then and he pulled Miki's sleeve back and put the cold, strained hand on the hood of the car.

Cernan nodded.

The larger man had a knife that caught the dull light for a moment.

Rita heard Miki's scream and then, through the windshield, saw the severed finger on the blood-streaked hood of the car.

Cernan held out a handkerchief. Miki wrapped his hand and the blood filled the white of the cloth. The large man picked up the finger and wrapped it in another cloth.

Rita cried then and it was loud but it was not louder than Miki's screams.

THIRTY-FIVE
Mannekin-Pis

The American agent walked up the street, swinging his left leg before him. It was only a little tender now. The bruises were deep and they would color his flesh for a long time but the swelling was nearly all gone. He scarcely felt the pain when he stepped on the leg.

He paused at the little shrine set into the corner of a building, almost hidden. The streets were empty of traffic because it was Saturday morning and it was too early for the stores to open. The sullen sky sprinkled gray light over the shabby blocks of buildings. Toward this part of town, the Arabs settled and the men had their coffee houses to meet in and the women had nothing but the hostile, wet climate and the frank stares of the Belgians who hated them. But now it was empty and the statue of the Mannekin Pis smiled impishly on the world he pissed on.

Brussels has become a very sophisticated city and it is slightly embarrassed about the Mannekin Pis, but the little naked boy with his paunchy baby fat and his perpetual bliss in pissing on the city from his fountain cannot be shut away. The story is that the city was saved from fire in medieval times by the little boy who pissed on the flames. It is a typical Belgian story because it mocks legends and heroes and times past and all that is sacred in the world.

A bell tolled in some church and a taxicab clattered over the uneven pavement on a side street. The streets were wet but it had not rained since just after midnight.

Cernan came down the hill toward the statue. His feet dragged and his button eyes focused on Devereaux from a long way off. When he got near, he did not look at the mocking statue above him.

"Your daughter is safe. She wants to go home."

"Where is she?"

Devereaux turned from the statue. His face was the color of ashes. "Rita."

"I have kept the bargain."

"Where is she?"

"In a car, waiting."

"And Miki?"

Cernan frowned at that. "Miki is not your concern."

"I want him."

"It is not your concern."

"He has to be."

"I ask you a question, Devereaux. What is the worth of Miki to you?"

"Nothing."

"Is it so?"

"I can tell you what he is worth to other people," Devereaux said. "To me, he was a little job. A little defection route that ran from Brussels to Zeebrugge and got hit along the way.''

''What would have happened to Miki if he had made his way to America?''

''He would have been milked,'' Devereaux said.

''Of course.''

''That's all.''

''You said I was the connection between Anna's disappearance and Miki,'' Cernan said.

Devereaux waited.

''Is it too much pain to walk a little way with me?'' Cernan said.

''No,'' Devereaux said. Slowly, down the shabby street, the two men strolled. They walked toward the center of the city. A police car cruised past and the policemen looked at them. For a long time, they did not speak. The street was cluttered with shops of stamp dealers and junk peddlers and little souvenir stands that sold statuettes of the Mannekin Pis. This part of the city seemed full of odd, useless enterprises.

''I am the connection,'' Cernan said. ''They wish Miki dead because of all he knows. And for this, they kidnap Anna Jelinak because she is my daughter. Is she not harmed?''

''She is harmed, Cernan,'' Devereaux said.

''How is she hurt?''

''In her mind,'' Devereaux said. ''She needs her father to talk to her.''

''Who does this to her?''

Devereaux said, ''Who wants Miki dead?''

Cernan slapped his hands behind his back and walked like a policeman on patrol. His shoulders were hunched and he frowned instinctively, a frown to frighten schoolboys.

"She said her father was killed by the police long ago," Devereaux said.

"Anna." His voice was sad. "She is a child of dreams. How can I tell her in all those years when I would see Elena that I am her father? How can I talk to her when I am too much a coward to marry her mother? I was young in the Party and full of ideals then. I was part of the new country, the new revolution to sweep aside the caste of privilege. Were you ever so?"

Devereaux stopped. They stood at the window of a tea room where people sat in the gloom of lush surroundings and ate delicate foods.

"Who wants you to kill Miki?"

"After you leave, I am made a visit by Colonel Ready. He wants this woman, your woman who loves you so much. I tell him he must get my daughter first. You see, I am not such a good person. I want something, I lie for it, I betray for it, it does not matter to me. I have so many ideals that I have no scruples. Do you understand me? I can see Anna from afar, I can see her stand by the Hradcany Castle where they make a film, and I say to myself, 'It's all right, Cernan, you have done your best for your daughter. You have opened all the doors for her and given her privilege. If you can't acknowledge her, well, that is just a little thing.' It is no little thing, Devereaux."

Devereaux saw the broken place inside the man. He decided to hurt Cernan, to make him give up Miki.

"When they had her," Devereaux said, "they abused her. They took her clothes off and made photographs of her. She told me that much. She said no one in the world loved her. Then, after a while, she said that God loved her. I just listened to her, but she had to tell me. She said she was sure God loved her, even if God let bad things happen to her. That's when she told me about the men who held her and made her take her clothes off.''

Cernan did not fight the tears.

He stood solid and alone and took the words like blows But Devereaux was not through.

"I listened to her all night long, all across the ocean. We were the only two people in the passenger section. She had to tell me things. She said that she had a statue of the Infant of Prague and that she saw the statue weep for her. She told me about her father being killed by the police, she said the woman who said she was her mother was not her mother. She said her real mother would have loved her.''

"What do you want from me?''

Devereaux stopped at the cry from the man. The empty, shabby street around them seemed frozen in this time and place forever.

"I want Rita and I want Miki. I want to know about Colonel Ready.''

"I told him to go after Anna, the same I told you. He said he had many contacts in America. I didn't trust you, I trusted no one. Except Gorkeho, who is now to be arrested. All the idealists get arrested finally, until there are no ideals left at all.''

"The man who wants to kill Miki took Anna and all the bad things that happened to her are because of him,'' Devereaux said. His voice had no mercy for the other man. "When they came to take her, they killed the lady who had taken her in. She said she asked them not to kill her. One of them hit the woman with a sledgehammer and knocked her down. They took Anna down to a car and they waited for the last one left in the apartment. When he came downstairs and got in the car, she said she looked at his eyes and she knew that the woman was dead. She's seen all this in the last four days.''

''You are a barbaric people. Americans kill and destroy and think nothing of it. Nothing is sacred to you, not even children,'' Cernan said. His eyes glittered in the dull morning light because of the tears.

''Who is the barbarian? The father who does not tell his daughter who he is? The man who kills Miki for a corrupt master?''

''Proof,'' Cernan said. ''He said he wanted proof. He wanted Miki's finger. He said to cut off Miki's finger when I killed him.''

Cernan took the little jewelry box from his pocket and handed it to Devereaux.

Devereaux opened the box. The finger was waxy and the ruby ring was now too large for it.

''Miki is dead,'' Devereaux said.

''So it appears,'' Cernan said.

The two men looked at the finger in the box and Devereaux closed it and handed it back to Cernan.

''The little girl is in a car in Brussels. Arrange for me to have Rita.''

''Rita is waiting,'' Cernan said. ''It is not so far to Zeebrugge. You know the way. You can be there in an hour. I think you know the way.''

Devereaux stared at Cernan. ''This isn't all, is it?''

''What is R Section?''

''It does not exist,'' Devereaux said.

''Miki said he wanted to go out, that he did not trust CIA because CIA is involved in this matter. I said to him, 'Why trust any of them?' But he had to trust this agency. R Section. What is it?''

''I don't know. It doesn't exist.''

Cernan put the box in his pocket. ''I have proof now

for Henkin of Miki's death. The proof is all that is ever required. So it is in every bureaucracy. Go to Zeebrugge now, Devereaux, and when you see Rita Macklin, you make your signal and Anna is delivered to the embassy at Brussels.''

Cernan turned to go.

Devereaux spoke his name.

Cernan looked back. His face was drawn, empty.

"The little girl wants one person in the world who belongs to her," he said. "I told her on the plane that her father was alive.''

"Why did you tell her?''

"Because she needed to know the truth. I told her that her father had been afraid for her for a long time and that now he wanted to tell her he loved her.''

Cernan made a small, wry smile. "I do not expect this of you, Devereaux.''

Devereaux did not speak.

"You said that if Rita Macklin is harmed, then you will kill Anna. It was not so, was it?''

Devereaux stared at him with level, gray eyes. "Yes, Cernan. It was so. I would have killed her and then come to kill you. Don't misjudge that. Even now, don't misjudge that.''

The smile faded. Cernan thought a moment and shrugged, then stopped and turned back.

"You talk to her all night?''

"Yes. She fell asleep when the first light came near Ireland.''

"Then you tell me: this miracle. This was all an arrangement? Was this false too?''

"I don't know.''

"The men who kidnap her—''

"I don't know.''

"Did she see a statue with tears?"

"She said she did."

"I cannot understand."

Devereaux said, "Neither can I."

"It is too much for my years," Cernan said.

"She said 'God seized my soul.' "

Cernan was suddenly overwhelmed with sadness for the world. They stood apart on the sidewalk and it began to rain. They were creatures of sensibilities and they had too many years to carry around. Too many bad thoughts and bad deeds.

THIRTY-SIX

Run

The North Sea was heaving and gray. It pounded the concrete walls of the harbor at Zeebrugge and moaned in front of the shuttered cottages and old hotels.

It was one hour by car from Brussels and the Mercedes-Benz had eaten the miles at a stately eighty-five miles an hour. The day was gray but the clouds scudded furiously across the sky. Now and then, sunlight shattered on the roadway.

Miki's face was white with shock and pain. He sat in the backseat, next to Cernan. Rita Macklin sat in the front seat next to Karl. None of them spoke and it seemed odd to her not to hear Miki's chatter. Miki's left hand was wrapped in a bandage that Karl had fashioned.

She felt so tired. She stared at the grayness of the countryside and it exhausted her.

Cernan spoke once to her, in polite English: "You come

to even give up your life for that man. Would that man do that for you?''

She had stared at him for a long time, and in the end she didn't respond. What could she say? That she didn't know?

She could explain that he loved her, that she knew it in her bones, but that when you asked her questions about him, she couldn't answer them. He was always a stranger to her. His touch was always unexpected. When they made love, it was always for the first time. When he spoke her name, she knew it was the act of a lover, but all the other places in him were hidden. Hidden from her, perhaps hidden from himself as well.

Zeebrugge was the most savage place in the world this day. It was cold and the harbor entrance was filled with trucks and buses and cars, waiting for the next ferry to England.

The big gray car pulled down the road that ran along the beach side and Rita Macklin saw him, standing in the doorway of the café. He disappeared inside. Cernan said, ''Now we wait a little while.''

They waited in the damp silence of the car. Now and then, Miki moaned. He rolled his eyes. His hand was swollen with pain.

''All right,'' Cernan said to Karl.

Karl got out of the car and went into the café and made the call on the public phone. The embassy assured him the child was unharmed. He went to the window and nodded to Cernan.

''All right,'' Cernan said with immense weariness. ''Go now. He is waiting for you.''

She couldn't believe it. She had adopted the guise of a prisoner killing time and now it was over. It seemed unbelievable for the gate to open.

She pushed the door open and felt the stiff wind slap her face.

She slammed the door and ran across the road to the café and he was standing in the doorway. She buried her face in his coat. She said his name.

Karl went back to the car.

The door opened again in the car and this time it was Miki who was shoved out. Miki stumbled, fell on the walk.

The Mercedes pulled away.

For a moment, Miki did not understand. Then he saw the American approach, the man who had tried to take him across once before. The American stood over him and helped him up.

"We finish the train journey now," Devereaux said to Miki.

Mrs. Neumann and the director of National Security and the director of the Federal Bureau of Investigation sat in her office with the door closed for a long time. Hanley waited in his bare, windowless office down the corridor with the familiar feeling in his belly. He wanted to retch but that would only make him feel worse. He sat behind his desk and arranged pencils and waited. The whole bill was $112,560, not counting slush that would have to be used to pay Denisov. Devereaux never told him everything all at once.

It was just after four P.M., which meant it was night in Paris. Devereaux would be in Paris by now. He would be pumping it all out of Miki, not just the outline he had given Hanley on the telephone two hours ago.

Why did he have to take the Concorde back?

He liked to travel first class.

Why did he delay?

He wanted guarantees.

He would get them when he came home.

No. He would get them before he came home.

Didn't he trust Hanley?

The question wasn't answered; there was no need. Hanley had gone the extra mile for him, Hanley reminded him. Hanley's neck was on the block too. Hanley reminded him of loyalty and duty. Hanley realized it was pointless but it was something he had to do. When Hanley finished, Devereaux explained the guarantees he wanted. About the matter in Chicago and the illegal return of the little girl named Anna to her own country. History must be rewritten so that certain acts had never happened.

The telephone on Hanley's desk buzzed.

He picked it up.

Mrs. Neumann said, "Come in." Her voice was cold. She had not been pleased at all. She had told Hanley she was not pleased.

He knocked at the closed door of her office and then opened it. The director of the FBI was a thin, thoughtful man with sallow skin and dark hair. The National Security director was an Italian with an open face. He was so tough he did not have to look tough.

"Sit down," Mrs. Neumann said.

The FBI director looked with curiosity at Hanley. Hanley sat up straight in the straight chair.

"You presented us with a problem," the NSC director said.

"And an opportunity," the FBI director said. "No one wants to cause this administration any harm, but some very strange things were done, very strange. We were interested in the domestic side, in the Hollywood connection and the skim going on at Atlantic City. We had no idea this was so much larger."

Hanley said nothing.

The FBI director cleared his throat. "The problem is there was a crime committed in Chicago."

"Which one?" Hanley said. The voice was civil but the question carried the edge of sarcasm that Mrs. Neumann knew. She glared at Hanley.

"Kidnapping. Four homicides. Was this sanctioned by Section?"

"Section does not sanction killing," Mrs. Neumann said.

"Then I don't see what we can do," the NSC director said. He looked at Mrs. Neumann.

"Then you don't want Miki, is that it?" Hanley said.

"I don't think it's a question of that," FBI said.

"Do you want him or don't you want him? He won't bring him in, you know."

"So what is he going to do then? Adopt him?" NSC said.

"Sanctions," Hanley said.

"Well, if that's—"

Hanley pursed his lips. They were willing to drop it, both of them. They really didn't want a scandal thrown on their laps. He looked at Mrs. Neumann. He saw it in her eyes. She didn't like it either. The two of them were most involved in this and they were going to drop it. Let him kill Miki or let Miki go, but they weren't going to break the rules and regs to safe-conduct Devereaux back to the States. No sirree.

"There are no rules," Hanley said. He said it to Mrs. Neumann. She looked at him with sad eyes. Understanding brings sadness, Hanley thought.

Hanley looked at the tough one. That would be the National Security Council director. He really had not made himself clear.

Hanley spoke. "The agent we speak of was involved

because of a woman. A woman he lives with." For once, he did not wrinkle his Protestant nose when he described their relationship. "The woman is a journalist. She is accredited with several publications." He named a news-magazine, a prominent monthly magazine and a newspaper on the Eastern seaboard.

The tough guy understood right away.

"Presumably, she is safe now?" His voice had dropped a notch. The John Law tone was missing.

"Yes."

"Did he say anything about . . . leaking this to . . . to his girlfriend?"

"No."

"Why do you bring it up?"

"Because I put him on a train nearly three weeks ago and I didn't tell him everything. I didn't tell him the FBI wanted to talk to Miki. I didn't tell him that Miki had been flogging himself for months with no takers. I didn't tell him that this might be extremely dangerous. I said to him, 'Be careful.' It is something your mother might say to you. He got caught in the middle and it nearly cost him his life, not to mention costing us his services. He has made the best of a bad deal. He has repaired some of the damage."

"You call killing four men in cold blood repairing the damages?"

"They were nothing, Mr. Director. You know that and so do I. Let's stop dancing." Hanley flared and it was as rare as an earthquake in Kansas. "The girl wanted to go home to Prague. He told me that. He talked to her a long time on the plane." They did not know about the Section plane. There were matters they had no need to know.

"That still doesn't justify—"

"You are talking like a Philadelphia lawyer," Hanley said, though he had never met one. "I assure you of the resourcefulness of this agent. If you cut his string and put him outside, he won't run away. He'll wait for you. He has Miki and by now he has more information than Mrs. Neumann was able to give you in the last hour. Miki knew everything about the operations. He was a gossip and a gossip is inquisitive. I can assure you that this matter can be handled two ways: directly, quickly, by us; or you can bleed to death with a thousand cuts.''

NSC did not speak. FBI frowned but was silent. For a long time the four of them were silent.

"I can reach the President at Camp David,'' NSC said. "I'll have to explain it to him. Jules Bergen is one of his friends.''

"You don't have to tell him about that part yet. Just about the CIA and the operation,'' Hanley said.

"Yes. I suppose so. When do you make contact with your man?''

"He makes contact with me. I will have to see the paper.''

"You can take my word for it.''

"I'm afraid—''

"Hanley, are you questioning my integrity?'' said the director of the NSC. He had seen them all, Hanley thought, they come and go and for a little time, they strut onstage as though there were no more elections.

"He is,'' Hanley said.

"Damn him. Did you ever think of just lying to him?''

"Yes,'' Hanley said. "But that's what started the trouble, isn't it?''

THIRTY-SEVEN
Targets

"This is very bad," Jules Bergen said. He had said it once before, at the beginning of the meeting. No one pointed that out.

It was very late and the cleaning women were moving through the executive offices in their gray uniform dresses, polishing and emptying and wiping things down. The three men were in Jules Bergen's suite at the northwest corner of the forty-ninth floor.

Jules was away from the other two men. He stood, small and precise, at the window wall and stared down at the narrow crosstown street. The yellow river of cabs surged up Sixth Avenue and a private scavenger truck was making a noisy collection of trash from the bowels of the network building.

Jules turned and looked at Willis and Ben Herguth.

"The President called me," he said. "He said he had

received a disturbing report about me, about the CIA, he said he called out of friendship."

"What are we going to do?" Willis said.

"Anna Jelinak is on her way to Prague," Jules said. "That's because of you, Ben. I am really disappointed in you. That's a terrible thing. Do you know what I got by messenger three hours ago? A jewelry box from our friend in Prague. It contains a finger with a ring on it. A finger as token that Miki is no more. Except I don't think that's the case. Do you think that's the case, Ben?"

Ben felt utterly miserable.

"Julie—"

"Stop calling me that, Ben," Jules Bergen said.

"I'm sorry. Four guys got whacked in Chi. How do I know this guy is gonna knock over the place? I told you I got on it right from the start, told everyone to button down because this Devereaux guy was coming into the States. Then I got this guy who knew Devereaux in the old days, this guy Ready, he's after Devereaux now, I told him two hours ago the guy was holed up in Paris. All we gotta do is find out where. If he's—"

"Who is Ready?" Jules asked.

"Well," Willis broke in. "He's a contractor, very independent, his files are washed in the Firm and I can't get everything on him. . . ." Willis hesitated. Files on Ready were deliberately incomplete. "He knew about Miki, he knew all about him, I put him onto Ben and he said he would put the hit on Devereaux and Miki for five figures."

"Is this the way it's done?" Jules said.

"You gotta understand," Willis said. "Nobody at that end of the business advertises in the Yellow Pages."

"Anna Jelinak was trade," Jules said. "Devereaux got

Anna and gave her back to the Czechs in exchange for Miki. I got Miki's finger but the fucking government has got Miki's story. Your government, Willis, the one you guys are supposed to be in charge of. The FBI is on to our case and National Security is on your case. We are going to take the count together because of the incompetence of your agency, Willis. Why didn't you get Anna back to Prague in the first place? Why didn't you sanction Miki the moment he wanted to come across?''

''Nobody thought it would get this far,'' Willis said, echoing the words used by scores of his predecessors suddenly caught in the middle of a scandal.

''This was business. And you didn't take care of business. You had the contacts with Henkin,'' Jules said. ''And you helped us get favored treatment in exchange for 'muling' a few hundred arms every time we packed up our movie equipment and headed home from Prague. Henkin was greased, Langley got its arms to ship to Afghan rebels and we were . . . compensated. The money was cleaned very nicely in Prague. And now the FBI is going to want to know about casino gambling revenues and where they went. And the National Security Council is going to want to know what Langley knew and when Langley knew it about trading in arms with a Communist country. What a stupid idea, to take Czech arms and send them to the Afghans. . . .''

''Not so stupid,'' Willis said. ''The rebels knocked over an arsenal twenty-nine months ago, all kinds of Soviet and Czech weapons. The Soviets just don't have any idea of how many because they're nearly as fucked up as our own quartermaster corps. So we give the rebels Communist weapons. And Henkin makes money. And you get a chance to clean a lot of money while you're making movies. Don't bring this all down on the Firm, Jules. We can all share a little blame for letting this go so far—''

''*Where is Miki*?''

Jules never shouted.

Ben Herguth grabbed his own mouth and squeezed it until it hurt. When it really hurt, he let go. He said, ''Look, Julie, this is a bombshell, no doubt about it. But we know the source. It comes out of one guy. This guy Devereaux. All we do is whack him.''

''All we do is whack him,'' Jules mimicked. ''That's what you said about Kay Davis in Chicago. Is she whacked?''

Ben Herguth said nothing.

''She is not. If there had been no Kay Davis, there would have been no 'miracle' and there would have been no defection of Anna Jelinak and—''

''Look, Julie, you want her whacked, I'll whack her myself. And right now, I got the guy going in after Devereaux. He's in Paris, it's a matter of time, he hasn't come out yet. So just wait a couple more hours and—''

''What if we cover this up?'' Jules said. ''Henkin sends me a finger. But it's Henkin who is going to get the finger because we can't use him anymore, we can't go into Prague, we got twelve million dollars in contracts going down the toilet because we can't start shooting *Napoleon* in January and there isn't any snow in Spain. So if we eliminate the man in Paris, if we silence Miki, there's still going to be a lot of covering up to do.''

''But you get the source,'' Willis said in a quiet voice.

''You guys,'' Ben said. ''Why don't you whack Devereaux?''

''We're not involved in those things,'' Willis said. ''The agency does not authorize sanctions.''

Jules made a face. He felt impaled by incompetents. ''I reminded the President of my support for him. He's a sly old devil. He said he was a friend and would always be a friend but if there had been illegal . . . he said 'shenanigans,' by someone working for me, then I should be the first to know it."

He stared at Ben Herguth and Ben felt cold all over, even colder than he usually felt just coming to New York.

"Ben," Jules said. "You were in charge of production on this. If you look at the matter in the right way, it's because of you that so much has gone wrong."

Ben stared at Jules and hoped he wasn't hearing it.

"Ben, we will engage the best counsel for you," Jules said.

"I don't want to do no time," Ben said. "I'm old and fat and I can't do time."

Willis stared at him with professional coldness. The atmosphere of the meeting had changed.

"It is not a question of that," Jules said. "Someone has to be out front on this. If you have to be out front, then so be it. The FBI will take years trying to put this together and we have lawyers, Ben, dozens and dozens of them. There can be motions and writs and when it comes down to it, it's going to fall a lot harder on Langley than it will on us."

Now it was Willis' turn. He looked at Jules. "I followed orders. I did what I was supposed to do. We've been supplying arms to the rebels for years."

"But you haven't been doing it with laundered money. And they haven't been Czech arms."

"Who can prove that?"

"Miki," Jules said.

"Ben is going to get Miki and Devereaux," Willis said.

"Words," Jules said. "I want to see results, Ben. So

you sit here with Mr. Willis and make things happen. Find ways to make things happen between you. I have a board meeting tomorrow at eight sharp and I'm going home. I think you should think about how you're going to stop Miki from talking and stop Devereaux. Remember, you both have something riding on the results.''

THIRTY-EIGHT
The Sick Man

"He's in rooms 503 and 504 at the Hilton in Paris. It's next to the Eiffel Tower."

"I know where it is," Colonel Ready said. He sat in the telephone booth in the lobby of the Edouard VII Hotel on the Avenue de L'Opera. Late-night traffic pounded outside the lobby doors. He had been waiting in the bar for the call, drinking very large gin and tonics. His eyes were clear and he did not need to write the room numbers down. The bar had been a hangout for a long time for former Legionnaires and those who had been in the Army in Algeria. It's how Ready had first known the place, a long time ago, when he had been posted in North Africa.

"He reconfirmed with Air France a little while ago." Ben Herguth's voice was so clear he might have been in the next booth. "The priority is Miki. Take Miki out first."

"I understand. How did you trace him?"

"He booked the flight in Brussels and he booked the rooms in Paris at the same time. We ran it down. Rather, we had our friends run it down. You can do anything when they use credit cards. They still think it takes months to trace down credit-card charges overseas. We checked with the hotel and got the room numbers. We checked with Air France and got the reconfirmation. Whatever happened, the administration bought it in Washington and they're going to let Miki come in. So you hit them. I mean, you fucking hit them."

"I will," Ready said. He replaced the phone on the green cradle and got up. He opened the booth and dropped a few francs on the switchboard for the operator. He went back into the bar. It was just after eleven and Paris was beginning to come out of the theaters and go to the clubs for a late supper. He paid his bill and did not finish the last gin and tonic. He pushed through the side door to the narrow street and felt the breeze. It was warm for the end of November, he thought.

He was in time to talk to the night concierge for the fifth floor. The woman was flattered but a little afraid of the policeman with the scar on his face and the strange blue eyes. Yes, the sick man was in Room 503. Yes, he was bandaged here, on his hand.

So Devereaux was in 503.

The police officer smiled at the night concierge. The night manager asked him if there would be any trouble. He said he hoped there would not be but the man was a notorious hotel burglar and it was a pretense to check in with his hand bandaged so that no one would think he could have committed the burglaries. He stole jewels and took them out of the hotel in the bandaged hand. You see, he was in Nice and Antibes in the summer; now he has come to Paris for the season. Ready explained it all in his very good French, flavored with the Parisian accent. The night manager wrung his hands and the concierge was quite excited because nothing exciting ever happened on the fifth floor.

When they were gone, Ready looked up and down the hall. The corridor was carpeted in red and the walls were papered with Paris scenes done in line drawings. It was a very American hotel with bright lights and strong doors.

He had a pass card—the hotel did not use keys—and held it in his left hand. His right was now filled with a pistol of Italian make, fitted with a silencer. The automatic carried nine rounds. He thought of killing and his eyes glittered in the light of the empty corridor.

He pushed the card in the lock and the door swung open. The room was dark. He stepped into the narrow hall that led to the dressing room and bath and held out his pistol. He saw the dim form in bed.

"Devereaux," he said.

He fired two quick thumps and the body in the bed leaped under the covers and there was no other sound.

He stepped into the room and pulled back the cover.

Miki's mouth was open in death.

He said something and turned. There was no other sound. He went back to the passage door and removed the pass card. He stepped to the next room and inserted the card in the holder. He pushed the door open slowly with the barrel of the silencer. He went into the room, which was identical to the other but in reverse layout.

He pushed the light switch this time.

The bed was turned down with two mints covered in green paper on the pillows. The room was empty. There was no luggage, nothing. The room was not in use.

THIRTY-NINE

Safe Conducts

He called at dawn. It was just past one in the morning in Washington, in the apartment on Massachusetts Avenue at the juncture with Wisconsin.

"Is it safe?" Devereaux said.

"Yes."

"You have the paper?"

"Signed by the Man. It's an executive order, they had to put it in legalese, but it's safe. All your sins are forgiven you," Hanley said.

"Was there reluctance?"

"Yes. Not by Mrs. Neumann. But the administration was reluctant. They saw, in the end, the way it was."

"The way it was," Devereaux repeated. "How will they handle it?"

"Quietly. Do you think they intend to call a press conference?"

"They have to handle it, Hanley. They really have to follow through, you know."

"They will. We are the nudge. I don't think the FBI director thinks well of you either. He wonders how you found the girl so quickly."

"They were in Chicago, I told you. I was born there. You know about me, Hanley. I have friends in unsavory businesses there. The FBI talked to the wrong people. If they were really trying to find her, I mean."

There was a long silence after that. Hanley yawned into the receiver. "We buy arms from our enemies and give arms to our friends. I really don't understand."

"You're getting old. Or you believe too much."

"Yes, perhaps that's it. Both of those things. I never turn out to be as cynical as I would like to be."

"I milked Miki yesterday. He has all sorts of interesting stories. He's still a bit woozy. I bedded him down at the Hilton."

"You're not at the Hilton? I thought you were at the Hilton?"

"No. I have perverse tastes. I like small and noisy French hotels."

"Is Miki all right?"

"Yes," Devereaux said. "Why?"

"Colonel Ready," Hanley said. "Our passport surveillance said he was a step behind you. He came into the States through O'Hare Airport thirty-six hours after you."

Devereaux felt the cold again in himself. It was like passing into shadows. He said nothing.

"We'll be in Dulles by one," he said at last.

"I'll be there."

He replaced the receiver and went back to the bed. He looked down at her. Her eyes were closed and she breathed softly. After living on the edge all these days, they had made shuddering love in the large, soft bed. All of the lovemaking had rushed out of their bodies, released into each other. When he made love to her, he discovered her all over again. He never said a word to her, except to say her name.

Rita opened her eyes now. She smiled at him, reached for him.

"What time is it?"

"Seven-thirty."

"The days get short."

"It'll be warmer in Washington," he said. He sat on the bed next to her. She reached for him. He was naked and she was naked beneath the covers. She put her hand between his legs and touched him. There and there. He sat for a moment and looked at her hand. Each part of her was examined as a part: her mouth, the line of her upper lip and the line of her lower lip; the slight hollow of her cheeks; the eyes, cloudless and wide and very knowing. He studied her sometimes in the morning light as a painter studies his model, to see the beauty of the lines, with no more desire than a child yet with a child's delight at the appearance of beauty. In those moments—now—there was no reserve in him.

He reached across her body and held her as a child holds beauty. He felt his warmth press against her belly. He went into her belly and he made love that was not original or even very skilled. His real skill was the urgency of his lovemaking. Her skill was the savage thing that took over her body when he was in her.

After they made love and Paris became morning beyond the window, they lay apart from each other for a time, and when he spoke he did not look at her.

"There's only one thing we didn't talk about."

She put the palm of her hand flat on his belly. She made

little circles with her hand on his belly. She didn't say anything.

He stared at the ceiling. "Ready. One way or the other, we can't let it alone. He'll finish us or we'll finish him."

Rita said, "I was going to kill him with my little knife."

"Maybe he doesn't die," Devereaux said. "Maybe he's the evil that was loosed at the beginning of time and he can't die until time ends."

She smiled at his tone. "The ultimate booga-booga."

He touched her hair. She bent, kissed his nipple, put her head on his chest. But they were both thinking about it.

"He went after me when I went after Anna. He missed me, Hanley said he was right behind me. So he has to be back here. And when we leave here, he'll be wherever we go. In Washington, Lausanne, wherever we go."

"I want to go home, Dev," she said.

"Where is it?"

"At least D.C. I want to be with Americans again. We couldn't lose ourselves in the world, let's give it up and go home. Could you go home?"

"I could go with you. Anywhere."

"We'll take Philippe out of school at the end of term. He'd do well in Washington."

She spoke of the black child whom Devereaux had rescued from St. Michel, who went to school now in Switzerland.

"All right," he said.

She felt troubled.

The morning light filled the room and the noise was full of Paris: Men shouted in the street and someone played a radio too loud and parrots talked to lonely old women in apartments across the court.

"I love you," she said.

"I'll wait here for a while," he said. "Wait for Ready. He'll come for us. I'll wait for him this time and get him."

"Don't." It was voice to the premonition. She trembled and felt cold. He pulled the cover over her naked body.

"Come back with me. Let Section find him for you. They owe you that."

"David Mason. I didn't tell you. He walked into the embassy last night and Eurodesk debriefed him. He was conked on the head in Bruges by a policeman who saw he had a gun. He was trying to accost two men, the police said. He told Eurodesk it was Ready. With Cernan. He got into trouble with Stowe and I told Hanley to take care of it."

"I liked him. He was decent," she said. She invested the word with all sorts of properties of approval.

"Ready would have killed him. Ready is alive, Rita," Devereaux said. He said it as suddenly as if he had just realized it.

"He can't hurt us," she said.

They lay in bed, naked and touching, staring at the same cracked ceiling, thinking about the man who hunted them both. A woman began to play Bach on a piano and the city began its daily argument, full of shouts and laughter. He felt her hand in his.

He got up then without a word and went to the telephone and dialed the number. He asked for the room and waited. He listened to the voice and asked a question in French and was asked a question in return. He put down the receiver. He looked at Rita lying on the soft, wide bed.

The voice on the phone had belonged to a policeman. Ready was that close, he thought. And he thought he must not tell Rita anything yet.

But she said, "Miki?"

He stared at her.

Rita understood. "Oh, God," she said. "Oh, God. Oh, come and hold me, please."

He sat down next to her.

He held her. Naked, they clung to each other.

The plane banked against the clouds above Bohemia and descended through them by bumpy steps.

Anna held her father's hand though she was not afraid. It was a luxury to seem to be afraid.

Her father, a ferocious man with a sad face, had told her many things in the past four hours and she thought they were all true. He had told her he was not a brave man and that he had made many mistakes but the worst mistake of all had been in nearly losing her. He told her many things.

Anna believed everything.

She saw the clouds like smoke streak past the windows. The plane smelled of home, the voices were of home, the smiles and faces were home. And her father was a handsome man and he cried once, when he first saw her in the embassy at Brussels.

"I love you, little one," he said again. He had said it many times in four hours, to make up for all the fourteen years he had not said it at all.

He knew that Gorkeho was arrested and that Henkin had received the finger and that, by now, it would become apparent that Miki was loose in the West. Goddamn Miki and the United States, Cernan thought. At least it was clean and there was an end to it. He might suffer from Henkin, but what could Henkin do to him?

He did not think to tell Anna what Henkin could do to him.

Gorkeho, that honest one-legged soldier who had guided him through the thickets of the political life, was lost and

Cernan might as well end up at his side, even in prison. But at least, for one moment, Anna would know there was a real father and that he loved her and if he was taken by the police and killed, well, then it was not just a dream but a real father who had died.

"And what did you see?"

"The Child," she had said in the embassy. "He wept for me."

"I do not think I could see that. I mean, you have seen it and I believe you, but I do not think I could have seen such a miracle."

"But, Father, you must believe what you see," she had said. "I saw the tears of Christ."

"Perhaps it was a trick of the Americans."

"And Stephanie. You would have seen that Stephanie did not make tricks. She loved me, Father."

"I am glad."

"I saw tears," Anna had said in the embassy.

All right, Cernan thought. Perhaps it was true. Perhaps, in time, miracles become too cynical for belief. What had he ever believed except in the perfectability of man in the State? An ideal, Gorkeho would have said and smiled. But where was Gorkeho now and when would Cernan join him?

"I do not say I love you, Father, because it is so soon since I've met you," Anna said. "Will you give me time?"

His heart broke as they bumped through the clouds. The earth came up to them.

The miracle came when they opened the door and he went to the stairs and looked down at the man waiting at the bottom of the ramp. Then he understood the possibility of things.

It was Gorkeho.

He was smiling.

FORTY
Without Illusions

They were all going to Acorn on Oak Street after the ten-o'clock local news. She was just a little late because she had to scrub off the makeup or she would have an allergic reaction in the morning.

Kay Davis walked out of the station shortly after eleven and there were no cabs and it didn't matter. Acorn bar was only a few blocks west. She started down the street, heels click-clacking on the pavement. The night was bright with the red city sky and the streetlamps and the doormen were in their cubbyholes in the lobbies of all the high-rise condominiums.

Al Buck was being transferred to Adelaide. That was in Australia. He had gotten a raise, of course, and the kids were keen on meeting Crocodile Dundee or someone very like him. That's the face Al Buck put on it.

It was hilarious. There were notes on the newsroom

bulletin board, the one management pretended not to read. No one knew very much about Australia but everyone tried to make kangaroo jokes.

Kay smiled at that. She walked along in the normal, aggressive urban manner, her head driving her body forward, her steps very businesslike. It was a grand illusion and every woman in every city knows it.

The man passed her and grabbed her purse.

She turned, held on.

And the purse-snatcher showed his long, thin knife and slashed once and twice and Kay Davis felt first warmth and then blood. Blood on her face. She held the strap of the purse and touched her face and there wasn't any pain. She stared at his face but he had let go of the purse, he was running up the street.

There was no pain.

She thought of herself as she had seen herself thousands of times, the pretty girl on television in Des Moines and Chicago and, next step up, the Big Apple. Pretty Kay Davis.

Felt the warmth of her own blood on her face.

And began to scream.

"That's done," Herguth said to Jules Bergen.

"My work is not as cut and dried." It was one in the morning and they were at the network apartment on West 56th Street. The room was done in vague Oriental colors and there was a samurai warrior's set of swords on a wall in an inner room that might have been a den. Ben's girl was in bed in the next room, sleeping off the booze and pills.

"Well, you got the patience."

"I have whatever has to be had," Jules Bergen said.

He stared out at New York and began to hum the Sinatra song very softly. It kept his spirits up. The city was cranky in the early morning, squawking to itself.

"You did good, Ben," Jules said.

That made Ben feel better. If Julie thought it was good, then it was. Like coming to him with an idea for a show: If Julie said something would work, then it would work, never mind if it bombed in the ratings. It would still be a go because Julie said so.

"Cunt'll never work in television again with a face like chopped meat," Herguth said. "I liked that. I liked that part of it."

"Did you ever consider you're a sadist?"

"Everyone on top is a sadist." Herguth smiled. "It's part of the perks, like getting keys to the gold washroom."

Jules said, "I didn't even give Kay Davis a second thought the other night."

"I know that, Julie, I know that but I had my pride. I told you a thing was gonna be taken care of and it wasn't and that made me feel bad."

"Henkin was arrested last night in Prague."

"And Miki was shot dead in Paris." Ben Herguth smiled. "My man didn't get the G man, but he got Miki and that means we are halfway home free. No Miki, no snitching."

"But we're still out all that money in contracts, set design, scripts—"

"I'm working on that too, Julie," Ben said. He was full of himself, he felt good, better than he had in years. "Prague is out for now, I appreciate that, but we're already starting to make progress. I been on the phone all afternoon. How does this grab you?"

Jules waited. Ben gurgled like a kid.

"Belgrade," Ben said like a present.

"Belgrade?"

"Yugoslavia. Belgrade looks exactly like Moscow used to look when they burned it down. Further, my man says we can get all the Yugoslav Army extras we need. And the cost gets down as low as Prague, maybe even lower."

"Belgrade," Jules repeated.

"Even snow isn't a problem, they already got six inches of snow there," Ben said. "They said they can handle the whole cast the month of January as long as we get out when the party congress starts February third."

Belgrade didn't make any impression on Jules. He closed his eyes and tried to think of it but it was no good. Jules had never seen the city, never set foot in Yugoslavia. He opened his eyes and Ben was grinning at him. Ben was making up for a lot of mistakes. Miki was whacked, he had gotten rid of Kay Davis in Chicago. . . . Jules grinned back.

"Why the hell not?" Jules said.

FORTY-ONE

The Untouchables

The scandal, if that is what it was, broke in little waves.

Miki was dead. His existence continued as 114 minutes recorded on both sides of a cassette tape. The voice was scratchy, at times incomprehensible. The voice of the questioner was plain and flat and the answers were fascinating.

Miki talked about the details of how Henkin routinely helped launder the money that poured into Prague from the production companies. There were kickbacks along the way to Henkin and various other cronies, including Miki. There were numbered Swiss bank accounts—and Miki knew some of the numbers because he handled all sorts of sordid details. The FBI made its request to the Swiss banking authorities through the State Department, and the Swiss, reluctant as always, honored it in time.

It was a dull financial scandal and no part of it touched

Jules Bergen. Naturally, a few questions were asked in the network boardroom but the answers were satisfactory. The target of the investigation was Benjamin C. Herguth, president of BH Productions of California and a supplier of network fare. Herguth was overseeing the scheduled shooting of *Life of Napoleon*, which was to be a 29-part mini-series the following fall. It would be shot on location in and around Belgrade, Yugoslavia.

In the Senate, two young Democrats on the Senate Oversight Committee asked questions about possible involvement of the Central Intelligence Agency. Miki on tape alleged that the CIA mingled funds with the production companies that used Czechoslovakia and bought arms from the burgeoning Czech arms industries and then smuggled these arms out of the country through the film company. All location shootings of any size involved vast logistics requiring tons of equipment ranging from cameras and sound booms to basic kitchens.

Where did the arms go?

For two days, one television network insisted the arms were smuggled to the contras in Honduras. This story was not only vigorously denied by the head of the CIA but was proven false when the Sandinista leadership denied it as well. As for the Czechs, they said nothing. A stony winter silence fell over Prague and there were reports of trials held in secret and of the execution of a high-ranking member of the bureaucracy named Henkin. But these were rumors, gathered at the usual listening posts in Vienna and Berlin.

The scandal had no life to it. It had no beginning and no end. The scandal could not be summarized neatly at the end of the evening news.

The Central Intelligence Agency was slightly shaken but no damage had been done. After all, the scandal came down to the scratchy allegations played on a tape made in a Paris hotel room.

Miki was dead; where was the proof of what he said? Certainly the government at Prague was not willing to come forward to support the story of the defector.

A federal grand jury in Baltimore returned six counts of an indictment on charges of income tax evasion against Benjamin Herguth in January. At the time, he was out of the country, overseeing production on *Napoleon*. He returned to the United States and posted bond. His attorneys assured him the case against him was weak and that it would take months to come to trial in any case.

Ben Herguth told his attorneys he wasn't worried.

She had called the number while she was still in the hospital. She had left her name and waited for him.

Kay Davis had the sympathy of all her colleagues who were still before the camera. There was no question of Kay Davis returning to the camera. One of the radio stations made her an offer; another television station asked her to sign on as a producer. People were kind to her in that special way that separates them from the unlucky one.

The scars were healed. One was across her cheek, below her left eye. The second one was a jagged line from her temple to the edge of her mouth. The surgeon had been skilled; the scars were traces. "They will fade further," he said. And there was the chance of more cosmetic surgery in time. It was a matter of time.

He came before Christmas. The city was bright with the holiday. The great tree was lit in the square between city hall and the courts building. On Michigan Avenue, thousands of little Italian lights winked on the bare trees.

Kay had been home to Iowa and everyone there was

very kind. They were also kind at her old television station. No one offered her a job.

A woman from *People* magazine had written a story about her that was touching. They ran her photograph. A millionaire insurance executive offered her money for more cosmetic surgery.

She thought she would kill herself before Christmas. She thought she would sit in her bath and cut her wrists and let her blood mingle with the warm water until she was dead.

But he came to see her six days before Christmas and she let him into her apartment on Chestnut Street and she told him everything that had happened. It wasn't very much really but she told him everything and told it to him over and over.

Devereaux listened to her and sat with her for a long time. Afternoon became evening. She made him a drink and then another one. They sat together on the couch and looked out the window wall at the city. He had given her the number, to call him if she needed any help, if she got into any trouble. The premonition had filled him from the moment he met her. He was full of premonitions this winter. He thought of Ready every morning when he awoke. He would open his eyes and he would see Ready in his mind. Stowe and Eurodesk said Ready had disappeared off the face of the earth. Rita Macklin said, "Perhaps he has gone back to hell."

Devereaux held Kay Davis' hand and when she cried —she cried several times—he held her and let her cry against him.

Devereaux had given the tape to Hanley and filled out a complete report and Hanley had said that it wasn't enough.

"These are big guys," Hanley had said. "It just isn't enough to get them on anything."

"So nothing happens," Devereaux had said.

Hanley had shrugged. "It happens," he said.

Win some, lose some.

He felt her tears against him. They sat in silence when she stopped crying.

"Why did it happen to me?" Kay Davis said. "I wasn't important to them, was I?"

You were someone's afterthought, Devereaux said in his mind. You were a butterfly and someone tore your wings off. You might have been ignored.

"If I hadn't gone to the church that morning . . ." she said. "I think about killing myself."

"Are you going to kill yourself?" he said.

"I don't know."

"Don't kill yourself," Devereaux said.

"I can't tell you what it's like. The worst part is the kindness. Everyone is so goddamn kind to me."

"Like me."

"I called you," she said.

He was holding her. It was an act of comfort. "You called me and I was late. I'm always late now. There's nothing anyone can do." He knew he was feeling sorry for himself and he despised himself. He wanted sympathy from her and that was despicable. He suddenly got up and went to the window wall and looked down at the city. Ready, he thought. He's already won. He freezes all my thoughts, my life. I can't even act to save myself, he thought.

He felt Ready all around him, grinning in the darkness, watching him, mocking him.

Rita had set up a place in Georgetown off DuPont Circle and Philippe was coming to Washington at the end of the holidays. He watched Rita as though he was no longer part of her because she could not share the part of him that saw Ready all around, in everything, in every room, at every moment.

"I'm glad you listened to me," she said.

He turned and saw her on the couch in the darkness. He smiled. "Do you believe in weeping statues?" he said.

"Yes," she said. "I saw it."

"The same as Anna."

"I'm glad you got Anna back. I'm glad someone turned out all right in this."

"What do you need, Kay?" he said.

"What do you mean?"

"Do you need money? Would money help?"

She smiled. "Money always helps."

"And revenge," he said.

She stared at him. She understood.

"Yes," she said. Her voice was changed; the self-pity was gone.

"All right," he said. "I don't know about the money. But I can get the other thing."

"Will you tell me?"

"You'll know," he said.

Jules Bergen turned the corner from Sixth Avenue and crossed the plaza to the front of the network building. He felt good. Ben was back in Belgrade and the indictments, well, what the hell were a few tax indictments? The whole thing had blown over. When network stock went down six points on the first rumors, Jules bought ten thousand shares and rode the swing back up when the rumors died. Some people knew how to make money out of anything, Ben had said to him with admiration.

Jules Bergen and the messenger got on the elevator

together and rode up together. The messenger carried a package of videotapes and he wore a Sony Walkman and sunglasses, even though the day was bleak and gray.

Jules did not really see him. No one really sees messengers. He wore a stocking cap pulled down tight to the sunglasses and a battered Army fatigue jacket.

Ding. Jules stepped out on 49. The messenger came behind him. They went into the executive suite together. Jules and the messenger pushed into the outer offices and Jules said good morning to someone and stepped down the corridor to his own office.

The messenger was behind him.

That's when Jules noticed him.

Jules Bergen turned and said, "Can I help you?"

"Yes," the messenger said. He closed the door. They were in the office together and Jules saw what it was. He went to the desk to press the intercom. The messenger slammed him onto the couch. Jules said, "You can't do—"

"Shut up," the messenger said.

"Who are you?"

"The messenger."

"Messenger from who?"

"Messenger from God," the messenger said. "Gimme all your money."

Jules took out his wallet and money clip and handed them to the messenger. The messenger put the videotapes on the desk. The messenger stared at Jules through the sunglasses. The mouth was straight, the shoulders hunched.

"What are you gonna do?" Jules stammered.

"Ben Herguth," the messenger said. "Got a message from Ben."

"Ben is in Yugoslavia."

"I know where the fuck Ben is. Don't interrupt me. I'm the messenger."

"What's the message?"

The messenger smiled. "Ben says he's tired of you letting him take all the gaff. He says you got to stand out there by yourself on some of this. He says he's gonna make a deal with the G and give them you. You know why he wants to tell you this? Because he says if you don't quash those fucking indictments through your friends in the White House, he's gonna cut all your fingers and toes off and then your nose and then he's gonna let you hang on a meat hook until you go crazy or dead, that's what the message is."

Jules trembled. He was in his own office on the forty-ninth floor in the middle of Manhattan in the middle of the morning and he was listening to a madman with a Sony Walkman and headphones.

"I don't know what you're talking about," Jules said.

"That's what Ben said you'd say. So I do the second part of the message now."

"What are you going to do?"

The messenger picked up Jules by the shirtfront.

"I'll yell," Jules said.

"I know," the messenger said.

Actually, there was no pain at first. The little finger of his left hand was detached quickly with a sharp cut of the scalpel in the messenger's hand.

"Now you can scream," the messenger said. He picked up the finger and put it in a videotape box and closed the box. "Bye, Jules. Don't forget the message."

And walked out the door.

All the screaming a moment later just added to the confusion. And when Jules described the attacker to police, the story made the evening news on all the network shows. It was so uncivilized, New Yorkers said to each other: You can't even trust messengers.

The next afternoon, Ben Herguth was back in New York but he couldn't see Jules. The afternoon after that, Ben Herguth was in Washington, D.C., talking to a thin man from the Justice Department, talking about Jules and about Jules wanting to kill him and what kind of a deal could Ben Herguth make.

The scandal, moribund so long, finally got sexy.

The whole country started following it, including Kay Davis in Chicago.

"It is a filthy matter," Mrs. Neumann said to the man seated at the lunch table across from her. Hanley bit into his cheeseburger. His old Greek friend, Sianis, had lost his place on Fourteenth Street but found another storefront off DuPont Circle, near a bookstore that served booze. It was a strange neighborhood for someone like Sianis, but the cheeseburgers tasted the same to Hanley.

"They are all filthy matters. Ben Herguth has made his deal and Jules Bergen will receive some sort of punishment."

"But who was the messenger?"

"Yes," Hanley said. "Well, perhaps we should not probe too carefully."

"Devereaux," Mrs. Neumann said.

"No. I have it on good authority—from Stowe—that Devereaux is in Europe. In fact, he is in Chartres of all places."

"The pilgrim," she said.

He studied her. The winter had aged her. The filthy matters had aged her. She was a woman who saw good in the world and did not temporize.

"I don't want to know who the messenger is, I don't want to know about Jules or the CIA," Hanley said. "The matter of Miki was a failure in the end. It came to nothing. We were lucky not to lose our agent in the end."

"The matter isn't resolved. There is still Ready. Somewhere," she said.

He put down his cheeseburger with finality. "That," he said, "is not my concern. That is a matter that does not concern Section."

"Come on, Hanley," she began.

"Mrs. Neumann. The matter of transporting Miki was as straightforward as I put it to Devereaux that afternoon in the cathedral at Chartres. I could not be expected to know that Ready stalked the train, had changed the driver, had subverted our private contractors in Brussels. Ready was driven to kill Devereaux and that was a matter that Devereaux set in motion himself with his childish act of violence on St. Michel, when he cut Ready's leg instead of sanctioning him. Devereaux is a man of logic but not when it concerns Ready. There is blood between them, blood spilled and blood ties. There are two sides of the same coin, yin and yang, whatever you want to call it. Except Ready is the stronger side.

"Ready wanted to kill Devereaux, that's why he hit the train. Miki was a bonus to him. He wanted to ship Devereaux across the wall. He got as cute as Devereaux had been. Well, it is stupid and childish and we have no part of it."

"And Devereaux is sitting at Chartres all winter, waiting for him."

"Yes. If Ready doesn't know where he is, it is because Ready is dead."

"He isn't though."

"No. I am sure he is not," Hanley said. "Ready stalks Devereaux to see if it is a trap."

"Is it a trap?"

"No. Devereaux is waiting. I think he is waiting for his own death. I put my faith in the wiser of the foxes, the one who was hunted and escaped his hunters. Devereaux was very good."

She felt the horror of the cold words.

"He was very good and he is going to die. There is nothing we can do about it. Don't tell me about filthy business, I know how filthy it all is. Devereaux knows he is going to die as surely as I do."

"Why?"

"He settled Rita Macklin, he settled the boy, Philippe, he settled one last score, a quixotic gesture no doubt for some distressed damsel. Well, all his accounts are settled, his bill is paid, the will has been written. He waits in Chartres. Why there? I don't know, I don't want to know. Perhaps because it began there and it has to end there." His voice was rising. He paused. "Devereaux awaits Armageddon. It is poetic but it is nonsense. It is merely two enemies who are going to meet, and one of them is going to die at the hands of the other."

"And Devereaux will die."

"Assuredly," Hanley said. He had lost his appetite but the rush of words forced him to go on. "He's thrown in his hand, Mrs. Neumann. I can see it, Miss Macklin can see it, surely you can see it. He waits like an old man. And what is Ready if not pure hatred, pure evil, with all the vitality of evil. He's more than that: He is mad. The gods don't make men mad before they destroy them; they make men mad to destroy other men. You can't hurt madness or threaten it or reason with it. Being mad is the final advantage. Madness, Mrs. Neumann, finally rules the world because madness is so damned sure of itself.''

She had known Hanley ten years and never heard him speak this way. He spoke as certainly as a preacher.

''You don't want this to happen,'' she whispered to him in her raspy voice.

He blinked at her. He would not speak to her.

''You don't want this,'' she said.

''Devereaux once saved my life but he cannot save his own. He has lost the will. He sees Ready in every shadow. Ready has not lost, cannot lose, and Devereaux cannot resist the inevitable anymore. He is in Chartres waiting for the end of things.''

He blinked again.

Now, at the edge of his eyes, she saw the wetness.

FORTY-TWO
The Last Thing

He left the cathedral at the same time each afternoon. It was a little visit really and he never thought to pray. He sat in the silence of the great church and he stared at the walls or at the windows or at the huge vaulted ceiling. He thought of men climbing wooden ladders set on wooden trestles, men carrying up stones one by one, putting them in place, wondering if they would live to ever see the finish of it.

Sometimes, in the darkness of the afternoon in the church, he could see Ready. Sometimes, in the darkness in his room at the hotel, he could see Ready. Ready stood at the edge of the bed. Ready stood grinning at him.

Rita Macklin wrote to him. He had never thought of letters. The letters touched him more deeply than the sight of her. The words were formed so perfectly, he thought. He could never say such things or use such words. He only knew her name.

He called her now and then because she wanted to hear his voice. She said that he should come home. He would tell her there was a final assignment and it would take a little while longer. He did not tell her he waited for Ready. He did not tell the boy, Philippe. He had closed the apartment in Lausanne on the Rue de la Concorde Suisse and it was just as well because the Swiss were in one of their periodic anti-foreigner moods and the woman who owned the building had decided to ask them to move in any case. Rita wrote to him and told him about daily life in America, about living again in Washington, about her happiness and her yearning for him. America sounded so strange, he would think after reading her letters. In all his life in Section, in all those years, he had lived out of the country so much that America seemed a vague, slightly old-fashioned idea rather than a real place.

He waited in Chartres because Ready would want to find him there. The trail was just plain enough to follow. He chose Chartres because of the beauty of the great church and because it comforted him to contemplate it. He saw no ghosts, no gods, no signs or wonders; he only saw the cathedral and the men who had built it, but they were not ghosts, only figments of imagination. Sometimes, when he thought he saw Ready waiting for him, he knew it was only fear.

He was very afraid.

He thought he had been afraid before but this fear was more real to him. It was more than a physical fear. He thought of a word: Dread.

He had dread. It soaked into his bones.

A taxi almost hit him once. It was only an accident. Would it be that way?

Another time, a man followed him back to the hotel. When he confronted the stranger in the shadow of the street near the hotel, he discovered that the Frenchman was only a homosexual, looking for a lover.

Dread woke him in the mornings after the night of dreams. He always dreamed. The dreams filled his mind the moment he fell asleep and they hammered at him furiously all night long, night after night, so that when he awoke, he was exhausted. Once in a while, he dreamed of Rita Macklin and he awoke with greater dread than he felt after the other dreams.

The season of Christmas proceeded into the season of Lent. The season of Lent began on Ash Wednesday and all the people of Chartres wore ashes on their foreheads that day. The day was blustery and gray and the faithful came into the cathedral and knelt before the priest at the railing around the high altar and they received the ashes. The ashes were made from the palms that had been burned on Sunday. The palms came from the palms of the previous year, given to the people to remind them of the entry of Christ into Jerusalem and the way in which the people had greeted his entry. The Church calendar rolled in cycles like the seasons, and Devereaux watched the changing calendar and the change from winter to spring and he thought it would be very soon now and he thought Ready was very close. On Ash Wednesday, he went to the church and watched the people trudge forward and receive the smudge of the ashes on their foreheads while the priest repeated, over and over, "Remember, man, that you are dust; and unto dust, you will return."

Devereaux received no ashes. He sat in the Café Au Depart near the station as he always did in the afternoon. Today, the proprietor thought he should put out the tables because it was going to be spring. The French are very optimistic about spring and always put out their tables too soon.

Devereaux sat at the table and drank his café noir and watched the world. He saw Ready at the entrance of the little station and he knew that this time he was not seeing his fear. He was seeing the dread of reality.

He did not have his pistol. It was in the hotel room. Had Ready watched him for days? Or was this just chance?

Ready crossed the plaza in front of the station and went to the café and stood over the table. He looked down at Devereaux.

"Pistol is cocked and aimed," he said and grinned. "You made it a little hard but not too hard."

"You're a wanted man," Devereaux said. "You should turn yourself in to the police."

"I thought he was you. At the Hilton in Paris. I mean Miki. The concierge said he had a bandaged hand. I thought it was you."

"It doesn't matter. The tapes were made."

"Where is our girl? I miss her."

"Away."

"Well, I can always find her."

"Sit down and have some coffee," Devereaux said.

"I'm going to kill you, man."

"That's what I supposed."

"Aren't you afraid, Devereaux?"

Devereaux thought about it. "Up to this moment, I was afraid. I think it was seeing you finally and hearing your voice. Sit down, Ready. You've got time for coffee."

"Come on or I shoot you where you sit."

"All right."

He got up and put coins on the tip saucer. He said, "Where do we go?"

"I rented a car. Over in the car lot by the station. We'll go out to the country and that's where it'll be."

Devereaux got in the car and sat in the driver's seat. Ready sat next to him with the pistol in view. It was long-barreled and automatic.

"Go south," he said.

Devereaux drove carefully through the town to the sign that divides the world neatly in every place in France: One part of the sign has an arrow that says "Paris" and the other part an arrow that points to "*Autres Directions.*"

They found a gray place in the gray countryside and they stopped the car at a dirt road. Devereaux sat with his hands on the wheel and Ready got out of the car. Then Devereaux got out on the other side. They stood on either side of the little Renault.

"Get on your knees," Ready said.

"No."

"If you won't get on your knees, I might have to shoot you in the belly instead of in the head. Chop, chop, just like Nam, Devereaux. One behind the ear. What do you say?"

"All right," Devereaux said.

He got down in the mud on his knees. The wind was cold. It was too early in the season to put out the tables. Ready came around the car and stood in front of him.

"Why did you wait at Chartres?"

"I wanted to understand something."

"What?"

"It doesn't matter."

"Did you get it figured out?"

"Yes. In a way."

"I go after the girl next," Ready said. He smiled. "I don't care about the nigger baby, but I owe the girl something."

"She's safe. She's watched."

"No one is safe," Ready said.

It was perfectly true. They were apart from each other for a moment, listening to the North Sea wind howl over the brown, broken fields.

"Chop, chop, just like Nam," Ready said. He smiled down at Devereaux on his knees. Madness glittered in his blue eyes.

"You want to die," he said. "You have the look, the sleep look. You wait to die." His voice was a little awed by what he saw in Devereaux's face.

He took a step to Devereaux's side.

Devereaux raised his right hand and touched him. "Please," he said.

Ready half turned toward him.

It was the perfect position.

Devereaux drove the blade of the Swiss army knife high into Ready's liver, through flesh and bowel. The knife pierced the pancreas in that demonic thrust. It was all shoulder, arm, hand, leveraged into the body from the man on his knees.

Ready blinked and saw bloodred at the edge of blackness. He blinked again and fired.

The shot made a thump through the silencer and tore a bloody chunk from Devereaux's shoulder. He fell back, toward the ditch, but he held the knife and it snagged at the ribcage and he dragged Ready on top of him.

They were falling in a dream. They fell around and around, fell to earth and beneath the earth, and could not touch the sides.

In this dream of falling, Devereaux raises the knife above his head and plunges it into Ready's right eye and Ready begins to scream. The scream rises and Devereaux, so slowly, pulls the knife out of the blood-soaked eye and the other eye is staring and he plunges the knife into his neck, slowly, beneath the chin, rending the voice box. The scream becomes a slow, gurgling bubble of blood foaming on his lips, but the face stares at him, judges him, and Ready is laughing still in silence as they fall together.

In the dream, Devereaux raises his knife again and again, slashing at the dread beneath him. Ready holds him as they fall and if he can cut him away, perhaps the falling will stop. He plunges the knife down and it is covered with blood, his hand is covered with blood, their blood comingles.

His breath comes in sobs and he opens his eyes and there is no dream. The dread is beneath his body, is covered with blood. Ready's mouth is covered with blood and his mortality can be seen in the one staring eye which sees nothing.

Devereaux rose in the ditch, covered with blood and mud. He stood in the mud and looked across the empty fields. Some of the fields were turned for planting and others covered with the brown haze of rotting stalks. He stared across the fields, dumb and in pain, and he saw them. At the horizon were the twin spires of the great church against the low sky. It was the view of the peasant eight hundred years ago; it was the vision of the pilgrim, coming to Chartres to find his faith. He stared at the spires of the church in the distance and then, after a long moment, turned and climbed up to the road.